STARING DOWN THE DEVIL

PETER BRANDVOLD

WHEELER PUBLISHING
A part of Gale, Cengage Learning

GALE
CENGAGE Learning·

Detroit • New York • San Francisco • New Haven, Conn • Waterville, Maine • London

GALE
CENGAGE Learning

Wheeler Publishing Large Print Western.
The text of this Large Print edition is unabridged.
Other aspects of the book may vary from the original edition.
Set in 16 pt. Plantin.
Printed on permanent paper.

LIBRARY OF CONGRESS CATALOGING-IN-PUBLICATION DATA

Brandvold, Peter.
  Staring down the devil / by Peter Brandvold.
    p. cm. — (Wheeler Publishing large print Western)
  ISBN-13: 978-1-59722-701-8 (softcover : alk. paper)
  ISBN-10: 1-59722-701-3 (softcover : alk. paper)
  1. Large type books. I. Title.
  PS3552.R3236S73 2008
  813'.54—dc22   2007043719

Published in 2008 by arrangement with The Berkley Publishing Group, a member of Penguin Group (USA) Inc.

Printed in the United States of America
1 2 3 4 5 6 7 11 10 09 08

For Eli

1

It would be remembered forever in the annals of the Slap & Tickle Saloon as the night a pretty whore goaded Lou Prophet into wrestling a bear.

"Oh, come on, Lou," the girl pouted before the infamous event. "It's not a very big bear."

Prophet was playing poker with four other gents at one of the Slap & Tickle's four gambling tables. The game was stud, ten cents the limit, and the dull-eyed houseman had a bad case of the yawns. Prophet had been trying to fill in a straight when the girl had come into the gambling den and poked a wet finger in his ear, voicing her request.

She was a short, round-faced girl with a delectable rosebud mouth and large breasts doing all they could to wriggle out of her skimpy purple dress. Skin like cream and hair like corn silk. A fake pearl necklace was looped several times around her neck, spilling over the ridge of her bosom to her waist. That, her snakeskin headband, and the feathers in her hair lent an added exotic flair.

Tillie Azure was the sexiest whore in Denver. Prophet had never had the pleasure of her pleasures before, but she'd assured him earlier the night was his. Now he was trying to earn enough money to afford her. He'd come to town two days ago fairly flush, having apprehended a bandit named "Walleye" Ned Whitcomb with a two-hundred-and-fifty-dollar bounty on his head, but Cherry Creek's pleasure girls and poker tables had cleaned him out.

"I don't care how big he is," Prophet said around the cheap cheroot in his mouth, chuckling dryly, "I ain't wrastlin' no bear."

"It's a black bear, not a grizzly," Tillie said.

"Good for him."

"What's the bear's name?" asked the traveling drummer sitting to Prophet's right.

Prophet looked at him. "How could that make a difference?"

"Curly," the girl said.

"Oh, Curly." The drummer grinned.

Prophet frowned. "You know him?"

"That's ole Cal Dyson's bear. Dyson's an ex-mountain man. Raised the bear from a cub. Dyson's old, kinda stove up from layin' traps in all that snowmelt, so now he and the bear just hang out here at the Slap & Tickle, and the old coot makes money off chumps who wanna wrestle his bear."

"You mean," Prophet said, his forehead creased with incredulity, "men actually pay to wrestle the bear?"

"No," said the stocky miner to Prophet's left. "They bet they can beat him."

"Some can," the drummer said, "some can't."

"He's old," Tillie said.

"Well, I ain't bettin' I can take no bear, old or not," Prophet told the girl. "And that's that."

"Well," Tillie said, crossing her arms over her ample breasts and stomping one heel on the floor, "I just bet fifty dollars you could. And if you don't go in there and wrestle that bear, Lou Prophet, you won't be spending this or any night with me."

Prophet looked at her, his mouth open, about to tell the girl that Ma Prophet of Murray County, Georgia, hadn't raised no fool and that she could go to hell. But then his eyes ran down her soft, curvy figure before returning to her sexy indigo gaze, and he imagined how she would look, wearing only the headband and the pearls. . . .

"Step right up here, Mr. Prophet," the old mountain man said, his right fist full of bills. Turning to the bear sleeping in the corner, he said, "Curly, get up here now. You got work to do!"

"What's the matter with him?" Prophet asked, indicating the man passed out on the floor behind Dyson's chair. The man had a pained snarl on his face.

"Oh, he'll be all right," Dyson chuckled. "He just wasn't ready for Curly's turnip twist, is all."

"You mean he wrestled the bear?"

"Always does." Dyson chuckled and wagged his head, thumbing through the bills, his grizzled gray hair falling from beneath a greasy wool hat with a narrow, upturned brim.

Men and pleasure girls had gathered around Prophet. The bartenders had paused to watch from behind the mahogany. When he'd entered the room from the gambling den, the room had erupted in applause, and Tillie had marched him over to the mountain man's corner, cheerily leading her lamb to the slaughter.

"What the hell's a turnip twist?" Prophet

10

wanted to know, scowling with apprehension.

"Curly, get up now, damn ye!" Dyson said, prodding the bear with his gnarled hickory cane. "You got work to do."

The bear's head lolled, and it swiped at the cane with a heavy paw. Dyson prodded the animal again, and the bear lifted its head, its deep brown eyes blinking and clearing as it rose out of its stupor.

Again, Dyson prodded the beast. Prophet watched skeptically as the animal yawned and stretched and slowly gained its feet. It ambled over to Dyson and regarded Prophet dully.

It was a big bear, but Prophet had seen bigger. Prophet weighed about two-twenty in his birthday suit, and all his horse riding and owlhoot chasing had chiseled every pound to hard muscle. The bear weighed probably double that, but Curly had big jowls and flabby shoulders and hips, and he moved awkwardly, swaying on his back hips, as though his bones were stove up from lying too long on the cold saloon floor. Also, he had a sizable paunch. Glancing at the floor where the bear had been lying, Prophet saw a pie tin of what looked like beer.

Prophet grinned as he stared into the bear's glassy eyes. Curly was not only fat

11

and stove up. He was drunk, to boot.

Dyson gave the bear's rear a swap with the cane and said, "Don't just stand there, Curly. Have at it. And keep your claws in. And for god sakes leave the poor man's nose alone."

"Nose?" Prophet crouched as he moved toward the bear, feeling like an idiot, not quite sure what to do with his hands. He'd never wrestled a bear. Maybe he should have sought the counsel of someone who had. . . .

"And leave off with the turnip twist!" Dyson ordered as the bear shuffled toward Prophet.

Prophet looked at the mountain man, who reclined in his chair like a lord, his boots crossed on the table on which his money, beer glass, and notebook lay.

Anxiously Prophet asked, "What the hell's a turnip twist?"

Several onlookers chuckled and elbowed each other. Dyson's brows furrowed. He scribbled something in his notebook.

Whatever a turnip twist was, it was too late for Prophet to back out now. The bear had closed on him, the animal's eyes dark and dumb but deep with feral purpose. He smelled of beer and the wild, musky-sweet smell of bear.

"Go, Lou!" Tillie Azure cried from a group of several other doves, clapping her hands. "I know you can do it. See, he's not a very big bear at all, and he's been drinkin' all afternoon!"

Prophet moved in. His best strategy would be to act quickly and take the bear by surprise. As the beast rose up on its hind legs, Prophet ducked under its flailing paws, pivoted around behind it, and jumped onto its back, crooking his arms around its neck.

The bear cried out with surprise as Prophet tightened his hold on its neck and dug his boots into Curly's gut. Giving another cry, the beast lost its balance, stumbled heavily, and fell with a boom.

"Go, Lou!" Tillie cried.

Gaining confidence, Prophet scrambled onto his heels, bolted off his feet, and dived onto the bear's shaggy belly, pinning one hairy leg with both his knees while holding the other down with his arms.

Curly gave an angry wail, jerking all his limbs at once, and suddenly Prophet was airborne, flying head over heels, brushing an onlooker, and plunging through a chair. He hit the floor hard on his ass. Staring at the rafters, he gulped air into his battered lungs.

"Lou-oo!" Tillie complained with more

disgust than concern. Several others, including Dyson, yelled and clapped for the bear.

"Get that son of a bitch, Curly!" a man yelled. "Get that son of a bitch!"

Prophet turned to see the shaggy beast awkwardly gain its feet, head swinging, smacking its lips as though hungry, its eyes as dark and dumb as before but with a vague glitter deep in the pupils, like a small flame at the bottom of a well. It lifted its front paws eagerly, giving Prophet an indignant glare.

Knowing he couldn't remain on the floor without the bear sitting on him or worse, Prophet gained his feet, staggering, red flares flashing behind his eyes. The bear approached, chuffing and growling and working its nose.

Prophet raised his fists, intending to smack the bear, which stood about Prophet's six-four. But the idea somehow seemed ludicrous. Who in the hell ever heard of punching a bear? What in the hell would you aim for — its nose? You'd only break your hand if you tried smacking that thick skull.

The hesitation was a mistake.

As Prophet tried to skip around the brute, the bear turned quickly, lunging and bowling into Prophet with what felt like the weight of an overloaded dray. Prophet went down, the back of his head slamming the puncheons and igniting a chorus of hoarse trumpets in his ears.

Sucking back the pain, he scrambled to his haunches. The bear got down on all fours and rammed Prophet with his shoulder. The weight and force was too much. Flat on his back once again, his head feeling like a smashed pumpkin, Prophet again found himself staring at the rafters.

"I give . . . I give . . ." he mumbled, trying to be heard above the crowd's din.

The bear rested its forearms on Prophet's chest, forcing the air from his lungs. Prophet struggled against the enormous weight, desperately kicking his legs. The great beast lowered its head, its eyes dark and flat and gold-flecked with rage. The toothy mouth opened, then closed over Prophet's nose.

"Owwww!" Prophet yelled as the teeth dug in. By instinct and reflex more than cunning, he brought his right boot up hard into the animal's crotch.

The bear opened its mouth, releasing Prophet's nose. It tipped its head back and cut loose with an indignant roar so loud that the hanging lamps shook.

The crowd fell silent as Curly sank to his butt, stubby back legs straight out before him, and dropped his paws to his injured groin. With a more hurt, indignant look than Prophet had seen on the face of man or beast, the bear wailed again, its eyes glaring at the rafters, its head wagging from side to side as if asking why, why, why?

Prophet scrambled back on his butt and glanced around. The crowd regarded the bear sadly. Several incriminating looks were directed at Prophet. Heads wagged.

"Jesus, what an awful thing to do!" someone exclaimed.

"He kicked him in the balls," someone else said, as though he could hardly believe his eyes.

As Curly wailed again, still holding his crotch, Prophet said, "Well, what in the hell did you expect me to do? The damn brute tried bitin' my nose off!" He grabbed the appendage in question and his fingers came away stained with blood — not a lot, but enough to know his kick had been justified.

"Oh, Lou!" Tillie cried, gazing at Prophet reprovingly. "How could you?"

"What?" Prophet raged. For god's sake, the bear had tried to bite off his nose.

"Lou!" Tillie cried again, stomping her foot. Turning to Dyson, who'd come out of his chair to check the damage to his bear, she said, "I'm sorry, Mr. Dyson. I never

16

should have suggested an uncouth brute like that" — she jerked her head at Prophet — "wrestle poor Curly. I just didn't know he'd fight like a damn . . . *girl!*"

With that, Tillie lifted her skirts, wheeled, pushed through the crowd, and marched haughtily up the stairs at the back of the room. The other girls gave Prophet angry glares and followed Tillie's lead.

"You okay, Curly?" Dyson asked the bear, hunkering down to get a look at the brute's crotch.

The bear only glowered at him and snorted, then pushed the man away and climbed to all fours. Wobbling like an off-balance Gypsy cart, it ambled back to its place in the corner, gave one last bereaved sigh, and lay down. Kicking one leg out, it planted its snoot on the floor and snorted, staring balefully at a knot in the worn puncheons.

Prophet looked around the room in exasperation, unable to believe all the nasty looks directed at him. "What in the hell did you expect me to do?" he yelled, his indignant voice breaking on the high notes.

"I know what you can do, mister," a burly man in miner's garb declared, stepping forward. "You can get the hell out of here right now."

17

"Yeah, you're not welcome in the Slap & Tickle anymore, Prophet," one of the bartenders told him.

"Now, wait a minute . . ."

Before Prophet could say more, three other men came forward. Two took his arms and two took his legs. Deaf to his objections, they carried him like a battering ram across the room and through the batwings.

"Now maybe you'll think twice before fightin' cheap again!" one of the men said as he and the others threw the bounty hunter headfirst into the street.

It had been raining, and the mud was a foot deep, laced with a healthy dose of horse dung. Prophet slid halfway into the street before he came to a stop. He lifted his face from the mud and dung, spitting the foul ooze from his mouth, blinking.

A pair of lady's cloth boots and the hem of a heavy wool skirt, held above the mud, appeared before him. To the right was a pair of men's ankle-high, calfskin shoes below the hemmed cuffs of pin-striped trousers. A black frock brushed the man's knees.

"Well," said the woman with cool disapproval, "that was a very attractive display." She spoke in an Old World brogue, pronouncing her *w*'s like *v*'s.

"Yes, very attractive," said the man. His

voice bore the same accent as the woman's. "Very attractive indeed, Countess. Are you sure he is the one we are looking for?"

"No," the woman said crisply. "But bring him anyway."

2

Prophet grumbled and cursed, spitting mud and dung. He rose up on his arms, his hands buried in the mud.

The man before him squatted down and peered at him skeptically. He was a stocky, blocky-framed hombre, round-faced, with a carefully trimmed mustache, goatee, and long sideburns.

"He does appear to be the one," the man said in his heavily accented English. "Are you all right, Mr. Prophet?"

Prophet stared at him, curious, his nose hurting and his eyes burning from the dung and mud. "Do I know you?"

"I am Sergei Andreyevich," the man said. Glancing up at the woman, he added, "This is Countess Roskov."

"No kiddin'," was the only response that came to the bounty hunter's reeling, beer-fogged brain.

"Dean Senate sent us," the man called

Sergei informed him. "We met him in Kansas City. He said you might be able to help us."

Prophet climbed to his knees and scrubbed mud from his left eye with his right sleeve. He eyed the round, hairy face before him, his drunken incredulity having been aroused by the name. Dean Senate was an old friend of Prophet's — an ex-mountain man who now owned the plush Ozark Hotel in Kansas City.

"Help you do what?"

"Sergei," the woman said, "this is no place to talk." The words hadn't died on her tongue before a phaeton rolled past, missing them by only a few feet and splashing them all with mud.

"No, it is not," Sergei agreed. He straightened and grabbed Prophet's left arm. "Here — let me help you up."

Prophet felt rickety and tired and dazed from the alcohol and his bear-bit nose. His back and neck were sore.

"~~Goddamn~~ bear," he groused as they approached the boardwalk.

"What bear?"

"The damn bear that bit me. 'Oh, he ain't a grizzly bear, Lou!' Pshaw! Grizzly or no, I never shoulda let that tart talk me into wrastlin' a bear."

"You wrestled a bear?" the woman asked with surprise. She stood facing Prophet on the boardwalk, between two lighted windows, one of which belonged to a hotel, the other a small café. Occasional miners and townsmen swerved around them. Buggies and wagons clattered on the street, horse hooves and wagon wheels making sucking sounds in the mud.

Prophet steadied his gaze at the woman, sizing her up. She was probably in her mid-twenties, her long chestnut hair worn in a stylish bun, with tendrils framing her heart-shaped face. Her eyes were rather startling in their blueness and in the way they slanted, almost like those of an Oriental. Her skin was pale and smooth as cream. She had a heavy brow, which gave her a severe look. She could have been the churchgoing wife of a politician or a military man. She was dressed for it, too, in a conservative purple dress and a black cape hanging loosely about her shoulders.

"Guilty as charged, ma'am," Prophet said, openly embarrassed. "I wrastled a bear. But it was my first one, so that should count for something."

The woman frowned. "What happened to your nose?"

"He bit me."

"That doesn't sound fair," Sergei said with a trace of irony in his voice.

"That's what I said. So I kicked the bastard in the —" Prophet stopped and looked at the woman. "Anyway, they kicked me out."

Tossing a disdainful glance back at the Slap & Tickle, where behind the two large, brightly lit windows a piano was pounding, men were yelling, and women were laughing, he added, "And they can all go to hell as far as I'm concerned. I'll do my drinkin' elsewhere. There's other girls. Tillie Azure ain't the only dove in Denver."

Regarding the two foreigners unsteadily, he asked, "Who'd you say you were again?"

"I am Countess Natasha Roskov. This is Sergei Andreyevich. And you, I believe, need a bath." Her intense blue eyes drifted down his muddy frame and back up again, acquiring a humorous light. "I believe I saw a bathhouse just down the street. . . ."

Prophet looked down at his sopping, filthy clothes. The stench of manure nearly gagged him. "Yeah, I reckon I could at that. Problem is," he added with chagrin, "I don't have any money. Reckon I'll just head down to Cherry Creek."

He gave the Russians a friendly nod. "Pleased to make your acquaintance, Sergei,

Countess. . . ." Still disoriented from the beer and bruising, he turned away.

"Uh, Mr. Prophet, the countess and I would be happy to treat you to a bath."

Prophet kept walking. "Thanks for the offer, but I don't beg money off strangers. Besides, Cherry Creek ain't that far. I've bathed there before; I reckon I can bathe there again. I'll lick my wounds under the cottonwoods."

The countess followed him, her eyes wide with pleading. "But, Mr. Prophet, Mr. Senate sent us here to find you. He said you might be able to help us."

"Oh, yeah, I remember. Sorry. I've had a few drinks. Just pulled into town." He grinned devilishly. "Like to kick up my heels a little, whenever I'm in town. Whenever I'm in any town, for that matter," he added with an exaggerated laugh, throwing back his head.

He regained his composure and gazed at the countess and Sergei with renewed curiosity. "So you know Dean, eh? What was it he thought I could help you with?"

The countess smiled patiently. "What do you say we treat you to a bath, and then we will discuss it . . . over coffee?"

"Coffee, eh?" Prophet thought it over, glancing once more with disdain at the Slap

& Tickle. "Make it coffee and whiskey, and you got a deal."

"All right." The countess brightened. "Coffee and whiskey it is."

"And we'll call the bath a loan."

"If it pleases you . . ."

"It pleases me."

"Right this way, then."

A boiler ticked and groaned at the rear of the bathhouse, on a large cast-iron range. Two of the five wooden washtubs were occupied by burly, red-faced men with fish-belly-white shoulders where their shirts had shielded the sun. The men were talking loudly, drunkenly, as they passed a bottle.

Boldly, the countess led Prophet and Sergei into the room. The proprietor was hammering a leg on an overturned bench. He looked up at the countess with wary surprise in his washed-out eyes. "Y-yes, ma'am?" He glanced at Prophet and Sergei.

An earsplitting whoop cut off her reply. "Come here, my sweet, and wash me back!" one of the bathers called to the countess.

"Mine, too!" yelled the other. "Mine, too!"

Both men guffawed. The countess ignored them, her nostrils flaring slightly.

"This man needs a bath," she told the proprietor sternly, indicating Prophet.

Regarding Prophet, the proprietor raised

his brows and tongued his cheek. "Well, I reckon he does. . . ."

The countess opened her small beaded reticule. "How much do you charge?"

"Four bits for four buckets."

The countess plucked several coins from the purse and dropped them into the man's hand. "That should take care of it."

She had turned and was about to speak to Prophet when one of the Irishmen said, "Hey, get yourself over here, me little piglet. You haven't washed me back yet!"

The countess wheeled to the man, and in a tone of strained tolerance, she said, "I have no intention of washing your back, sir. Now, if you'll please, I've business to attend."

One of the men turned to the other. "Hey, ain't that a Dutch accent?"

The other man shook his head. "Nah, sounds more like Polack to me, Pat."

"You know what they say about them Polack women, Joe."

"Ahhh, but I do, me friend. But I do!" Lifting his florid gaze to the countess, Pat dropped his hand between his legs and said with a lusty leer, "Come on over here, me little Polack. Me dong needs ascrubbin'!"

Sergei, who had been regarding the men with the same strained tolerance as the countess, strolled casually over to the Irishmen, who watched him approach with a jovial cast to their eyes. Sergei stepped between the two round wooden tubs, crouched down, and hooked the index fingers of both hands.

The Irishmen regarded each other, wary. Frowning, they leaned toward Sergei, each cocking an ear.

The stocky Russian crouched between the two men, smiling, and then in a blur of movement, he grabbed each man by his neck and smacked their heads together with an audible crack.

Pat and Joe were out like blown candles, sagging like rag dolls in their tubs.

Sergei stood, casually flicked water from his coat, and strolled back to the countess, Prophet, and the bathhouse proprietor. The latter two had watched the proceedings with mute amazement. The proprietor's jaw hung slack. The countess had acquired the expression of a vaguely amused spectator at an event staged for her entertainment.

Now she turned to Prophet, continuing where she'd left off. "When you are finished here, Mr. Prophet, have a cab take you over to the Denver House Hotel. A room will be waiting for you there. Sergei and I will be in the saloon. I will leave money in the office here for your cab." She turned to the bath-house man. "Have his clothes cleaned, as well. I will send a clean suit over from the hotel."

She turned to her companion. "Let us depart, Sergei."

Prophet stared at the figures retreating through the steam. "Hey, wait a minute!" A vague indignation had swum up through the alcohol and body aches. It was one thing to buy him a bath and a whiskey, but a room in the poshest hotel in town? He was beginning to feel like a puppet.

Sergei glanced back at Prophet, gave a funny little half smile, touched his hat brim, and followed the countess outside. The door closed behind them.

"Hey, wait just a ~~goddamn~~ minute!" Prophet yelled again, but with less vehemence this time. The couple was gone. It was just the proprietor, the two unconscious Irishmen, and himself, sopping wet and stinking to high heaven, his vision blurry from too much beer and whiskey and an ill-fated fight with a drunk bear.

And he'd spoiled his chance for a night with the prettiest dove in town. . . .

"~~Goddammit~~," he groused under his breath.

"Well, what do you say, mister?" the bathhouse proprietor said. He'd limped over to the boiler and indicated one of the steaming copper kettles with a grin. "The Polacks are buyin', and I'd say if anyone ever needed a bath, it was you."

"Yeah," Prophet said. "But what's it gonna cost me?"

A quarter hour later Prophet climbed out of the tub.

"These are the duds that Polack gal sent over," the bathhouse manager told him. The man set the clothes on the bench and checked on the two Irishman still out cold in their tubs.

When Prophet had toweled dry, he turned to the clothes — a charcoal suit of the same cut Sergei had been wearing. The underwear and socks were silk. Prophet cursed. He hated suits. He could count the times he'd worn one on his left hand.

As soon as he'd climbed into the underwear, he saw there were going to be problems, and things didn't get any better until he was standing before the mirror, the coat and frilly puff-sleeved shirt stretched so taut across his frame that the gold buttons bulged, threatening to pop. The pants hung three inches above his ankles but sagged across his ass and through his hips. The bowler hat looked just as ridiculous, perched as it was atop his broad, sun-wizened face, two sizes too small.

Only the shoes fit, soft as lamb's skin.

"~~Goddamn~~ them to hell, anyway," he groused in the mirror. The uppity foreigners were becoming sharper and sharper thorns in his side. He wanted to rip the ridiculous clothes off his back, but what else could he do? His own trail duds wouldn't be washed and ready to wear again till morning, and he doubted the proprietor had any spares that would fit.

"Listen," he told the bathhouse man on his way out, "I want my duds shipped over to the Black Stallion Livery Barn as soon as they're done, understand? Don't tarry. Goin' out at night like this is one thing, but I will not — repeat *will not* — be seen like this in daylight."

He frowned at the bathhouse proprietor, who was guffawing in his desk chair as he ran his eyes from the bowler down to the hemmed trouser cuffs riding Prophet's shins, then back up to the ruffled shirt and jacket, the sleeves of which were practically gathered about the sunburned bounty hunter's elbows.

"Understand?" Prophet repeated.

Shoulders jerking as he laughed, the man flicked his left hand in acknowledgment and bounced back in his chair, wheezing.

"Glad ye think it's so damn funny," Prophet groused as he opened the door and stepped cautiously onto the boardwalk.

He stayed back in the shadows against the bathhouse until a cab appeared. He waved it down and crawled in, keeping his hat over his eyes and slouching down in the seat.

"The Denver House," he called to the driver. "Pronto, for chrissakes!"

3

The Countess Natasha Roskov and Sergei Andreyevich regarded Prophet bemusedly as he marched across the dining room, an indignant set to his jaw. He removed his hat and chucked it on the table.

The countess arched her brow, a humorous light in her frosty blue eyes. "I didn't realize how much taller you were than Sergei."

Sergei chuckled into his napkin.

Ignoring them, Prophet pulled out a chair and dropped into it. "Just out of curiosity, you understand, what in the hell do you two want from me?"

The countess had removed her cape to reveal a purple satin traveling dress with white stitching at the seams. The dress was buttoned all the way up to her throat and then some, and was secured at her long, aristocratic neck with an ivory brooch. "Would you like a drink? The liquor here is very good — for a frontier town."

"No, thanks."

She turned to Sergei. "Tell him, would you, Serg? It might sound better coming from you. Mr. Prophet is apparently aroused by women."

Prophet doubted that *aroused* was the word she'd meant to use. In spite of himself, he chuckled and turned to Sergei, who ran his thumb and index finger through his shiny, raven goatee and sipped his brandy.

Setting the glass down before him, he entwined his stubby fingers around it and leaned over the table. "As I mentioned before, this is the Countess Roskov. I am Sergei Andreyevich, her manservant and bodyguard. We are from Russia originally but now reside in Boston. We have come west in search of the countess's sister, Marya."

"We met your friend Mr. Senate in Kansas City," the countess said. "He told us that you might be able to help us. He told us, in fact," she added, with a trace of patronizing humor, "that if anyone could, it is you." She glanced at Sergei, as if wondering if Senate had been off his rocker.

"I'm a bounty hunter," Prophet said, giving the cravat an irritated jerk. "I only go after people with bounties on their heads."

33

The countess studied him coolly. "Mr. Senate said that you would probably be in Denver in the early winter. We've been waiting for you for several weeks. I hope we have not waited in vain."

Prophet scowled. "You have. I'm a might later than I expected. How did you find me, anyway? Denver's become a pretty big berg."

"We asked around at the — how do you say? — cathouses." The countess's expression was matter-of-fact, but the knobs of her cheeks flushed slightly. "A helpful young lady said that sooner or later we could find you at the house where she works or in the Slap & Tickle Saloon."

Prophet's cheeks warmed with chagrin as the countess continued. "We just happened to check there after dinner this evening, and there you were, flying out the door."

A smile tugged at her lips, and she glanced at Sergei Andreyevich, whose hairy hands were still entwined around his glass. He had a ruggedly handsome face. The carefully trimmed goatee lent a formal, almost military touch. A humorous light shone in the broad Russian's lustrous brown gaze.

"Mr. Senate described you perfectly," the countess said, a note of admiration tempering her amusement.

Prophet finally removed the annoying cravat and tossed it on the table with the hat. "Sorry, I can't help you." He slid his chair back and stood.

"Can't?" she asked. "Or won't?"

"Both."

"Why?"

"I told you, I'm a bounty hunter. If your sister don't have legal paper on her, I won't mess with it. Just simpler that way. I like things simple. I'll leave the clothes at the Black Stallion Livery Barn in the morning. It's by the Cherry Creek bridge."

Before he could turn away, the countess nodded at Sergei, who removed a fat, brown envelope from his jacket and set it on Prophet's side of the table.

"I can offer you one thousand dollars at this moment," she said. "Another thousand when we've found Marya."

Prophet looked at the envelope. As much as he needed the money, he couldn't do it. He didn't work for people, only wanted dodgers. Life was just more livable that way. Besides, these people took too much for granted.

"Sorry," he said again. Leaving the hat and cravat on the table, he headed for the door.

As he headed east toward the livery barn,

he stopped in a tavern for a bottle. Back in the fresh night air, he dug the cork from the bottle with his pocketknife and drank, enjoying the burn of the whiskey in his throat.

Two thousand dollars. Damn.

He took another drink, corked the bottle, and continued walking east along Denver's downtown flats. He was halfway down the block when a string of horses appeared, walking slowly around a closed leather goods shop, heads hanging with fatigue. At the head of the string was a short, long-haired hombre on a tall, black horse. All four horses behind him carried riders draped belly down across their saddles, their heads, arms, and feet jerking stiffly as the horses tramped through the mud.

Prophet frowned at the man on the lead horse. In the darkness compromised by only the buttery glow from saloon windows, he couldn't see the man's face, but something about the man — the set of his narrow shoulders and the way his hands gripped the bridle reins, chin in the air — looked familiar.

"Well, I'll be ~~goddamned~~," Prophet said aloud to himself, his face cracking a grin. "That ain't no man atall!" Stepping off the boardwalk as the rider approached, he yelled, "Hey, you there! Where the hell you think you're goin'?"

Faster than Prophet could blink, the rider brought her horse to a halt and clawed her six-gun from her holster. Thumbing back the hammer, she brought the revolver to bear on the bounty hunter, aiming down the bore with one eye squinted. "Wherever I please, sir, and what are you going to do about it?"

Prophet lifted his hands and bottle above his head, and grinned. "Don't shoot, Louisa. It's Lou."

The girl frowned and leaned forward, her blond hair falling across her shoulders. She wore a man's flannel shirt, sheepskin vest, tight jeans, and plainsman hat thonged beneath her chin. They were a man's clothes, all right, but the slender curves and high bosom were all woman. Or those of a well-built eighteen-year-old girl.

She was close enough that Prophet could see her gazing at him, surprised. "Lou?"

"In the flesh, little darlin'," Prophet said with a chuckle, dropping his arms. "What in the hell brings you to Denver?"

"Lou!" the girl cried, depressing the hammer of her six-gun and sliding the pistol back in her holster. "I didn't recognize you in that suit."

Quickly she slipped out of her saddle, dropped her reins, and ran to Prophet, wrapping her arms around him and burying her face in his chest. Her hat slid off her head and hung down her back by the thong. "Oh, Lou, it is you!"

Prophet hugged her. "Sure is good to see you again, girl. Yes, siree . . . mighty fine. I been worried ever since we split up back in Nebraska." He looked at the horses strung out behind her black Morgan, all tied tail-to-tail. "But I guess I don't have to ask you what you've been up to."

She pulled away from him and followed his gaze to the dead men on the horses. "That's the Kelly Gang," she said, her sonorous schoolgirl's voice turning hard. "Or what's left of them. They held up a stage near Cheyenne. They massacred all the passengers, including the father of five children and a mother of two. I tracked them to just north of Denver, caught them all bathing in Stony Butte Creek."

"They decided not to come peaceful, I take it."

Louisa Bonaventure, whom Prophet had once dubbed the Vengeance Queen on account of her quest for the gang that had murdered her family, shook her head. "I couldn't convince them I was serious, in spite of the fact I had my Winchester on them and they were all standing naked as jaybirds in the water. They just laughed and went for the guns they'd left on the bank." She shook her head as she regarded the dead men thoughtfully. "It was just like shooting ducks on a millpond."

Prophet chuckled at the girl. She had the angelic face and countenance of a pious farmer's daughter from Nebraska, which she was. Circumstances, however, had turned her into an improbably formidable manhunter. The combination, wrapped as it was in such an attractive package, was astounding and not a little discomfiting. To their everlasting regret, hardcases didn't take her seriously.

"Law, Miss Bonnyventure," he said, "you are a caution!"

"Someone needs to rid the earth of evil men as these," she said, suddenly pensive as she studied the bodies draped over the horses. "You can't do it all yourself, Lou."

"No, I reckon not," Prophet allowed. "Where you headin' now?"

"I was looking for a place to keep these men until the sheriff's office opens in the morning and I can file a claim for the bounty on their heads. I need oats for the Morgan, and trail supplies."

"I know just the place." Prophet untied the second horse from the Morgan's tail and mounted behind the dead man.

Louisa watched him with a puzzled smile. "What on earth are you doing?"

"Why walk when I can ride?"

She grunted a laugh as she appraised his garb. "Do you realize your suit doesn't fit?"

"I'd just as soon not get into that, if you don't mind. Come on."

"Where we going?"

"To the livery barn where I got Mean and Ugly stabled."

"I have money, Lou. We don't have to stay in a barn."

"Well, I don't, and I'm a little sensitive about it at the moment," Prophet said. "Come on. Let's go bed your vermin down as well as ourselves."

Louisa grabbed the Morgan's reins and swung onto the saddle. "Lou Prophet, are you trying to sweet-talk me into sleeping with you tonight?"

Prophet grinned. "Is it working?"

Louisa gigged her horse down the street. "The good Lord frowns on heathens and fornicators, Lou."

"Yeah, but we'll have a good time, anyway," Prophet said.

4

Prophet and Louisa laid out the dead outlaws near a woodpile behind the livery barn. Prophet didn't think the Mex swamper, stretched out in the barn's tiny rear office, sound asleep in the arms of a drunk dove, would mind.

When they'd stalled the horses, Prophet led Louisa into the hayloft, where Prophet spread his soogan. Louisa spread hers out next to Prophet's, and they sat down, resting against the hay mound looming behind them.

Prophet had brought up a bull's-eye lantern, and its buttery glow offered the only light from its nail on a ceiling joist. The air was rich with the smell of hay, horses, wheel grease, and wood smoke from the stove in the Mexican's office below. Outside rose the night sounds of distant, muffled voices and the occasional, artificial squeals of a working girl leading some miner off to her crib.

"Drink?" Prophet offered, uncorking his bottle.

"You know I don't drink that stuff, Lou," Louisa said. Fishing around in her saddle-bags, she produced a slender bottle. "Cherry soda. Picked it up in Cheyenne. I've been saving it for a special occasion."

"You sure know how to kick up your heels, girl," Prophet said with a grin, studying her doll-like, peaches-and-cream features in the wan glow from the lantern.

Her face was a perfect oval, the skin smooth as fresh-whipped cream and tinted almond by the sun under which she rode, stalking the West for evil-doers, like those who'd killed her family, as if somehow she could single-handedly purge the world of villainy and even the odds against the devil.

It was a hopeless cause, but Prophet knew she had to make the effort. It was all she had. He hoped she'd get it out of her system someday, and live the kind of life a girl like her was meant to live — an ordinary life in some small town, with a husband and kids and a house with a porch and a lazy dog asleep by the well pump.

"Oh, I'm tired," she said, unlacing her boots. "It's been one long ride from up north. The Indians are causing problems up there, so I had to be extra careful. Sometimes I only rode at night. And those boys" — she curled her button nose — "were getting a little ripe."

"I'll say they were," Prophet said, having smelled the bodies himself. He shook his head. Anticipating his thought, she touched a finger to his mouth.

"Don't tell me it's no life for a girl, Lou. I don't want to talk about that. I just want you to hold me real tight, okay?" She stared into his eyes, her own eyes wide and moist with ancient loneliness.

He placed his hands on her shoulders and pulled her to him. She scooted down on her blanket, curling her knees under her and snugging her cheek against his chest, holding him tightly around the ribs.

"Nightmares again?" he asked, remembering she'd been racked by them — searing images of death and destruction following her family's slaughter.

"Sometimes."

"Should ride with me for a while."

"I can't."

"Why not?"

" 'Cause you're a loner, Lou. And so am I. You know it's true. Besides, if we started depending on each other, we'd likely come to harm. You told me that yourself."

43

Prophet shrugged. "Bounty hunting's no life for a girl."

She lay against him, breathing softly, and he thought she was asleep. But after a while she lifted her head and gazed up at him.

"Can we do it?"

"I thought you didn't want to."

"I didn't say I didn't want to. I just said the good Lord frowns on it when you're not married."

"Then why do you want to do it?"

"I figure with you it's different. We pret' near are married — wouldn't you say?"

Prophet smiled. "I reckon we are at that, Miss Bonnyventure."

"It's Bonaventure — without the *y*," she said. "You'll never get it straight."

"Nope."

She lifted his head and stared into his eyes, her own eyes wide hazel orbs in the flickering light of the lantern. "You always make me feel so good, Lou."

He reached up and smoothed her honey-blond hair back from her cheek. "Honey-girl," he said, "the way I make you feel ain't nothin' like you make this old Georgia Rebel feel."

He smiled and sat back, unbuttoning his shirt. She stood and removed her clothes. When they were both naked, she knelt beside him, her hands over her breasts, a shy expression on her face — an expression he had seen when they'd made love before. It was a bashful, coy look — a look that said, "Here I am; I'm just a girl. I'll do my best, but I hope you don't expect too much." It was such an innocent look that his heart twisted a good three inches counterclockwise, and his desire burned.

He took her face gently in his hands and kissed her, barely touching his lips to hers. Then he held her away, drew her hands away from her breasts, lowered his head, and kissed each delicate pink nipple in turn. She sighed softly as he worked his tongue over her pert young breasts. He lifted his head and kissed her more hungrily this time, but with a gentleness he reserved just for her, this Nebraska cherub turned bounty-hunting vengeance queen.

A moment later he laid her gently on his blanket and parted her knees with his legs, lowering himself gently between them and closing his mouth over hers. She folded her arms around his back, lifted her knees, and groaned with passion as he began moving very slowly, very gently. . . .

When he finally rolled onto his back, drawing her against him with a sigh, she crooked a leg over his and nuzzled his side, her hair fanned across his chest.

"Oh, Lou, I love you so much. I wish we could be together always."

"Well, we could be," he said, though he knew it wasn't true. He could never promise himself to one woman, though if he could it would be to Louisa.

"Shh," she admonished. "Let's don't talk." She ground her face into his side, smelling him like some frisky animal. She ran her fingers lightly across his genitals and fell quickly asleep in his arms.

When he woke in the morning, she was gone. Sitting up, he saw she'd taken all her gear and vanished. The soft dawn light knifing through the cracks between the wall boards revealed several greenbacks on his saddle. Angrily he reached for them.

Fifty dollars.

"Goddammit, Louisa!" he complained.

He felt like a damn whore. Didn't she know a woman didn't leave money with a man? Didn't she know what such a thing did to his pride?

No, she didn't, he decided as he sat naked in the hay and scratched his bristly jaw. She'd known he was broke and was simply doing him a favor, lending him enough to stake him through to his next bounty.

Damn, but his self-respect had been

abused lately!

Remembering the thousand dollars the countess had dropped before him on the table, as an advance for honest work, he leaned back in the hay and rolled a smoke. When his clothes were delivered to the livery barn a half hour later, by a blond boy in knickers whom Prophet tipped with a nickel he borrowed from the Mexican hostler, he dressed quickly and stuffed Louisa's fifty dollars in his shirt pocket with an annoyed chuff.

He needed a job and he needed it fast, and as soon as he saw Louisa again, he was going to return her damn fifty dollars!

"Sorry to wake you," he said after he'd pounded on the countess's door in the Denver House.

She'd answered holding a silver-plated derringer and wearing a black silk wrapper that molded to her body, which was shapely and amply bosomed, he was a little surprised to discover. She'd removed her chestnut hair from its bun, and it hung straight down her shoulders. When she wasn't all starched and fastened and trussed-up like an undertaker's wife, she looked damn sexy.

She blinked at him groggily and gave a start as he thrust the suit into her arms.

"I've decided to take the job."

She just stared at him through sleep-glazed eyes.

Prophet heard someone breathing behind him. Turning, he saw Sergei Andreyevich standing in the doorway wearing a striped sleeping gown and nightcap, an English-styled .45 revolver in his big right hand, aimed at Prophet's head.

"Serg," the bounty hunter said, pinching his hat brim.

"How are you this mornin'?"

The next day Ed Champion sat in the Slap & Tickle Saloon, staring grimly out the window while he stewed over his recent poker loss.

He'd walked in three hours ago with fifty dollars left from a bank heist he and the boys had pulled in Julesburg several weeks back. But that fifty dollars was gone now, forty of it padding the snakeskin wallet of a sober-faced cardsharp from Abilene and the last ten having gone to the house when his craps dice turned up snake eyes.

Champion cursed and glowered at the beer the bartender had bought him. He thought the man felt sorry for him, but really the barman had wanted to avoid a temper tantrum. Champion was known in half the saloons in Colorado for busting chairs and jaws after losing at poker.

He was known to tear up a place pretty bad, and it wasn't hard for him, standing six-feet-four as he did, and broad as a barn door, with arms and fists like mallets. He'd once skinned mules and placer mined for a living, and both occupations had banded the muscles on him like scales on a fish.

When the door opened, he looked up to see two compatriots swagger in, shit-eating grins on their hard, unshaven faces.

"What the hell you two grinning about?" Champion growled as the men approached.

"We just got laid," Earl Cary said, kicking a chair out from the table and collapsing into it. He was skinny, about five-ten, with little round eyes under the floppy brim of his filthy bowler hat. "What's eating you?"

"I just lost my poke."

"All of it?" asked Bobby St. John, a lanky river rat from Tennessee. He had a patch over the eye socket a Cherokee whore had emptied with her fingernails in a Tennessee riverboat saloon.

"Yeah, all of it," Champion grunted. "I got fleeced by a damn sharpy that had the good sense to light out after the game, before I had time to think it over."

"Don't worry about it, Ed," Earl Cary

49

said. "I'll treat you to that pretty little whore I just did the mattress dance with. She's only three-fifty, and man, can she buck! Helluva time!"

"I just poked a bean-eater," St. John said. He waved to the barman and ordered a rye. "She was the best I had since we got to Denver."

Cary was about to say something else when Champion stopped him with, "Shut up." Champion was staring out the window.

"What is it?" Cary said, frowning and following his leader's gaze through the dirty plate-glass window, on which "Slap & Tickle Saloon" had been stenciled in gold-leaf lettering.

Champion's attention had been snatched by the stagecoach sitting before the Denver House Hotel. He'd thought it odd that a stage would be stopped so long before the hotel, when the stage station was just around the corner. But now he'd finally figured out why.

It wasn't really a stage. Or, to be more exact, the auburn Concord coach no longer served a stage line. It appeared to be privately owned. That much Champion had figured out because the only people gathered around it were a young woman in a cream traveling dress and a stocky, dark-

50

featured gent with a black goatee. The man wore odd clothes — strangely cut twill trousers with large pockets running down both legs, a cream flannel shirt with the sleeves rolled up his hairy arms, a string tie, buckskin vest, and moccasins. He also wore a beaver hat. He was stowing steamer trunks and carpetbags atop the carriage and in the rear boot. The woman supervised from the boardwalk.

Nearby a rangy hombre in a buckskin shirt and flat-crowned Stetson sat a hammer-headed dun. The man was rubbing his jaw and eyeing the Concord like he'd never seen one before.

"That's those Russians," St. John said.

"Russians?" Champion asked.

"Sure. They been staying at the Denver House, waitin' on some bounty man named Prophet. They were askin' around town for him about every two days. Looks like he showed. That's him there — the big bastard on the mean-eyed dun."

"So that's Prophet," Champion said, absently fingering an old scar on his cheek. He'd heard of the Confederate-turned-bounty-hunter, the exploits of whom — regarding women as well as men with bounties on their heads — were gaining fame and legend throughout the West.

51

"Yeah, that's him," St. John said, sipping his rye. "I for one would like to put about two rounds in his hide. He's trouble for men like us. Always has been, always will be, till someone beefs him."

"What's he doin' with those two furriners out there?" Champion asked.

"You got me," Cary said, shrugging.

St. John threw back his rye, slammed the shot glass on the table, and motioned for the barman to bring him another. "They're lookin' for the woman's sister down south somewhere. That's what the dark-haired gent told me one day I ran into him right here, after he asked if I'd seen Prophet in town."

Champion was still staring out the window, his horseshoe jaw hanging. The foreign gent was moving a trunk from the boot to the coach's roof. The woman was talking and pointing, fully in charge. Prophet just sat on his horse grinning and shaking his head.

"She's sassy," Champion said, staring at the woman. "A damn polecat. Look at her." He chuffed an admiring laugh.

Cary shook his head. "She orders the gent around like a Mississippi slave."

Champion's broad nostrils flared and his massive chest heaved, straining the buttons of his blue plaid shirt. "She's cute. I like 'em perky."

"Cute and perky?" St. John said. "Nah, she's stiffer'n a damn church pew."

"That's how I like 'em," Champion grumbled lustily. "Kinda fun, makin' 'em do what I say — after they're done screamin', I mean."

Cary laughed. "That's sick, Ed!"

"Yeah, it is," Champion agreed, nodding dully. "Why they lookin' for the girl?"

"I don't know," St. John said. "That's all the man would tell me."

"Looks like they have money," Champion said.

"Well," Cary said, "they did stay pret' near a month in the Denver House. And look at that private coach. They have to have money!"

Champion and the other two men stared quietly out the window for several minutes. Finally the stage pulled away, the stocky gent driving, Prophet following along behind. St. John looked at Champion. He offered a rare, knowing grin.

"Are you thinkin' what I think you're thinkin', Ed?"

Champion followed the stage and Prophet with his eyes, till they were both out of sight. Champion's nostrils flared as he snorted and ran a paw over his head, bald and pale as an egg.

"Get the other boys," he said absently, still staring out the window where carriages, phaetons, and rockaways hustled.

But he was still seeing the coach with all its steamer trunks and the curvy little foreign woman who'd climbed on board and primly closed the door behind her. He imagined how it would be, having her kowtow to him under threat of death, pouring his coffee and rubbing his back and shedding her clothes when he told her to . . .

"Get 'em now," he told St. John and Cary, his voice rising urgently.

As St. John and Cary headed swiftly for the door, Champion called, "Have them ready to ride in twenty minutes, you hear? Twenty minutes!"

5

Having second and third thoughts about accepting the Russians' offer to guide them to Arizona, Prophet clutched his Winchester in both hands as he made his way through a crevice in a rimrock, frowning and gazing around warily.

He and the Russians had been on the trail for nearly a week. He figured they were about a hundred miles south of Denver. They had several weeks of travel ahead, and Prophet thought it pure loco that they had not taken a train as far as Durango. The countess, however, had nixed the idea as soon as Prophet had voiced it. She wanted to be in control of her own schedule. Besides, she didn't like American trains. They were noisy, smelly, and congested with "simple people."

She'd bought the coach from the Ellison-Daniels stage line in St. Louis and outfitted the rig to her own specifications. That's how she and Sergei had traveled to Denver and how they intended to travel throughout the West, Sergei in the driver's box, she in the coach reading and napping and sipping afternoon cordials while smoking her French cheroots.

Prophet thought it the most decadent thing he'd ever seen. The Russians acted like they were on some extended rich man's picnic. Already one of the stage horses had thrown a shoe, another had almost pulled the whole contraption — countess and all — into a ravine, and Sergei had almost snapped an axle when he'd rammed the coach into a rock.

To top it all off, neither the countess nor Sergei had told Prophet why they were looking for the countess's sister. All he knew was that Marya Roskov was somewhere in Arizona and that the countess Natasha wanted to find her and bring her back to Boston.

That was all he knew and, as the countess had informed him in her highfalutin tone, all he needed to know for now. If it hadn't been for the thousand dollars he'd already pocketed and his humiliating morning with Louisa Bonaventure, Prophet would have told these uppity royals where they could drive their wagon. Before he started a job, he wanted to know what the job — the whole job — entailed.

He wasn't sure, though, that in this circumstance he really wanted to know. Deep down, he had a bad feeling. Anyway, he'd be south for the winter. He'd never liked snow.

It was seven o'clock in the morning of their fourth day on the trail. From his watch atop a nearby ridge overlooking their camp, Prophet thought he'd seen movement. He'd worked his way over to investigate while the countess and Sergei slept.

"Shoulda woke 'em up," Prophet thought. "Let them do a little worryin' for a change. Damn foreigners . . ."

He came to the end of the crevice and stepped into a box canyon of sorts, lined with strewn boulders appearing milky in the dawn light.

Prophet looked around, listening. It was too quiet. He half-turned to his right in time to see a figure leaping from the rocky escarpment above him. He didn't have time to raise the Winchester before the Indian was on him, plunging a knife toward his chest.

Prophet dropped the Winchester as he reached for the knife, the force of the leaping savage bowling him onto his back. The

Indian landed on top of him, howling, cursing, and punching Prophet with his left fist while trying to wrench his right free of Prophet's grasp.

Prophet fought for the knife, but the young Ute had an iron grip. Holding the kid's right hand with his own left, Prophet dropped his right hand to his Colt, whipped it out of its holster, and stuck the barrel in the kid's ribs.

The brave froze, staring with sudden terror into Prophet's eyes.

"You done bought it, kid," Prophet said through gritted teeth.

The shot was muffled by the brave's belly.

The kid jerked, giving a startled cry and groan. He slumped sideways. Prophet gave him a shove, scrambling to his feet.

Two more braves appeared before him, crouched and firey-eyed, long black hair whipping in the morning breeze. They wore cotton shirts, hide loincloths, and beaded moccasins. One was a few inches shorter than the other's five-eight or-nine. The shorter brave wore a soldier's faded blue kepi.

Prophet brought the gun up.

Seeing the Colt, the braves hesitated. They were armed with nothing more than the knives in their hands. Prophet hoped that, seeing the score, they'd have sense enough to run.

Their doubts did not last, however. Black eyes dancing with fury, they leaped toward the bounty hunter at the same time. Prophet stepped back, crouching, and triggered the Colt twice, the reports echoing off the rocks. Screaming, both braves stopped, jerked back, and fell. The blood bubbling from their chests turned bright red in the climbing morning sun.

"Damn younkers," Prophet griped, scowling at the bodies.

He leaped atop a boulder pile and swept his gaze around, looking for more would-be attackers. He saw little but rock, purple shadows, and sage tufts, but there had to be a larger band around here somewhere. He just hoped they hadn't heard his pistol shots. If they had, there would be more braves here in a minute.

Deciding he had little time to spare, Prophet left the bodies where they lay, and hurried back the way he had come. He slipped and slid in the gravel as he descended the last ridge, and saw that the Russians were up and about — Sergei building a breakfast fire and the countess sitting on a canvas chair by the coach, brushing her hair to a keen shine.

"Load up," Prophet said as he approached, a little breathless. "We got Injun trouble."

"Injun trouble?" Sergei said, squatting by the fire.

"That's what I said." Prophet grabbed his saddle. "Load up, and be quick about it."

"Are you sure, Mr. Prophet?" the countess asked him. "It seems so peaceful out here." She looked around with an ethereal expression, appreciating the morning with its birds and freshening breeze.

"I take it you didn't hear my pistol shots?" Prophet asked, his irritation building.

Sergei and the countess looked at each other blankly. "We heard nothing," the countess said.

"Three braves jumped me a couple of ridges over. I don't know if they've been following us or just happened onto me this morning, but we need to assume the worst — that there's a larger band nearby — and fog it out of here."

He turned toward his horse, his saddle in one hand, rifle in the other.

"Lou, are you sure you did not fall asleep and were dreaming?" Sergei asked with a patronizing smile. "I mean, we heard no shots. . . ."

Prophet turned to the big Cossack, anger

burning his gut. "For one thing, mister, I don't fall asleep on night watch. For another, I don't dream up trouble for the fun of it. Now, if you didn't hear those pistol shots — good. Maybe no one else did, either. But it would be pure loco to assume they didn't. So if you and the royal wouldn't mind" — he glanced at the countess still sitting in her canvas chair, ivory brush in her hand — "haul ass!"

Face red with exasperation, Prophet whipped around and stalked off toward his horse. Sergei glanced at the countess Natasha and shrugged. "I think our Mr. Prophet is dreaming, for I heard nothing and I have the ears of a young wolf," he told her in French. "But let us humor him this morning, eh, *ma chèrie?*"

"I suppose that would be best," she agreed, rising, the corners of her mouth turned down. "But we'll have to stop for tea later. I simply cannot live without my tea. . . ."

They rode that day and then another, and Prophet, keeping a keen eye on their back-trail, saw no more Indians. He knew the Russians thought he'd been imagining things, and for that reason he almost wished they would see some Utes — a whole warrior band bearing down on them from a rimrock, arrows notched and lances ready to fly.

But that would have been cutting off his nose to spite his face. . . .

These Russians could sure be irritating.

That night they camped in a narrow canyon sheltered by pines and junipers and cooked the deer Prophet had shot earlier.

The next morning Prophet climbed a hill above the canyon and raised his field glasses. Slowly he made a hundred-and-sixty-degree scan of the surrounding countryside — broken prairie bathed in morning sunlight, with the first front of the Rockies looming sagely on his left, their peaks mantled in snow.

A chill wind whistled through a scraggly pine. Prophet lifted the collar of his sheepskin coat. It was cold this high in the foothills, and it was bound to get higher and colder before they descended into the Arizona desert.

Swinging his gaze back to the camp, he watched with disbelief as Sergei washed the coach with a sponge and soapy water from a wooden bucket. White sleeves rolled up his arms, a stogie jutting from his mouth, the Russian scrubbed away as though on a general's polished rockaway.

Meanwhile, the countess reclined against one of her half-dozen steamer trunks beneath a fringed silk parasol. She smoked a cheroot while reading a leather-bound book the size of a hatbox.

"Jesus H. Christ," Prophet grumbled.

Why did he always find himself in the most outlandish situations? Was it that pact he'd made with the devil years ago, after the War? He'd vowed to shovel all the coal ole Scratch desired down below, as long he could live and drink and fornicate to his heart's content on this side of the sod, forgetting all about those he'd seen killed and mangled at Chickamauga and Ringgold and Kennesaw Mountain.

"Maybe I shoulda read the fine print in the contract," Prophet mused, watching the Russian washing the coach. "I shoulda known that deal was just too good to be true."

He lowered the glasses and started down the ridge.

Ed Champion trotted his coyote dun over the lip of the ridge and descended the draw. The horse snorted and blew as its hooves bit deep in the loose clay. At the draw's brushy bottom, Champion reined the horse right and soon smelled the fire and the aroma of scorched coffee.

Wade Snelling stood before the fire, his Spencer rifle in his hands, a wary expression on his face. When he saw it was Champion, his shoulders relaxed and he told the others squatting around the fire, "It's Ed."

"What took you so long, hoss?" Earl Cary said to Champion, lifting his little round pig eyes over the rim of his smoking coffee cup.

"Took me awhile to find their camp. That bounty hunter has them bedded down in a little ravine. I think it's doable, though."

"You sure, Ed?" Bobby St. John asked snidely. "Sure you don't want to wait another week or two? Maybe they'll ride up to us and invite us to all their money and whatever gold they have, and, hell, maybe they'll throw in the girl while they're at it."

Champion scowled. "You think I'm over-cautious, that it, Bobby?"

"Oh, I didn't say that, Ed," the one-eyed St. John said. From his perch on a rock, he grinned into the fire.

"I didn't see any reason to rush things," Champion said. "They're goin' in our direction, for chrissakes. Why not wait till the opportunity seems right? That Prophet — he's savvy. I can tell by the ground he chooses for camping every night. And the Russian don't look like no tit-suckin' calf, neither."

St. John sipped his coffee, adjusted the patch over his right eye, and continued grinning into the fire.

"Buford, bring me a cup o' that coffee," Champion demanded, still steaming over St. John's jibe.

The bastard didn't have any respect for Champion — that was obvious. St. John was too new to the group to realize what happened to those who questioned Champion's authority, not to mention his brass. Well, maybe he'd just find out — sooner rather than later.

When young Buford Linley had brought Champion a mug of coffee, Champion took a sip, blowing ripples. "Well, what'd I just say?" he yelled. "We're gonna do it. Now! Move your sorry asses! You, too, St. John!"

All the boys around the fire jumped to their feet and hustled over to their horses tied to a picket line several yards away. All but St. John, that was.

The one-eyed cowboy from Texas sat on his haunches another thirty seconds, took another two ponderous sips from his coffee, then tossed the dregs in the fire. Only then did he stand, stretch, kick one foot out as if to clear the creaks from his knee, and saunter over to his horse. He dropped the cup in his saddlebags.

Champion watched him, his broad nostrils flared in a snarl. "Proddy son of a bitch," he muttered, lifting his hat and running a hand brusquely over the bald dome of his head. "He's gonna rue the day he ever galled my ass . . . that's for damn sure."

A few minutes later all the men were mounted. They gathered around Champion, who was still drinking his coffee.

He said, "They're in a little ravine about two miles south. Follow me and stick close and for god's sake keep your traps shut, and no smokin'." He looked at St. John. "Understand?"

St. John looked back at Champion and smiled, showing all his teeth.

The others said they understood, casting cautious glances at the silent St. John, then shuttling them back to their leader. With a grunt, Champion tossed out his coffee grounds, stowed the cup in his saddlebags, and reined his horse back the way he'd come.

It was getting dark, the first stars appearing. The eight-man party rode slowly up the side of the ravine, onto the ridge, and out across the rolling prairie, heading south. Fifteen minutes later Champion reined his horse to a stop at the mouth of a dark ravine opening onto a gurgling creek swathed in beech trees.

Quietly he told the men his plan. Then he and young Buford Linley rode out of the ravine, turned left at the creek, and followed the meandering game trail downstream. They rode side by side in silence as the last light bled from the sky and a beaver slapped the water, flushing a grouse from a thicket.

As they rode, Champion released the hammer thong over his Colt and loosened the revolver in his holster, getting set for the dance, as they say, and imagining what that pretty little Russian bitch would feel like under his blankets tonight.

6

As hard as Prophet, the countess, and Sergei rode that day, they made little better than twenty-five miles, the bounty hunter guessed. If it hadn't been for the plodding coach and the countess's frequent stops, they could have gone twice that distance.

Near dark, they made camp in a grove of scrub oaks along a creek. While Sergei built a fire, Prophet scouted around, making sure they were alone, then led Mean and Ugly down to the creek. He picketed the dun in the tall grass near the water and far enough from the bays that Mean couldn't pick any fights.

He was brushing the line-back dun when he heard grass rustling and turned to see the countess making her way toward him. She was strolling, her hands clasped behind her back, enjoying the evening.

She approached him slowly and stopped a few feet away, a pensive little smile on her lips. Prophet turned back to his job, grooming Mean with the curry brush and picking the loose hair from the bristles. He was disgusted with this pair's uppity airs and didn't feel like being friendly. If she wanted to talk, she could start the conversation herself.

Silently the countess watched him curry the horse. He was definitely a strange one to her. She'd been in the West only a few weeks; still, she'd thought she'd seen every kind of man there was to see out here — farmers, miners, Indians, cattlemen, river men, train men, and townsmen. But she hadn't, until the other night when he had been unceremoniously shown through the doors of the Slap & Tackle Saloon, laid eyes on anything like Lou Prophet.

In his dusty trail garb, his buckskin shirt straining across the slabbed muscles of his chest, and his perpetual wolfish half-grin, he reminded her of Sergei's people. The Cossacks of southern Russia were fierce warriors and expert horsemen, on the order of the best of the American Indians. As honorable as they were savage, as cunning and shrewd as they were chivalrous, they would fight to the death any man who moved against them, or threatened their territory or way of life, or slandered their bloodlines.

They liked stories and strong drink, and they loved to laugh. Also, they were the gentlest, most creative lovers on earth.

The countess knew this from firsthand experience, though not from Sergei, whom she loved like a brother. But a few years ago, when she still owned the innocence of youth and was traveling with her father to the remote regions of the Caucuses, she'd been in love for three blissful days with a stocky, sunburned farm boy named Mishenka.

Lou Prophet would be a lover not unlike the rustic Mishenka, she thought now as he moved toward her. Against her will, she imagined how it would feel, running her tongue over his lips, to be wrapped in those muscular arms, to feel those taut buttocks in her hands as he thrashed between her legs. . . .

My god, it had been so long since a man had shared her boudoir!

She shook her head to clear the lust fog. Reminding herself what she had walked over here for, she extended a worn piece of paper that fluttered in the chill breeze. "Tell me what you think of that, Mr. Prophet."

He turned to her, frowning. When he'd set the brush on the horse's back, he took the leaf and leaned against Mean, tilting the page to the weak light.

It was a map of sorts, inexpertly drawn in pencil on cheap tablet paper. Jagged lines presumably marked mountains, serpentine lines must have been creeks or washes, and the bold X, of course, marked some meaningful spot.

At least, it must have been meaningful to someone. To Prophet, it was just an X amidst squiggly lines on cheap tablet paper.

He shrugged and said as much to the countess.

"My sister sent it to me."

"Why?"

"For safekeeping."

"What is it?"

"It is a map, is it not?" the countess said, arching her brows patiently. "Marya says it marks the location of a secret treasure her friend had discovered in the desert."

Prophet looked at the paper again and nodded passively. So-called treasure maps were a dime a dozen in the West. Most were sold by confidence men to unsuspecting tinhorns. In the Southwest you could find them in dozen bundles for less than a nickel.

"Where did it come from?"

"The postmark on the envelope was from Broken Knee, Arizona."

"Broken Knee? Never heard of it."

The countess looked at him hopefully. "But you can find it, can't you?"

"Probably," Prophet allowed. "Is that where your sister is?"

"That's where the map came from," the countess said with a dainty shrug. "I don't know where else to look."

"Wait a minute," Prophet said, frowning. "You mean, you don't know for sure?"

"Marya didn't tell me." The countess stared back at Prophet. "You see, Marya ran away, against our mother's wishes, when she traveled West. She has always been an adventurous girl. After reading many books about the frontier, she decided to come here herself."

Prophet was baffled. "She didn't tell you where she was headin'?"

The countess shook her head. "Marya knew she could confide in me — we were close, she and I. But she also knew that our mother could get the information out of me and probably send someone West to escort Marya back home. So all I know are the sketchy details she included in her letters — that she met an old prospector somewhere in Arizona and went off with this man, looking for gold!" The countess's voice had risen with exasperation.

"How old is your sister, anyway?" Prophet asked.

"Four years younger than I — eighteen."

"Well, that explains a lot," Prophet mused aloud. He was a little surprised to learn that the countess was only twenty-two. By her regal, haughty demeanor, he would have said she was in her late-twenties, early thirties. But then, her skin did appear awfully smooth and firm, he'd noticed with manly interest.

She continued. "Not long after this time, I received that map in the mail. Along with the map was a brief note from Marya saying only that she wished for me to keep the map safely for her and to not show it to anyone. She said that if all went well, she would send for it."

Prophet stood beside his horse, frowning curiously. "If all what went well?"

"I do not know. But she has not sent for the map, and we have heard nothing from her since she sent it. A couple of weeks ago, when my worry got the best of me, I decided to come to Arizona to look for Marya. And, if possible," the countess added with a sigh, "bring her home."

"What did your mother say about that?"

"She did not like it, but in the end she agreed that I should go, accompanied by

Sergei. I have always been the most respon-sible child in the family. Besides, Mother, too, is very concerned about Marya."

"Why didn't you tell me this before?"

The countess looked demurely down at her shoes. "Because I didn't think you would help us, after hearing such a crazy story."

"I got to admit, it does sound a little loco."

The countess clutched her shoulders and turned away, looking back toward the coach. It was nearly dark. Stars sparked to life in the violet sky above the black, spindly branches of the oaks.

Sergei was gathering wood for a fire. Birds chattered. To the north and west, the mantled peaks of the San Juans turned salmon.

"Marya is a . . . a black goat, is how I believe you say it in English."

"I believe that's 'sheep,' " Prophet cor-rected with an inward smile.

"Yes, sheep," the countess agreed. "She always sought adventure, even before our father was killed and we came to this coun-try."

Prophet's frown lines deepened in his forehead. "How was your father killed?"

"He was a nobleman and an officer in the Russian army. He had a very prestigious

74

position. Many others were jealous." The countess shrugged her shoulders, lifting her hands and dropping them. "So he was killed — shot while crossing the street to his favorite bakery. That happens in our country."

"What brought the family here?"

"We were afraid that the men who had killed my father would try to kill us, as well. That is also a danger in my country. People disappear, you see. Whole families. So Sergei — who had fought with father against the Tartars and had become Father's personal secretary — escorted us to Boston. Sergei lives with us. We have an apartment. It is a quiet life — much too quiet for Marya." Prophet heard the smile in the woman's voice.

Prophet allowed a contemplative silence to seep in around them. Finally he turned, grabbed the brush off Mean's back, and tossed it in the air, catching it and staring thoughtfully into the darkness. "So your sister's in Arizona . . . somewhere."

"Yes," the countess said, turning around to face his back. "Will you please help us find her, Mr. Prophet?"

Slowly Prophet nodded. "I already agreed to that, didn't I?"

"But I thought after you had heard how

crazy she is, and wild — and about the treasure map — you might have decided that we were all too crazy to —"

"Listen, Countess," Prophet interrupted, turning to face her. "I done took the job. It ain't my way to back out halfway in. Or even a third in. True, I would have appreciated knowin' all the details up front." He squinted one eye at her. "I just hope there's nothing else you're holdin' back."

"Nothing," the countess said, shaking her head reassuringly.

Her voice thinned. "I am worried about my sister, Mr. Prophet. I am certain she is in trouble. What kind of trouble I cannot imagine."

Prophet nodded and sighed. "I reckon you're right." Any girl alone in the West was in trouble. One that had run off with some old desert rat after buried treasure in Apache and *bandido* country was most likely already dead.

The countess stepped toward Prophet and placed her hand on his arm. She must have read his mind. "I am worried about Marya, Mr. Prophet," she repeated. "She is young and headstrong. I want to find her and take her home."

"I think you're all little headstrong, if you don't mind me sayin' so," Prophet said with a cantankerous smile. "And that coach is pure-dee bullshit."

Her chin rose. Her nostrils flared. The proud royal was back. In a taut voice she said, "I need you, Mr. Prophet, but I am not fond of your impertinence."

"Tough titty."

Her eyes flared, and she took one startled, angry step backward. "What?"

"It's an old expression that means I don't give a shit about how you feel about my attitude. The way I see it, you loco royals have gotten far too accustomed to giving orders and doing things your own way, whether they make sense or not. Now, I'm not going to run out on you, because for some damn reason that has only a little to do with money, I feel obligated to help you find your sister. You can keep your ~~goddamn~~ coach since it means so much to you to travel in style, but from now on no more day stops other than those to rest and water the horses. We keep movin'. No hour-long stops for lunch and afternoon tea. We move. Understand? The faster we've found this Broken Knee, the better off we'll be."

The countess's eyes flashed. "And the sooner you'll be rid of us, no?"

"You got that right."

He stared at her. She stared back, the skin

stretched taut across her face. The sky's last light boiled in her slanted eyes. Suddenly she bolted toward him, and for a moment Prophet thought she was about to slap his face.

But then she was in his arms, rising up on the toes of her delicate shoes and clamping her mouth over his. Befuddled, he just stood there while she kissed him, wrapping her arms around his neck, pressing her bosom against his chest. He could feel the heat of her thighs against his own.

He was lifting his own hands to hold her when she stepped back as suddenly as she'd pounced, as though she'd been jerked away by a taut rope.

"Oh, my god," she said, her voice quaking, pressing a hand to her breast. Her cheeks had flushed strawberry red. "I am sorry!"

She turned, grabbed her skirts in her fists, and hurried through the brush toward the camp.

Prophet stared after her, wide-eyed, open-mouthed, bewildered.

"Well, I'll be damned," he said, shocked. He rubbed his open hand across his mouth, then looked at the wet palm, frowning.

Sure enough, she'd really kissed him.

"Well, I'll be ~~goddamned~~," he said again,

still unable to believe it.

Slowly he shook his head, stooped to pick up his rifle and saddlebags, and started toward the fire, dazed.

7

"Countess, where have you been?" Sergei asked the countess as she approached the fire. "I was getting worried."

"I took a stroll to stretch my legs."

"Ma chèrie," he said, gently chiding, "do I need to remind you of the dangers of this country?"

The most dangerous thing in their camp at the moment was none other than the countess herself, she thought as she made a beeline for the coach. She could not believe that she had just thrown herself at Lou Prophet. My god! How could she ever face him again?

"No, Serge. I am well aware of the dangers here."

"Where are you going?"

"To bed. I'm suddenly very sleepy."

"But, Countess, you have not eaten supper. You must —"

She stopped and wheeled toward the big

Cossack, her skirts flying. "Oh, please, Sergei!" She was poised to continue the outburst, but stopped herself and took a deep, calming breath. "I am sorry. I am just . . . I have a headache. I am going to turn in early tonight."

"But I have not made your bed. Certainly you can eat something. . . ."

"No, I am not hungry. I will make my own bed this evening. Thank you, Serge. Good night."

When she'd disappeared into the coach, the Cossack twisted the ends of his double-barreled mustache as he considered the Concord, which jounced and squeaked as the countess prepared her bed.

Hearing brush thrash behind him, he turned and slapped the revolver on his right hip.

"Easy," Prophet said, moving toward the fire the Cossack had built. "Just me."

"Ah . . . yes," Sergei growled.

Prophet saw that the barrel-chested Russian was watching him suspiciously. He must have witnessed the countess's distress and been wondering if Prophet was to blame. They'd both come from the same direction.

Just Prophet's luck. A woman throws herself at him, and he gets blamed!

Prophet glanced at Sergei, grinned innocently to put the man at ease, then reached for the coffeepot steaming on a rock in the fire. "Is there anything better than a cup of hot coffee after a long day on the trail?" he asked with as much affability as he could muster.

He sipped the brew and cast a cautious glance at Sergei, who was swallowing none of Prophet's charm. He regarded the bounty hunter darkly, one hand on the butt of his revolver. On his other hip he carried an English-made LeMatt. The combined six-shooter and single-shot scattergun could make a hell of a mess at close range.

Conversationally Prophet said, "Nothing like a cup of Arbuckles to cut through the trail dust and lift a man's spirits. Join me?"

The Russian stared at him. Finally he gave a snort, turned, and climbed to the coach's roof, apparently mucking around for his bed gear.

Later, Prophet reclined against his saddle, gnawing jerky and drinking coffee. Sergei squatted across the fire, preparing his teapot.

"Hello the camp," rose a man's cry in the quiet twilight.

In an instant Prophet's Colt was in his hand. He bolted to his feet. Glancing across the fire, he saw that the Russian was standing also, having dropped his teapot in favor of the stout LeMatt in his hand.

Prophet stepped back from the fire so he could see clearly into the thickening shadows of the oaks along the creek. He was vaguely aware of the Cossack doing the same, as though they were mirror images of each other — two men from separate countries but with similar instincts no doubt based on similar experience.

"Identify yourselves," Prophet called.

"Name's Ed Jones," came the man's pinched voice. "My partner's hurt. Can we ride in?"

Prophet glanced at Sergei, who returned the wary gaze. Prophet threw a hand up for the Russian to wait, then he wheeled to the coach and opened the door.

"What are you doing?" the Russian asked, his voice a taut, angry rasp.

Prophet didn't take the time to answer. He reached into the dark coach, said, "Countess, take my hand."

"What's happening?" she asked groggily.

"Take it!"

She did, and Prophet pulled her brusquely out of the coach. She was dressed in gauzy blue nightclothes with a thin cotton wrapper. She needed something warmer, but she didn't have time. Quickly Prophet led her through the brush and into a jumble of rocks at the camp's rear.

"Stay here and keep your head down."

She gazed up at him, frightened. "What is happening?"

"Probably nothing." She'd be safer in the rocks than in the coach, the thin walls of which bullets could easily penetrate. "Just a precaution."

He wheeled and trotted back to the fire. He grabbed his Winchester leaning against his saddle, and cocked it. "All right, come on in."

For several seconds there was only the sound of the breeze in the branches. The fire snapped. The slow clomp of hooves rose and grew louder until the silhouettes of two horses and two riders appeared in the trees along the gurgling stream. One man rode straight in his saddle. The other leaned low over his horse's neck, his head down.

"What's wrong with him?" Prophet asked.

"Snakebit," said the one who'd identified himself as Ed Jones. He was big, raw-boned, and slab-shouldered. He wore a black vest over a grimy shirt missing buttons and bearing a torn pocket. He appeared to be bald under his broad-brimmed hat. He wore twin Colts in tied-down, border-draw holsters.

Dismounting his paint pony, Jones dropped the reins and turned to the other horse. He put a gentle hand on the injured rider's shoulder. "You still kickin', boy?"

"Yeah, but I'm hurt pretty bad," the young man said in a shaky voice. A rifle stock poked up from his forward-canted saddle sheath, and the kid wore an ivory-gripped Remington on his right hip.

Prophet's eyes lingered over these details as he stood frozen near the Cossack. His heart beat a steady, wary rhythm.

"Where's he bit?" Prophet asked.

"Belly," Jones said. Light from the guttering fire revealed the lines in his craggy face. Prophet guessed he was in his early forties, though his mustache was pure black. "He leaned down for a drink of water, and didn't see the diamondback coiled under a rock."

"Ouch."

"Yeah, ouch," Jones agreed. "Would you help me get him out of his saddle and over to your fire, mister? I'd sure appreciate it."

"No." It was Sergei. He'd turned his head to direct his reply to Prophet. His voice was low, level, and tight.

"What do you mean, 'no'?" Jones said, scowling with indignation. "I told you, he's snakebit!"

Prophet gave the two men the twice over,

trying to see what Sergei had seen and which had prompted the Russian to deny the man's request for assistance.

As he did so, a gun barked, making Prophet jump and extend the Winchester. Jones's head went back, and he staggered against the young man's horse. The horse jumped, and Jones fell, but not before Prophet had seen the round, dark hole in his forehead.

Prophet glanced quickly at Sergei. The Russian's LeMatt was smoking.

"What — ?"

Before Prophet could say another word, the snakebit rider's head came up, his eyes wide. The kid clawed at the gun on his thigh while trying to steady his horse, which had commenced prancing and shaking its head at the shot.

Sergei's LeMatt barked and flashed again.

The kid screamed and crouched over his saddle horn. His head dropped to the horse's buffeting mane just before the horse jerked to the left, throwing the kid from his saddle. He hit the ground with a groan and lay grinding his boot heels into the ground while clutching his wounded belly. His horse and Jones's paint galloped back the way they'd come.

"Countess, stay down!" Sergei yelled as

he wheeled and ran across the encampment.

Running and yelling in Russian, the Cossack fired the LeMatt and his second revolver into the darkness. Prophet wheeled then, too, and took off after the crazy Russian, vaguely confused but also knowing with a sick feeling in his guts that the night was about to explode.

8

The night did, indeed, explode. The gunfire came from behind. Whoever the owlhoots were, they'd intended to distract Prophet and Sergei with the "wounded" kid and storm the camp with guns blazing from the other side.

Sergei was shooting at the gun flashes in the shrubs, yelling again for the countess to stay down. Prophet ran toward the shrubs, dropping to a knee every few feet and firing the Winchester, hearing the attackers' bullets whistling around him and plunking into the grass before him.

One burned his right cheek. He cursed as he levered another cartridge into the Winchester's breech, picked out a gun flash, and fired.

The Winchester's report was followed by a startled cry of anguish.

Prophet fired again, noticing that Sergei's guns had quieted. When his own rifle clicked empty, he dropped to a knee, set the rifle down, and drew his revolver. As he thumbed back the hammer and raised the gun, he froze, frowning into the darkness.

The shooting had stopped, the silence descending even heavier than before. The stench of powder smoke filled the air. From far off he heard muffled yells and clomping hooves. Closer by, a man groaned and cursed and groaned again.

"Help, damnit! I'm hit *bad!*"

A shadow moved to Prophet's right. He jerked the .45 toward it and called, "Sergei?"

"Do not shoot." Sergei moved into the brush about thirty yards before Prophet, toward the groans of the wounded owlhoot. Brush crunched under his moccasins.

"Careful," Prophet called.

"They are gone," Sergei replied. He stopped. Moving toward him, Prophet frowned curiously as Sergei's arm came up.

"No, wait!" the wounded man cried. "Stop!"

The LeMatt flashed in Sergei's hand. The report was a sharp thunder clap. Prophet stopped, startled by the Cossack's cold execution of the wounded man, then continued through the brush, stopping where the body was sprawled out in the grass, fresh blood gleaming in the starlight.

Sergei was hunkered down, going through the man's pockets.

Prophet frowned. "Why'd you kill him?"

"He attacked us."

"You might have tried to find out why and who the hell he was before you beefed him."

The Cossack stood, stuffing the man's revolver behind his cartridge belt. Dully he looked at Prophet. "Why?"

Not waiting for an answer, he walked back toward the coach. Watching him go, Prophet had to admit the Russian had a point. Still, it wouldn't have hurt to try to find out how many were in the group and what exactly they were after.

Prophet also had to admit that Sergei had sniffed out the trap before he had. Sergei may have dressed like a dude and exhibited a fetish for cleanliness, but the Russian was a warrior to ride the river with. That much was clear.

Another revolver report shattered the stillness. Prophet snorted and shook his head. The Russian must have finished off the kid who'd ridden into the camp with Jones.

"Law," Prophet said, "that Russian's colder'n the devil at Easter."

The bounty hunter walked over to the rocks where he'd hidden the countess. She stood before them now, looking around warily, her chestnut hair framing her pale face. She looked pretty and soft and vulnerable, the bounty hunter thought, his pang of lust coinciding with his memory of what had transpired between them less than an hour ago. She wasn't nearly as upright and dour as she liked people to believe.

"It's all clear," he told her now.

"Who were those men?" she asked slowly, watching Sergei crouch down and go through the dead kid's pockets.

"I don't know. Didn't get a chance to find out," Prophet said with an edge in his voice. "But I have to hand it to your bodyguard there. He sniffed out the trap before I did."

The countess gave Prophet a self-satisfied smile. "Sergei is a warrior as well as a gentleman," she said meaningfully. "You see, one does not have to exclude the other."

"It was you pret' near jumped down my pants awhile ago, Your Majesty," Prophet said with a mocking chuckle. "Is that how ladies behave over there in Russia?"

Cowed, the countess turned away and said softly, "It was a momentary lapse. I didn't know what I was doing. I do hope, however, that you will forget it ever happened . . . as a gentleman would."

"Sure, I'll forget it," Prophet added with a grin. "As long as you can."

She turned in a huff and made her way to the coach.

After dousing the fire, Prophet and the Russian sat up the rest of the night. Sergei took a position in the trees across the creek, not far from the coach. Prophet sat near the crest of the northern ridge, where he had a good view of the surrounding terrain and would be able to spot any more attackers. He doubted the same group would try two raids in one night, but it never paid to let your guard down. Besides, the gunfire may have attracted Indians.

He sat on his butt, rifle across his knees, just down from the ridge's crest. Above him the stars winked and flickered, impossibly clear in the arid sky. Hat tipped back on his head, Prophet smoked and swept his gaze around, keeping the coal cupped in his palm, his ears alive to the slightest unnatural noise.

What the owlhoots had wanted was obvious — money, valuables, and no doubt the countess. She would have been good for a few hours of fun out here where women were few and far between. She'd bring a nice price down in Mexico, too, where women were bought and sold like cattle.

"Well, here's where you earn your money, old son," the bounty hunter told himself, taking a deep drag off the quirley.

At first light Prophet built a small fire and boiled coffee. He and Sergei went over Prophet's map of the Southwest, Prophet pointing out the trail he thought they should take — a trail that joined up with a stage road near the village of Limon, New Mexico.

The countess appeared from the coach looking as fresh and haughty as always in spite of last night's festivities. Prophet smiled at her over the rim of his coffee cup. She flushed and turned toward the creek.

"Tell me," Prophet said to Sergei. "What made you savvy the trap last night?" The bounty hunter's pride was bruised.

The Cossack smiled pridefully and shrugged, inflating his big chest. "I just had a sense, my friend Prophet," he said, flicking dead ashes off his black cheroot. "Just a sense."

"A sense?" Prophet said, irritated. "That was it? You had a sense?"

"Yes, I had sense. Besides, it is an old trick, no? The Tartars I fought tried such ruses all the time."

"Well, I sure am glad your sense proved to be right," Prophet said wryly. "Otherwise, I reckon we'd be cold-blooded killers."

The Cossack apparently found this one of the funniest things he'd ever heard, for he threw his head back and guffawed loudly. Rising, he slapped Prophet's back so hard that the bounty hunter nearly tumbled face first into the fire. Strolling off toward the horses, the Russian began singing merrily in his mother tongue.

Prophet tossed his remaining coffee in the fire and saddled Mean and Ugly. " 'A sense,' " he grumbled.

A few minutes later they were on the trail, the sun rising over Prophet's shoulder, extending rock and cactus shadows westward. The stage clattered behind him, the Cossack in the driver's box urging the four matched bays up grades and around rimrocks.

Prophet thought ahead, to when he'd be rid of these loco royals and luxuriating in Phoenix or Tucson or Mexico, enjoying the sun-washed village plazas and buxom señoritas while waiting for the snow to melt up North.

First he had to find the countess's sister, which meant he had to find some town called Broken Knee. Since he'd never heard of the place and since the town wasn't marked on his map, he'd have to ask around — when he found someone to ask, that was.

"Have you seen anything of our attackers, Mr. Prophet?" the countess called out the stage window later that afternoon.

Drifting back to ride even with the stage, Prophet was surprised. The countess hadn't said two words to him since their embarrassing moment on the ridge. She seemed to have recovered from it now, however, for she regarded him directly out the window, squinting against the westering sun.

"No, ma'am," Prophet told her. "I've ridden ahead and lingered behind and made a big loop around the coach, and I haven't seen so much as a dust plume. But that isn't to say those long riders aren't following us. I'm hoping they've decided we're more trouble than we're worth."

"Yes, it is better to be safe than sorry," the countess Natasha said. "That is the expression, is it not, Mr. Prophet?"

"That's it, ma'am."

"What happened to your cheek?"

"Bullet creased it last night. Just a scratch. Goes with my nose."

"Your nose is almost healed," she said, smiling amusedly at the faint tooth marks. "But your cheek — it should be covered. You've gotten dust in it."

Prophet shrugged. "Like I said, it's just a scratch."

"Tonight I'll clean it for you."

"Better not, Countess," Prophet said. "We get too close, I'm liable to get Sergei's dagger in my hide."

She laughed, her face opening beautifully, her cheeks coloring. Her slanty eyes turned downright pretty. "He is a bit overprotective," she said above the creaking wheels and squeaking leather thoroughbraces. "We were through a lot together, Serge and my family. On his deathbed, Father made Sergei promise to keep the family safe."

"I reckon you couldn't be in safer hands," Prophet allowed, remembering the Cossack's quick, decisive action the night before.

"Yes, though he does tend to get a bit . . . zealous, shall we say?"

Prophet smiled. "I reckon he just wants to make sure you and your sister make it home safe, is all."

"Nevertheless — I will clean your cheek for you tonight." She dropped her chin and smiled demurely. "But I promise not to embarrass myself further."

Prophet looked at her, flushing. "That's all right," he said. "To be frank, you can throw yourself at me anytime you want . . . as long as he's not watchin'," Prophet added, tipping his head to indicate Sergei in the driver's box, yelling at the horses as they climbed a grade.

The countess lifted her slanted eyes to him again. Now her timidity was gone, replaced with a brassiness that turned Prophet's middle to jelly. He noticed that her shirtwaist wasn't buttoned up so high, revealing a spray of freckles angling down toward her cleavage.

"I will take that under consideration," she remarked.

"That mean you're not mad anymore?"

"I am not mad," she replied. "You were right, Mr. Prophet. The coach is an unforgivable luxury, especially when I should be making haste to reach Broken Knee to find Marya. I am afraid we Roskovs have a lot to learn about humility and practicality."

"Looks to me like you're already learning," Prophet said with a smile.

The countess returned the smile, which grew thoughtful. "Do you think Marya is alive?"

He looked off and pursed his lips, not sure what to say. Then he looked at her again and shrugged, trying not to look too grim. "I don't rightly know, Countess."

She nodded slowly. "Call me Natasha."

"If you call me Lou."

With a parting grin and a pinch of his hat

brim, he gigged Mean and Ugly past Sergei and the team. He scouted the trail ahead for half an hour, then rode back to the coach. Riding abreast of the big Russian smoking a black cheroot in the driver's box, Prophet said, "There's a stage stop ahead."

"A what? A stop?"

"We're on a stage road. Stage companies have lodges here and there along the road, where coaches can stop for the night and to switch teams. They call these lodges stops or way stations. We'll stay there for the night, if the station agent will have us. It'll be safer than the trail, and I'm sure the countess wouldn't mind sleeping in a bed for a night."

"No, I am sure she would not," the Cossack agreed. "To be honest, Mr. Prophet, I would not mind a bed myself. This old Russian has gotten spoiled since coming to your country."

"It's settled, then."

Before Prophet could ride ahead, Sergei held up a hand to waylay him. "I feel I must remind you, my friend Lou, that the countess is . . . how do you say . . . ?"

"Off limits?" Prophet asked with a tight smile.

"Yes," Sergei said, returning the smile as cold as a Russian winter. "Off limits."

"Isn't that rather up to the countess?"

"No," was the Russian's taut reply.

"I see," Prophet said. Heeling the dun into a lope, he added under his breath, "I just wonder if she does."

"How you doin', Barstow?" Bobby St. John asked the wounded rider as he pushed off his hands into a sitting position. St. John had been drinking in Two-Boulder Creek, and now he adjusted his eye patch over the empty socket and loosened his bandanna.

"My knee's all shot to hell," Barstow complained. "Look at me bleed! I'm like to bleed dry!"

Barstow was a hefty lad with straight brown hair cut high around his scalp. His face was flushed and perspiring, his eyes bloodshot, from the pain of his bullet-shattered knee.

"Just hold on, Bar," Ned Jamison said. He was sitting with his back to a rock, cleaning his Winchester.

Two other survivors of their failed attack last night sat nearby. "Squirrely" Jack Nye was tending a flesh wound in his arm, and the other man, the huge, green-eyed mulatto, Kevin Kimbreau, was drinking coffee and eating jerky.

Counting Bobby St. John, a total of five

men had survived the attack.

"Hold on?" Barstow raged, wincing through his pain. "You hold on, damn your hide anyway! This hurts like hell. I need a doctor."

"We ain't got no time for a doctor," Bobby St. John said. "We got a job to do."

"Leave the damn coach!" Jamison said. "Can't you see Barstow's bleedin' dry?"

"Squirrely" Jack Nye, always cool as a November breeze, chuckled. "Hell, he's gonna die, anyway. Why waste time gettin' him to a sawbones? I'm with Bobby. I say we overtake that friggin' coach. I ain't passin' up that much money, not to mention that much woman."

Nye looked around the group. The others looked back at him. St. John was grinning. In spite of his earlier sentiment to the contrary, Jamison appeared to be considering it. Like St. John, the olive-skinned Kevin Kimbreau had already made up his mind. He sipped his coffee and chewed his jerky, blinking dully at Nye.

"No, ~~goddamn~~ you!" Barstow said. "You can't leave me here to die! Ole Ed wouldn't o' left one o' his boys to die!"

"Champion's dead," St. John growled.

"Yeah, he's dead," Kimbreau agreed.

"Stupid asshole fouled up good and true,"

100

St. John continued. "He an' that damn kid. Liked to get us all kilt."

"~~Goddamn~~ you sons o' bitches!" Barstow raged. "You can't do this to me. Me and Ed — we was the ones who started this group in the first place! You can't leave me here to die!"

Ignoring his friend Barstow, Jamison turned to St. John. "That Russian and that bounty hunter — they're a tough tangle."

"So you're sayin' we should let 'em go?" Nye asked accusingly.

"Yes!" Barstow yelled.

Ignoring the wounded man, Jamison shrugged his shoulders.

"I say we get the Russian lady," Kimbreau said. He grabbed his crotch and flashed his big, white teeth, his green eyes flashing.

Barstow turned over on his side, grabbing his bleeding knee and panting. "You can't leave me," he intoned, his voice growing weaker.

"All right, we won't leave you," St. John said. Casually, the one-eyed Texan removed his revolver from his holster and hefted it in his hand. He glanced at Nye, who smiled agreeably. Then St. John thumbed back the Remington's hammer and extended the gun toward Barstow.

"Jesus, Bobby," Jamison cautioned.

Barstow turned to St. John. Seeing the gun, his eyes widened and flashed with terror. "No! What are you doin'?"

"Don't worry, Bar," St. John said. "We ain't gonna leave ye here. Leastways, not alive. I'll put a forty-five slug right between your eyes."

"Better move closer," Kimbreau advised. "Might hit his other knee." The mulatto grinned.

Jamison turned his face away, wagging his head. "Jesus Christ . . ."

"I can get him from here," St. John said as Barstow slid clumsily away, digging the heel of his good foot into the sandy ground and holding his arms over his face. He screamed and pleaded for his life.

"Put your ~~goddamn~~ hands down, Bar," St. John urged. "I can't get a clean shot with you waving your arms all over the damn place."

"Noooo!" cried Barstow.

St. John aimed down the Remington's barrel, his good eye hard as steel. Finally the gun jumped and barked. A neat round hole appeared in Barstow's forehead, above his right eye. Barstow collapsed, dead.

For several seconds silence hung heavy over the group as each man studied the dead Barstow, blood trickling from the neat hole a half inch above his half-open eye.

"Didn't get him between the eyes," Nye said. "Got him above the right eye."

"Yeah, you did, Bobby," Kimbreau agreed.

"He shut up, didn't he?" St. John growled, flipping the loading gate open and replacing the spent shell. "Get off your lazy asses," he ordered. "We got a coach to run down."

9

Prophet rode up to the stage station at nearly six-thirty that evening. Behind him clattered the stage coated with seeds and gray dust, the equally dust-coated Cossack smoking his cheroot in the driver's box.

As Prophet was climbing out of the saddle, a portly, gray-haired gent stepped from the cabin onto the rickety porch. He had large, rheumy eyes and a knob-shaped, pock-marked nose. He carried a double-barreled greener down low at his side.

To Prophet's left, the barn was quiet, its doors closed. From the log shed beside the barn rose the tinny barks of a blacksmith's hammer. Sooty black smoke poured from the shed's tin stovepipe, flattening out against the roof. In the corral directly across the trail from the cabin, a half-dozen horses hung their heads over the top rail and twitched their ears at the strangers.

"Evenin'," Prophet said to the man.

The portly gent was giving the stage the twice-over. "Ellison-Daniels Stage and Express Company?" he read, scowling.

"Private coach," Prophet said. "We were wondering if we might impose on you for the night."

"Whose coach?"

"The Countess Natasha Roskov," Sergei said from the driver's box, reins hanging loose in his gloved hands. His sunburned face was clay-colored by dust, as was his hat, a tan plainsman to which he'd switched when the weather got warmer.

"Countess?" the old man said, wrinkling one nostril. "What in hell's a countess?"

"A Russian noblewoman," Prophet answered for Sergei, just to keep things simple. "This is Sergei, uh —"

"Andreyevich," Sergei answered for Prophet, who had not yet mastered the pronunciation of the Cossack's last name. "I am the countess's assistant."

Prophet said, "We've all been on the trail for over a week and sure could use a bed and some table food."

The old man gave Sergei a slow, suspicious appraisal, then slid his eyes back to Prophet, studying the bounty hunter cautiously. "Who in the hell are you? You don't look like no Russian. Why you ridin' with them?"

"I'm their guide," Prophet said. "I'm friendly enough. Lou Prophet's my handle. If we can stay, say so, Mr. uh —"

"Fergus."

"Mr. Fergus. If no, we'll fog it on down the trail."

The man studied the coach, Sergei, and Prophet once more, twitching his bulb nose. He shrugged. "I reckon it'd be all right," the man grumbled. "I don't have another coach due for two days. I have five cots in the cabin and a couple more in the barn."

"There's just the three of us."

"It'll cost you three dollars apiece. That's including food and a bed with a pillow. Liquor is more."

"I have to tell you," Prophet said, "we may be trailed by long riders. We were attacked last night in our camp. I haven't seen any signs of them today, but I thought I'd warn you just the same. If you want us to keep ridin', say so."

"Long riders, eh?" the station agent said, flaring his nostrils. "Well, I've dealt with road agents before. Out here, they're a fact of life. That's why I keep a half dozen rifles loaded and this here greener by the door. Light and tend yourselves. There's a basin inside."

"Much obliged." Prophet started to climb out of his saddle. Sergei set the coach's brake.

The man called across the yard, "Timmy! Jimmy! Get out here and tend this team!"

Prophet glanced across the yard, where two men appeared in the open shed door, their faces and coveralls black with soot. They both wore visored caps, both were in their mid-sixties, and both were the spitting image of the other. Twins. Their identical faces were long and sallow, their eyes vaguely haunted in deep, wizened sockets. One held a long blacksmith's tongs in his right hand clad in leather gauntlets.

"That's Timmy and Jimmy Miller," the station agent said. "They're twins, in case you couldn't tell." He wheezed a laugh. "They'll take good care of your horses, but the feed'll cost you another dollar."

"Sounds fair," Prophet said.

"Will they groom their coats, sir?" Sergei asked the station agent.

Fergus had turned to the cabin door. Now he turned back with a surly frown. "I reckon they can groom 'em, for an extra dollar."

Sergei appeared about to argue. Not wanting the agent's feathers ruffled, Prophet cut him off. "That's right generous," he said, looping his reins over the hitch rack.

When he looked at the agent again, he saw that the man was frozen before the door, staring toward the coach, a curious light in his owly eyes. "Well, hello there," he said, a smile wrinkling his mouth.

Sergei had opened the coach door, and the countess was disembarking, one hand in Sergei's, the other bunching her skirts above her booties. She blinked her eyes against the dust that was still sifting around the coach. Her sleek, lacy traveling attire with plumed hat was nearly as dusty as Prophet's and the Cossack's garb; the coach's canvas shades did little to prevent dust from seeping in the windows.

"This is the Countess Roskov," Sergei said very formally, when the countess had planted both feet on the ground and was gently beating her dress with her gloves.

"Countess . . ." Fergus said wonderingly. "Well, that sounds some highfalutin, it does!"

When neither the countess nor Sergei joined in his laughter, the manager flushed and sobered. He gave his gaze to Prophet, who arched his eyebrows wryly.

Nervously rubbing his hands on his shirt, the manager said, "Well, it sure will be nice to have a woman in the place for a change. It's been a couple weeks now since me and the boys have seen a woman. Ain't many that travel this country, what with the road agents and Injuns."

"And you are . . . ?" the countess asked the man, daintily extending her hand.

"Oh, I'm Riley Fergus," the manager said, giving his right hand another wipe before giving the countess's a rough shake. "I'm the boss o' this here crew," he said, nodding at the hostlers taking the bays off the coach. "If you call two old French bachelors, a half-dozen cats, and a fat ole coyote-dog a crew, that is." He tipped his head back and guffawed, but Prophet saw his eyes roving the countess's dress.

Apparently, Sergei had seen Fergus's scrutiny of the countess, too. The big Russian cleared his throat and said, "The countess is tired, and we're all very hungry. . . ."

"Oh, yes, of course, of course," Riley Fergus said, clumsily opening the door and stepping back, grinning moronically while the countess and Sergei stepped into the cabin.

"After you," Prophet said, waving the manager in ahead of him. He didn't like giving his back to strangers. Besides, he wanted to take a look around the station, make sure they hadn't been followed. He stood on the porch until he heard the countess inhale sharply.

"What is it?" Prophet said, hurrying into the cabin, his hand on his Colt's butt.

The countess stood looking silently around, a hand drawn to her mouth in horror.

Prophet followed her gaze across the two rough-hewn tables littered with dirty plates, cups, food scraps, and cigarette and cigar butts. Two cats were eating off the tables. The benches were covered with torn clothing and leather gear from the barn, which was apparently in the process of being mended. Cobwebs hung from the low rafters. The place was a dump.

The only sign of civility was a half-dead African violet perched on a windowsill, in a cracked stone pot bleeding dirt.

A calico cat, sleeping on a stack of yellow newspapers behind the door, lifted its head to scrutinize the strangers. A few seconds later it went to work, languidly bathing its left front paw.

"What's the matter, ma'am?" Fergus asked, confused.

The countess spoke in Russian to Sergei, who merely shook his head. To the agent, he growled, "The countess was not prepared for such squalid lodgings."

Fergus glanced around the room.

"Squalid! What the hell do you mean, squalid? I reckon I ain't the best house-keeper in New Mexico, but I don't think it's fair, you callin' it squalid!"

"Easy, easy," Prophet said, placing a placating hand on the manager's shoulder. "The countess has had a long, hard pull. I'm sure she'll be as happy as a duck in a puddle once she gets some vittles in her."

"Squalid?" Fergus grumbled, casting his injured gaze around the room again. "This ain't New York City! Who do they think they are?"

Prophet urged the man toward the kitchen, slipping him a silver cartwheel to smooth his feathers. When the man returned with a coffeepot and three cups, he point-edly ignored the countess and Sergei and said to Prophet, "You'd think foreigners would know enough to mind their *p*'s and *q*'s over here, wouldn't you?"

When he went away, the countess leaned toward Prophet, eyes narrowed. "What are *p*'s and *q*'s?"

Prophet got his makings from his shirt pocket and sighed as he began building a smoke. "He means you ruffled his feathers."

"What is 'ruffled his feathers'?"

"Never mind," Prophet said, tired of trans-lating.

111

She tilted her long nose toward the ceiling. "I will sleep in the coach."

"I wouldn't do that. You're gonna pissburn the gent but good."

She frowned, staring at the bounty hunter. "What is — ?"

"Oh, give it a rest, will you?"

She gazed at him, hurt. "You are angry."

"I'm not angry," Prophet lied. "I'm just tired."

"I will get water for your cheek," the countess said, rising from the bench where they'd taken a seat.

"The cheek's fine," Prophet assured her.

Ignoring him, she walked into the kitchen part of the cabin and asked Riley Fergus for a bowl, water, and a clean cloth.

"Oh, you want a clean one, huh?" Fergus said indignantly. "Reckon you want it starched and ironed, too?"

When the countess finally had a bowl of water and a relatively clean cloth, she returned to the table and sat down beside Prophet. She soaked the rag in the basin, wrung it out, and dabbed at the cut.

Prophet jerked back.

"It hurts?"

Prophet nodded. "A little."

She smiled, faint lines forming at the corners of her slanted eyes, which were more lovely than Prophet had thought. He'd never seen them this close.

"I will be gentle," she said softly.

"Why, thank you, ma'am."

Prophet grinned a smoky grin and began rolling a cigarette from his makings sack. He spared a glance at Sergei. The Cossack was staring at him, a skeptical cast to his hide-brown eyes below his black, furrowed brow. He puffed his cheroot aggressively.

Prophet returned his gaze to the countess, who was wringing the rag out again in the basin.

"Protective, ain't he?"

The countess's eyes sparked as she smiled and dabbed again at Prophet's face. "My father trained him well."

"I reckon he had his reasons," Prophet said, sprinkling tobacco on the paper while keeping his chin raised for the countess. "Not the least of which was havin' a pretty daughter."

She looked shocked. "Mr. Prophet, was that a compliment?"

Sergei grunted under his breath, as though his cheroot had grown nasty. The countess ignored him.

Prophet shrugged and rolled the quirly closed. He poked the cigarette in his mouth, struck a match on the table, and fired the cigarette. He canted his head to one side and regarded the countess through slitted eyes.

She did not shy from the gaze, but returned it with a brash one of her own, lids drawn a third of the way down, her hand dabbing gently at the crusted blood on Prophet's face.

Prophet lowered his gaze to her smooth, creamy neck, then down her chest to her ample bosom pushing at her finely cut white basque. He dropped it still farther, to her thighs straddling the rough bench, her sage-green skirt drawn tight against their firm suppleness.

As he ran his eyes back the way they'd dropped, he thought he could hear a slight catch in her breathing. He saw she was still gazing bemusedly at him, apparently unoffended by the scrutiny. In fact, it seemed to warm her cheeks, evoke a sheen on her brow.

The look stirred him, and to distract himself, he said, "Didn't figure you to play nursemaid."

She shrugged, licked her lips, taking awhile to answer. "I guess I just tired of seeing blood on your face. You said it was nothing."

"It is nothing."

"You could get infection. Then what would you do?"

"I got a strong constitution," Prophet said, inhaling deeply on his cigarette.

She withdrew the rag and gazed at her handiwork. She pursed her lips, pleased, then returned her sultry gaze to his. "I believe you do, at that."

Prophet's throat constricted with desire, and to temper it, he drew deep on the quirly and turned away from both her and the Cossack, whose eyes Prophet could feel boring into him.

She was wringing the cloth out in the bowl when Prophet heard a low whine. Suddenly Sergei leaped from the bench and grabbed the LeMatt from his holster. Prophet froze, thinking the Russian was going to beef him.

"Wolf!" the Cossack cried.

Prophet whipped his head to the door. A dog — or was it a coyote? — stood in the open doorway, hanging its head and looking in expectantly, wagging its brushy tail. Its bushy, burr-ridden coat was mottled gray, its nose long and sleek.

"No, no!" Fergus shouted. "That's ole Miguel, my ole coyote-dog. Raised him from a pup after I found him down by my trash hole one day, all by his lonesome."

The agent whistled. "Come on, Miguel.

Get your treat!"

The coyote padded through the door, its fat gut jouncing. Its toenails clicked on the wood puncheons as it entered the kitchen, where Riley Fergus bent over, a scrap of raw meat hanging from his mouth.

The coyote sat back on its hindquarters, raised its long, pointed snout, and gently took the meat in its teeth. Eyes bright with bliss, the coyote packed the meat quickly to the door and outside.

The station manager guffawed. "He just loves that trick, Miguel does!"

"What a hellish place this country is," the countess whispered, a hand to her chest. "They let wild animals eat from their mouths!"

Prophet was just finishing his cigarette when the sullen station manager brought three bowls of stew to the table. At least he called it stew. It looked like a few white disks of meat boiled in water with a smidgeon of rice. The biscuits were hard and stale.

"What is this, Mr. Prophet?" the countess asked quietly, so the manager couldn't hear.

"Stew," Prophet replied, just as quietly.

"I mean, what is the meat?" She poked at it with her spoon.

"Oh, that . . . that's rabbit," Prophet lied. He knew rattlesnake when he saw it in his bowl. It didn't bother him; hell, it had been a fast, easy meal for him many times in the past. He had a feeling the countess wouldn't approve, however.

"Oh, rabbit," she said. "I love rabbit." She spooned one of the disks in her mouth, chewed slowly, and nodded. "It is good."

Prophet eased a relieved sigh through his lips.

When they were through with the main meal, the station manager served apricot cobbler and coffee. The dessert wasn't half bad, Prophet judged, and the countess and Sergei appeared to agree, for they cleaned their plates. Nothing like traveling to make a man — or woman — hungry.

They were just finishing when the two old-timers, Timmy and Jimmy, came in, sat down at the other long table, rolled cigarettes, and broke out a deck of cards. They didn't say a word to each other or anyone else, giving all their attention to their cards and cigarettes. Occasionally the station manager wandered over to refill their cups.

After a while the coyote wandered in, a half-eaten rabbit in its teeth, and lay down by the fire in the stone hearth. It plopped one paw over the rabbit, rested its snout on the paw, and went to sleep with a weary groan. The cats were lounging here and there; one was eating a food scrap under the table.

"I believe I will retire now," the countess said, raking her dismayed gaze around the room and rising.

When she'd retreated to one of the cots and had drawn the blanket, partitioning herself off from the rest of the room, Prophet asked the station agent if he knew of an Arizona town called Broken Knee.

The agent ceased scrubbing a pan at the range and turned to Prophet, frowning. Prophet noticed that the twins jerked startled looks at him, as well.

"Broken Knee?" the manager said.

"That's where we're headed."

"What in the hell you want to go there for? Nothin' but cutthroats in that place. Cutthroats and Leamon Gay's men. One and the same thing."

Prophet considered the information and glanced at Sergei, who arched an eyebrow at him. The Cossack was drinking another cup of coffee and smoking another of his black cheroots. He'd loosened his shirt collar, and his chest hair was nearly as thick and black as his well-groomed goatee and mustache.

"Who is this, uh, Leamon Gay?" Sergei asked, taking the question right out of

Prophet's mouth.

"Nothin' but an owlhoot, through an' through. Used to hunt Indian scalps and sell 'em down in Mexico. Then he'd steal horses from the ranchos down there and smuggle 'em into Arizona, sell 'em to American ranchers. Used to steal arms from the Army and sell 'em to the tribes."

Prophet asked, "What's he have to do with Broken Knee?"

"A few years ago a man found gold in the Pinaleno Mountains. The prospector ended up dead — a so-called *accident,* if ye savvy my drift. All of a sudden Gay moves into the area with a hundred or so wagon loads of hard-rock miners and whores and builds him a town. Only it's his town, run his way, or he chisels ye a tombstone!"

One of the twins piped up, growling low, "Many a man, he goes to Broken Knee" — the twin ran a long, gnarled finger across his throat — "and is never seen again."

Prophet winced and glanced at the other twin, who corroborated the story with a dark nod, drawing deep on his quirly stub.

"I've heard tell," Riley Fergus said, "that Gay's responsible for the deaths of more than fifty men."

"Hellkatoot!" Prophet grunted, suddenly wondering what he'd gotten himself into.

"You folks don't want nothin' to do with him or Broken Knee, and they're one and the same thing. He's the devil, and it's the devil's town."

"We do not have a choice," Sergei said, consternation straining his voice. "We are looking for the countess's sister. The last the countess heard from her, Marya was in Broken Knee."

Fergus shielded his mouth with his hand, so the countess couldn't hear from her cot behind the blankets. "She a whore?"

Sergei looked angry but kept his voice down. "She certainly is not."

"Then what's she doin' in Broken Knee?"

"We think she might be lookin' for gold," Prophet said. Before Fergus could ask another question, Prophet asked one of his own. "What's the best way to get there?"

"There ain't no best way," Fergus said. "I reckon I'd go south through Lordsburg, though, and take Pyramid Mountain Pass. Then trail north along the San Simon River. With that coach you don't have much choice. Watch for Apaches, though. Ole Cochise ain't actin' up now like he was a year ago, but I'd still grow eyes in the back o' my head and do a lot of my travelin' at night. Should be a full moon soon. Apaches won't attack at night."

"Thanks for the advice," Prophet said, inwardly cursing the Russians again for not taking the train. Apaches rarely attacked trains. Stretching, he stood. "I reckon I'll keep first watch on the porch," he told Sergei.

"That sounds good, my friend," the Cossack said. "I'll take over in a couple of hours."

"You still expectin' those highwaymen?" Fergus asked Prophet. The station manager had gone back to scrubbing his pan.

"Have to," the bounty hunter said as he headed for the door. "That way we'll be ready if they come."

"Well, if they come, they'll be sorry. They might not look like much, but Timmy and Jimmy, they'll back you in a fight any day of the week, and by god, there'll be hell to pave and no hot pitch!"

Prophet glanced at the wizened old pair, over which a cloud of cigarette smoke hung, thick as twister dust. Nearby, ole Miguel, the fat coyote-dog, snored with one paw on the rabbit. The cat behind the door rolled onto its back, kicked its feet in the air, and yawned.

"That's right comforting," Prophet said, sharing a rueful glance with Sergei.

He went outside and led Mean and Ugly

off to the corral. Back outside, rifle beside him, he sat on the porch and rolled a smoke. He was thinking of the long ride he had ahead of him through hostile territory, wishing he'd never run into the Russians in Denver. But then he thought of the countess's bold gaze meeting his, and of her swelling bosom and flushed cheeks, and he felt a little better. . . .

10

To Prophet's relief, the night passed un-eventfully. In the morning he and the Rus-sians sat down to breakfast feeling relatively fresh.

It had been nice not sleeping on the ground for a change, and Prophet suspected that, while she never would have admitted it, the countess had enjoyed a night away from the coach's cramped quarters and lumpy leather seats. Fergus's cots hadn't been bad.

The same did not go for his breakfast, however. The eggs were too runny, the biscuits were burned, and the venison sausage tasted gamy as week-old deer liver, as though the station manager had aged the carcass too long in the sun. Prophet didn't say anything, however, and was happy that the Russians didn't, either. They appeared to be acquiring the humbling art of humil-ity, though they didn't clean their plates —

a transgression which would have made Prophet's mama scowl.

Just after sunrise Timmy and Jimmy harnessed the bays to the coach, and Prophet and the Russians were off, the fat coyote giving the coach's wheels a parting bark and nip. Prophet waved at Riley Fergus standing on his dilapidated porch, then cantered ahead of the coach to scout the trail. He figured their attackers of the night before last had given up on them, but it never paid to let your guard down.

In the coach Natasha Roskov rummaged around in several carpetbags until she found her silver cigarette case. Sitting back in her seat, she adjusted the pillow cushioning her back, opened the case, and removed one of the yellow French cigarettes she loved so well. Sticking the cigarette between her unpainted lips — what good did it do to wear face paint when dust covered it all, anyway? — she struck a match.

Before she could touch the flame to the cigarette, an arm snaked out of the luggage boot behind her. She gave a start, dropping the match, which died. Before she could cry out, the hand slapped tightly over her mouth and jerked her head back brusquely against the seat.

"Do you want to die, my lovely?" came a

man's low, breathy voice in her right ear. The hot breath smelled sour. Rolling her eyes around, heart pounding, neck aching, feeling as though she were suffocating, the countess saw the grinning visage of a savage-looking man wearing a black eye patch.

"Do you?" he asked again, tightening his grip on her mouth and bringing a wide-bladed, blood-crusted knife to her throat. She squeezed her eyes closed and ground her teeth together as she felt the razor-sharp blade slice slowly into her neck.

Prophet was on his second scouting trip of the morning when he swung left off the trail, keeping an eye skinned on the terrain around him while watching for horse tracks and other signs of recent riders.

It was a stark, beautiful country they were traversing now, heading south through New Mexico on their way to Lordsburg. The rolling plain was covered with buffalo grass with occasional cedars and greasewood thickets dotting the swales. The benches were spiked with Spanish bayonet, or yucca. In the west rose the velvety slopes of the Chuska Mountains, their higher peaks stippled with cedars and pines.

Prophet had visited this country several times, on quests for badmen and to escape the northern winters. Still, smelling the greasewood and tangy sage, and seeing this majestic landscape again swept with purple cloud shadows, his heart grew light. It was cold, though, with a bite to the piney breeze, and he raised the collar of his sheepskin and swung Mean and Ugly back north.

Suddenly he stopped and stared downward. Fresh hoofprints pocked the sandy, sage-tufted ground.

Frowning, lifting his head to scan the distance, then returning his eyes to the prints, he gigged Mean ahead, following the prints. They led into a shallow, rocky arroyo — a good place to get drygulched.

Prophet was just releasing the thong over his .45's hammer when two horseback riders rode out from behind a boulder. Prophet reined Mean to a halt and grabbed the butt of his revolver, but froze when one of the men said, "Unh-unh. Don't do it, *amigo*. Less you wanna die quick."

He was a big, dark-skinned man with a helmet of tight, curly black hair lying close to his scalp, under a wide-brimmed, dust-colored hat pushed back off his forehead. His eyes were green. He was holding a side-hammered saddlegun in one hand, aimed at Prophet's belly.

The other man was somewhat smaller

than the mulatto, with a wispy blond mustache and greasy, sandy hair spilling out from under his curl-brimmed hat. A white man, he wore a Mexican poncho, and two tied-down Colts with ivory grips. One of the Colts was in his hand, the polished gunmetal winking in the bright sun.

Prophet raised his hands halfheartedly, squinting against the sun, which the men had been shifty enough to get behind them. Prophet didn't say anything. Neither did the others for several seconds. Then the mulatto stretched a grin, flashing big teeth with a gap in the right side of his mouth.

"My friend, Prophet. Don't you remember me?"

Prophet studied him.

The mulatto, whose name Prophet remembered was Kevin Kimbreau, chuckled. "Oh, yeah, you remember."

"Remember what?" Kimbreau's partner asked him.

Kimbreau nodded at Prophet, his grin dying on his lips. "He run me down in a little roadhouse in Wyoming last year. Found me drunk after a night o' whorin'. Slapped the shackles on me and took me to see the judge in Whitestone."

"They shoulda stretched your neck, Kevin," Prophet said, canting his head so his hat brim blocked the sun, "for what you did to that poor schoolteacher and that kid."

"They were going to," Kimbreau said, laughing. "Had the gallows all built and everything. Then I tunneled out. Killed a farmer and stole his horse." He grinned crazily at Prophet, taunting him. "Cut his throat."

"That wasn't nice."

"Look who's talkin' nice. You wasn't nice, sneakin' up on me like that, then punchin' me after you had me shackled."

"You tried to make a run for it."

"I don't cotton to bein' punched, 'specially by a stinkin' Rebel."

Kimbreau's friend said, "Just shoot the son of a bitch."

"Maybe he'd like to punch me," Prophet said. "Is that it, Kevin? You wanna fight with fists?" Prophet smiled a challenge, buying time as well as an edge.

"Sounds good to me," Kimbreau said. He tossed his reins to the other man and slipped easily out of his saddle. "Make me feel real good to beat the holy hell out of you, Reb. Then I'm gonna go get me some o' that Russian gal." He lifted his carbine toward Prophet again and said, with all humor wrung from his flat-featured face, "Get off that there ugly horse and take off your gunbelt."

"Now, you can insult me all you want, Kevin, but it piss-burns me good when I hear my poor, defenseless horse slammed," Prophet said, his wry tone belying his concern for the countess and Sergei. He had a feeling the other cutthroats in the gang had stopped the stage. "He can't help how he looks." With no quick movements, Prophet dismounted, dropped his reins, and unbuckled his cartridge belt.

"Toss it over there," Kimbreau ordered.

Prophet tossed the cartridge belt with gun and bowie knife several feet to his right. "Now what about your own belt?" he asked Kimbreau.

"You ain't exactly in any position to set terms, are you?"

Prophet shrugged regretfully and fashioned a lopsided grin. "I reckon not."

Kimbreau tossed his carbine to his partner, who smiled over the neck of his buckskin horse, enjoying the show. Leaving his cartridge belt on his hips, Kimbreau shucked off his hat and buffalo coat, and rolled up his shirtsleeves. Meanwhile, Prophet removed his own hat and coat.

Kimbreau stepped forward and raised his mallet-sized fists, grinning. "This is sure gonna be fun."

Prophet stepped forward and raised his own fists. He and the mulatto circled each other several times. Prophet jabbed the air, feinting, shuffling his feet and staring deep into Kimbreau's eyes. The mulatto followed in a circle, feinting and jabbing, as though testing the air between them.

Kimbreau grinned. "You gonna throw a punch or just dance?"

"Well, I reckon," Prophet said. He stepped toward the big mulatto, bringing his right arm back as if for a haymaker. He checked the swing, stopped, and lifted his right boot instead, bringing it up and forward with venom, soundly burying the toe in Kimbreau's crotch.

The mulatto bent forward, wailing and covering his crotch with his forearms.

"Why, you — !" Kimbreau's partner raged.

"Sorry, Kevin, but I don't have time for a fair fight," Prophet said.

Before the man could level his six-shooter, Prophet reached behind his head for the Arkansas toothpick he wore in a slender sheath down his back. He sent the wicked-looking weapon tumbling end over end until the rider's chest impeded its flight, swallowing it right up to its leather-wrapped hilt.

The rider dropped his Colt and grabbed at the toothpick with both hands, grunting and cursing and trying to dislodge the weapon from his breastbone.

Meanwhile, Prophet swung his leg toward Kimbreau again, bringing the toe of his boot up savagely to the underside of Kimbreau's chin. The raging mulatto flew backward with another deafening cry and hit the ground on his back. He lay there like a landed fish, his neck broken, kicking his feet and swiping a hand toward the six-shooter on his hip.

Knowing he needed to hurry — the countess and Sergei were no doubt under attack by the other hardcases — Prophet stooped to grab his gun from his holster and shot the mulatto twice in the chest. He looked at Kimbreau's partner, who still sat his buckskin horse stiffly, both hands wrapped around the handle of Prophet's Arkansas toothpick, the poncho around the buried blade slick with gushing blood.

The light was leaving the man's eyes as his head fell slowly to his chest.

"If you'll excuse me," Prophet said, reaching up and yanking the knife from the man's chest, "I gotta run."

When he'd cleaned the blade on the man's denim-clad thigh, Prophet ran to Mean and Ugly and mounted up. He galloped off, hearing the thud of Kimbreau's partner hitting the ground.

Prophet had just spurred Mean into a wind-splitting gallop when several pistol and rifle shots echoed in the north, back where the stage would be. The bounty hunter cursed and spurred Mean even faster, hoping he wouldn't be too late to lend Sergei a hand.

But then the shooting stopped, an eerie silence descended, and Prophet had a bad feeling. . . .

He rode to the base of a stony ridge, swung down from the saddle, and shucked his Winchester '73. He scrambled up the ridge, using his hands to push himself up the steep incline, slipping several times in the shale. Near the top, he doffed his hat, then crawled to the ridge, easing a look over the lip and down the other side.

He drew his lips back from his teeth when he saw the stage halted on the trail below, behind the four sweat-shiny bays. One man in trail garb stood around Sergei, who was on his knees, one hand extended for support. The Cossack's bare head was tipped toward the ground. His free hand clutched his side, dark with blood, as was his right shoulder.

Holding a rifle in the crook of his arm, the hardcase was smoking and grinning up at the stage roof, where another man was cutting the ropes securing the Russians' luggage to the brass rails. Prophet couldn't see the countess, but he heard her screaming in Russian from inside the coach, which rocked and shivered and caused the bays to look back at it, ears twitching. One of them whinnied.

Sergei lifted his head and turned toward the coach. "Countess!" he shouted. The hardcase stepped toward him and casually swung his rifle butt against the Cossack's head, laying Sergei out on his back.

"You sons o' bitches," Prophet growled.

He levered a round in the Winchester's chamber, rested the barrel on the lip of the ridge, and planted a bead on the man nearest Sergei. He fired, and the bullet took the man through the back of his head, throwing him forward, limbs akimbo.

The man atop the stage looked up, clawing at the revolver on his hip. Prophet squeezed the Winchester's trigger. The man flew backward off the roof with a clipped shriek.

The Winchester's two reports echoed as one around the narrow canyon in which the stage was stopped. The echo finally died as Prophet hurried down the other side of the ridge, arms thrust out for balance.

He realized someone was screaming.

He'd just bottomed out on the canyon floor when a man burst through the stage door. He wore a patch over his right eye, and he clutched the other eye now with his hands. Blood was oozing from that eye and streaming down his face.

"You whore!" he raged. "You blinded me, you whore!"

He cursed and cried as he danced around blindly, clutching what had been his one good eye. Finally he stopped, clawed his revolver from his cross-draw holster and squeezed off two shots, swinging the gun around, trying to get his bearings.

"You whore! You blinded me, you ~~god-damn~~ *whore!*"

He was about to squeeze off a third shot when Prophet jacked a round, lifted the rifle to his cheek, and shot the man through the neck. The blinded hardcase flew off his feet and landed hard on his back. He gurgled and spat for several more seconds before his limbs relaxed and he gave a long, final sigh.

Prophet heard the thoroughbraces groan, and turned to the stage. The countess stood crouched in the doorway, her torn basque covered in blood, her cheeks smeared. In her hand she held a small dagger. From the slender blade, blood strung to the ground.

Seeing Sergei, she dropped the dagger, jumped to the ground, and ran to the Cossack who lay unconscious on his back.

"Sergei!" she cried. "Oh, Sergei — please don't die!"

11

Prophet made sure all the attackers were dead, then hurried over to Sergei, who was conscious now and groaning painfully as the countess knelt beside him, squeezing his hand and begging him not to die.

"Let me have a look," Prophet said as he knelt across from the countess and inspected the Russian's wounds.

"How does it look?" Sergei asked, lifting his head to study the blood on his shirt.

"I've seen worse," Prophet said. "The one in the shoulder doesn't look too bad; the bullet must have gone straight through. But there's one down low here in your side. It'll have to come out pronto."

The countess groaned, her face bleached with worry. Sergei squeezed her hand.

"Come out?" Sergei blinked at Prophet, groggy but dubious. "What do you mean it will have to come out?"

"Just what I said. Don't worry, I'm no

sawbones, but I've mixed lead before."

He told the countess to gather wood and build a fire. "I'm going to get my horse." He had a good surgical knife in his saddlebags, plus a bottle of whiskey.

"The countess does not build fires," Sergei objected as Prophet stood and started up the ridge for his horse.

"Oh, Serge, shut up!" the countess retorted, worry quaking her voice. "I can build a fire as well as any Cossack!"

In spite of the circumstances, Prophet grinned as he climbed the ridge, slipping and clawing at sage tufts.

When he'd led Mean and Ugly to the canyon floor, the countess had a small fire burning not far from Sergei, whose head now rested on a red satin pillow the countess had apparently retrieved from the coach. Prophet didn't like the Cossack's pale features and dilated pupils — he'd obviously lost a lot of blood and was probably in shock — but Sergei managed some wrath.

"Russian royalty does not build campfires!"

"Out here everyone is equal," Prophet said as he knelt down by the fire and spread out his possibles bag. "That's what I like about the frontier."

The countess fed a slender branch to the

growing flame she'd coaxed to life using pine cones and dead grass. "I am not as spoiled as you have tried to spoil me, Serge," she said, lifting her long straight nose as she babied the guttering fire.

Prophet smiled thinly as he knelt beside the Cossack and produced a slender skinning knife from an oiled leather sheath that bore a small silver disk in which the Southern cross had been engraved. The sheath had been with him since the war. He swept the blade through the fire several times, then offered Sergei a bottle and a chunk of rawhide.

"There you go, Serge. Take you a few drinks of that busthead there, and bite down on that leather when I start cuttin'."

"What does the leather do?" the countess asked, moving near to inspect the procedure.

"It will keep me from shattering my teeth when I lock my jaws," the Cossack growled. He grabbed Prophet's forearm in his meaty fist and heaved up off his shoulders, giving the bounty hunter a sinister glare. "If I die, it will be your duty to protect the countess from any and all evils she may encounter on your precious frontier. Do you hear?"

"I understand," Prophet said with a solemn nod.

"And keep your lusty frontiersman's hands off of her!"

Prophet nodded again, slipping the countess a furtive grin. "I'll give it my best shot, ole hoss."

Releasing Prophet's arm, the Cossack collapsed with a sigh and a groan. Panting, he said, "All right, cut away if you must." He shuttled his gaze to the countess. "Do not worry, *ma chèrie.* I am not going to leave you. I just wanted him to understand . . . as a precaution."

The countess nodded, her face in her hands, her frightened eyes peering at Sergei through her fingers.

Prophet cut the Cossack's shirt away from the wound.

"You ready, Russian?" he asked, his knife poised above the bloody wound from which dark blood bubbled.

Sergei bit down on the leather and tipped his head back. He gave the countess a comforting wink and said tightly, "Yes, American, I am ready."

Prophet probed the wound with his knife and fingers. Sweat popped out on Sergei's forehead. The Cossack grunted and cursed while biting down on the leather. The countess held his head in her hands, watching with a strained expression as Prophet poked around in Sergei's side, feeling for the slug.

Finally he felt his knife tip nick something solid that did not feel like bone. Wincing, he worked his right index finger and knife point around it, and pulled. He lost it, retrieved it, and carefully slid the bullet out the entrance hole.

"Got it."

Sergei lifted his head and gazed blearily at the bloody bullet in Prophet's fingers. He nodded. "So you did. And without killing me. Surprising . . ."

The Russian's lids slid down over his eyes, and his muscles relaxed. He passed out, his face and hair drenched with sweat.

"That's gratitude for you," Prophet groused, flipping the bullet into the brush.

"It is over?" the countess asked.

"My part's about done, anyway," Prophet said, threading a needle from his sewing pouch. "I reckon he'll be out for a while. That bullet was damn deep. We'll stay here for a time, give him time to rest."

The countess peered into the unconscious Sergei's passive, sweat-beaded face. "Will he live?" she asked softly.

"Hard to tell. I'll know better in a few hours."

"You have done this before."

"A few times, during the war. There weren't many surgeons on our side. If you wanted your friends to live, you had to doctor them yourself."

"Thank you for saving Sergei," the countess said, turning her moist brown eyes on Prophet and wrapping her trembling fingers around his arm. "I do not know what I would do without him." Her previous snobbery was gone. In its place was humility and genuine gratitude. Prophet thought it looked good on her.

"I haven't saved him yet," he said. With a reassuring smile, he added, "But I'll do everything I can."

Prophet moved the stage off the main trail. He hid it behind rocks up the canyon, near a runout spring, and picketed the bays there, as well.

He hadn't wanted to move Sergei before, but now that his wounds were tightly stitched and wrapped, Prophet rigged a travois using rawhide straps and canvas. He eased the Russian off the trail, into a pocket of shrubs and deep grass surrounded by boulders. There he made a soft bed of pine boughs and grass, and the countess covered the Cossack with a heavy blanket from the coach.

Prophet considered returning to the stage station, only a few miles away, but nixed the idea. He doubted Sergei could ride even that far. Besides, the Cossack would be nearly as comfortable in the coach as on one of Fergus's cots.

Prophet buried the dead hardcases in shallow graves, well away from the campsite. His next chore was to picket Mean and Ugly near the bays, though far enough away that Mean couldn't pick any fights.

By the time the sun had started falling, Prophet and the countess had settled in to wait for Sergei's fever to break. Prophet didn't dare move him far until he'd recovered some strength and had made up for his blood loss.

"What happened?" Prophet asked the countess as he washed from a wood basin near the fire. It was the first time he'd mentioned the attack directly.

She was sitting beside Sergei, whose head was resting on the red pillow. She'd drawn a blanket around her shoulders. There was a forlorn, worried cast to her staring eyes.

Slowly she said, "One of the men was in the coach. In the luggage boot. He held a knife to my neck and made me order Sergei to stop. When the coach stopped, Sergei climbed down to see what was wrong, and two of the riders shot him as they rode out from the rocks along the trail. Then the other man, the one-eyed man, took me back into the coach . . ." Her jaws grew taut and her face flushed with anger as she remembered. "They didn't give Sergei a chance."

"No, they wouldn't have." Prophet told her about the other two who had followed him away from the stage. "They wanted to separate us."

"They must have wanted us pretty badly, no?"

Prophet nodded.

He saw no reason to add that it had been her they'd wanted, specifically, as well as any valuables she was carrying. He figured she knew that much, and that a rig like this, carrying only two people and half a ton of steamer trunks, was bound to draw attention. No use getting fresh about it again. It was her way, however asinine to him. He hadn't had to take the job, but now that he had, he couldn't quit. Finishing jobs he started, the circumstances be damned, was his way.

"Are you . . . okay?" he asked her timidly.

"He did not rape me," she told Prophet, gazing at him with candor. "But he would have if you had not shown up when you did. And Sergei would be dead. . . ."

Prophet toweled his face dry and donned his hat. "I'm just sorry I didn't check the stage out before you boarded. I should have been expecting something like that."

"You can't think of everything, Mr. Prophet." It was the first time he'd seen what passed for a smile on her face in hours. "You are a good man to have around, as they say, in a fight."

Prophet grunted self-deprecatingly and poured a cup of coffee.

They sat around the fire for the rest of the night, the countess swabbing Sergei's sweat-burning face with a wet cloth, Prophet changing the bloody dressings every few hours.

They were sitting there the next night and the next night, too.

Finally the Cossack drifted back to consciousness the following morning, looking sheepish about how long he'd slept and asking for food. The Russian's appetite was a good sign, Prophet figured, and the countess fed him several spoonfuls of oatmeal, which he promptly vomited and then apologized for vomiting.

"Don't be silly, Serge," the countess said.

"A Cossack doesn't vomit in the presence of women," Sergei growled.

"What's wrong with that?" Prophet said,

trying to lighten the mood. "American bounty hunters do it all the time."

They let the Russian doze the rest of the day. The next morning Prophet decided Sergei was ready to ride in the coach, on the countess's bed. After dousing the breakfast fire and situating Sergei in the coach, Prophet tied Mean to the luggage boot and climbed into the driver's box.

"You know how to drive this thing, Lou?" Sergei called up from inside the coach.

"Well, if it was a six-mule team, I might have a problem," Prophet called back. "But since it's just these four bays, I reckon I can keep us on the trail. Hold on. You ready, Countess?"

"Ready, Mr. Prophet."

"Lou."

"Pardon?"

"Thought we agreed to first names?" Prophet released the brake and turned the bays onto the trail.

"Oh, yes," the countess called. "Lou."

"When did you agree to first names?" Sergei asked suspiciously.

"Never mind, Russian," Prophet said.

He grinned and clucked the bays into a trot.

Slowly the coach wound its way south

through New Mexico, avoiding the major mountain ranges. Just as slowly, Sergei regained his strength, until he was finally able to sit up.

That night he insisted he sleep on the ground, vacating the coach for the countess. Prophet figured that sleeping in the coach while a woman slept outside was just too much for the Cossack's pride to bear any longer.

Several days later, near the Arizona border, they stopped for the night in the yard of an adobe trading post run by a fat Mexican and his two buxom daughters, Nedra and Paulina. The man, whose name was Juan Santos, was a sloppy, good-natured gent who welcomed the company to his lonely outpost by roasting a whole javelina over an outdoor fire.

The daughters were pretty and smoky-eyed if a little heavy in the hips. Paulina hovered around Sergei during the meal, which they ate at a rough-hewn table near the fire. The girl was obviously enamored of the big Cossack, whose accent and military bearing she found amusing.

Several times she asked Sergei if she could caress his goatee, for she'd never seen one so thick and black and neatly trimmed. While Prophet had seen the Cossack appraising the girl lustily, he denied her request, flushing with embarrassment.

"If you want to sleep with one of my daughters, or even both," Juan Santos told the Cossack as he sipped from his wineglass, "it will cost you only one dollar for the oldest, Paulina, and two dollars for Nedra."

Prophet and the countess glanced at Sergei. The countess arched her eyebrows. Prophet grinned and nudged the Cossack with an elbow.

Formal as always, Sergei cleared his throat and lowered his eyes to his plate. "Uh . . . no. I thank you, sir."

Across the table the girls squealed with laughter.

Later that night, drunk on the Mexican's wine, Prophet and Sergei sacked out in the adobe barn while the countess made her bed, as usual, in the coach. Prophet had just drifted off to sleep despite the bleating goats, when he heard rustling near him in the stall which he and the Cossack shared. Moonlight slanted through the crumbling adobe walls, revealing the Cossack bent over and quietly stepping into his boots.

A few seconds later Sergei donned his hat, went to the barn's main door, opened it quietly, and stepped out. He closed the door softly behind him.

Prophet bit his cheek, curious. Where in the hell was the Russian off to? He wouldn't have needed his boots and hat just to relieve himself.

His curiosity getting the best of him, as well as his suspicions, Prophet went to the door and cracked it. Sergei was walking toward the trading post huddled in the moonlight, the milky light reflecting off the brush arbor out front. Nearby, the cookfire sputtered and sighed as it died.

Sergei mounted the porch steps and slipped furtively into the cabin.

"Well, I'll be damned," Prophet said through a grin. "He's going after that pretty Mex girl. Or both of 'em." Prophet's grin widened as he stared at the dark trading post and shook his head. "That Russian dog."

Then a thought occurred to him. He turned his gaze right, where the coach sat before the brush corral in which their horses as well as several of Santos's cayuses milled. The stage was dark, which meant the countess had finished her nightly reading and gone to bed.

Prophet grabbed his hat from the stall and dressed in his jeans. Bare-chested and -footed, he left the barn and headed for the coach, avoiding the chicken and goat dung littering the hay-strewn yard.

He tapped on the coach door.

No answer.

He tapped harder. "Countess?"

Rustling sounded within; the thorough-braces squawked as the coach rocked slightly. "What is it? Who is there?"

"The tooth fairy."

"Lou? What do you want?"

"Same thing you want."

Prophet opened the door and climbed into the coach. He pulled the door closed behind him. Then he turned to where he could vaguely see the dark shape of the countess reclining on her bed heaped with tasseled pillows and gold-trimmed blankets.

He sat on the edge of the bed and began removing his jeans, an awkward maneuver in such close quarters.

"What are you . . . what are you doing?" the countess asked with quiet bewilderment.

"I'm about to give you what you been wantin' and I been needin'," Prophet said with a grunt as he finally got his left leg free of the jeans. He turned to the countess. "Slide over."

"You are drunk."

"I been drunker. Slide over."

She didn't say anything for several seconds. Then she whispered, "Where is Sergei?"

"In the trading post."

"What?" It sounded like she was smiling.

"He went to visit those Mexican gals, I reckon. I think we'll be safe for a little while."

"Lou Prophet, what makes you think you can barge your way into a lady's boudoir and order her to make love with you?"

"The way you're lookin' at me now," he said, standing nude before the bed. He grinned. His eyes had adjusted to the darkness inside the coach, and he saw her smile.

"You could take off your hat," she said, throwing the blanket back and sliding over a few inches.

Prophet tossed his hat away with a quiet victory whoop and crawled into the bed. He wasted no time peeling the straps of her nightgown down her shoulders, planting his lips on her round breasts, and kissing the stiffening nipples hungrily.

She stifled a scream, throwing her head back, shivering beneath his touch, rubbing her hands brusquely through his hair.

He massaged and kissed her breasts and ran his tongue down her legs, pausing to explore her nooks and crannies, taking his time. When she fairly growled with passion and kicked the nightgown away, he mounted her and nuzzled her neck. She clutched at his back with her arms and legs and groaned as he entered her, mumbling something he thought was Russian though he wasn't paying much attention to anything but their ravenous coupling.

This was a hungry woman — a Russian thoroughbred — who hadn't had a man in a long time. As the thoroughbraces rocked beneath him, he had a feeling he wouldn't be leaving the coach anytime soon . . . and that didn't bother him a bit.

The next couple of hours passed as if in a heady, erotic dream. Then he slept like the dead, the countess's long, sweaty limbs entwined with his.

When he opened his eyes, it was still dark. He heard the thoroughbraces creak and realized what had awakened him. The countess was kneeling before the window facing the trading post, peering through the half-raised shade. Her hair fell down her slender back.

He was reaching out to run his fingers lightly down her spine to her buttocks, when she turned her head sharply toward him.

"Sergei," she said, her whisper shrill with alarm. "He is coming!"

"Huh?" Prophet said, blinking groggily as

151

he gently massaged her smoothly curving hip. "So?"

"Please, Lou — you must go!"

"Hey, we're all grown-ups here, ain't we?"

"No, you do not understand," she said, tugging on his arm. "My mother made Sergei promise to keep me chaste until I married. He must kill any man who dishonors me!"

"Oh, shit." What was it with Russians and honor? Prophet jumped up, grabbed his clothes, and scrambled out the door. Keeping the coach between himself and the trading post, he ran through the corral and entered the barn through the rear door.

The startled goats bleated and kicked their stalls as Prophet jogged, wearing only his hat and clutching his jeans in his arms, to the stall containing his bedroll.

Outside, Sergei glanced at the stage, dark under a milky sheen of moonlight on its roof. The countess slept peacefully. Sergei smiled. In spite of the ache of his healing bullet wound, aggravated by the rambunctious Mexican girls, he felt not only content but fulfilled. The images of the two lovely señoritas danced in his head as they had danced over and under him for the past two hours — all breasts and hair and legs and lips — while Juan Carlos snored in his lean-to room off the kitchen.

The Cossack had always thought the women of his own blood were the most bewitching lovers, but he didn't mind giving credit where credit was due. A Mexican girl could, as they said out here in the West, "haul his ashes" anytime.

He paused to scrutinize the coach, remembering that, in his desire, he had left the countess and Lou Prophet unattended. Shame pricked at the Cossack. Who knows what the American bounty hunter might have tried in his absence. Remembering the oath he had sworn to the countess's mother, he listened for telltale noises within the coach. Hearing nothing, he strode quickly to the barn. If Prophet was not in the barn, where Sergei had left him . . .

Jaws clenched tightly and his blood hammering in his temples, Sergei placed one hand on his dagger and made for the barn. Quietly he tripped the leather latch on the barn door, and stole inside. Just as quietly, he closed the door behind him. Blindly he fumbled through the darkness until he'd found the stall where he and the bounty hunter had bedded down.

He stopped and listened. His chest lightened when he heard Prophet's raspy breathing and low, muffled snores. He heaved a silent sigh of relief.

He was kicking out of his boots when Prophet's snores ceased. "Sergei?"

The Cossack muttered a Russian curse. He'd hoped the bounty hunter wouldn't wake up and discover Serge's shameful tryst with the Mexican girls. "Yes . . . it is only I."

"What are you doin' up at this hour?" Prophet asked.

The Russian's heart quickened with embarrassment. His mind raced for an excuse. "I was just — how do you always say? — 'shaking the dew from my lily.' "

"Oh, I see," Prophet said, rolling over on his blanket. Grinning, he added under his breath, "I bet it was one hell of a shake."

12

Young Marya Roskov awoke with a start as her bedroom door flew open. Opening her eyes, blinking sleepily, she saw him standing there in the open doorway, wearing nothing.

Morning light washing through the room's two windows set deep in the adobe wall revealed him in all his repugnance and horror — a tall, long-boned man with a bulging paunch. The top of his head was nearly bald, but the stringy, cloud-white hair on the sides hung to his shoulders. His heavy lids flapped over his eyes. He stepped into the room and closed the door.

"I'm back. Did you miss me?"

"Why would you ever doubt it?" she said, with enough playfulness to keep from raising his ire, but with enough scorn to tell him how she really felt.

He threw the covers back, revealing her in a silky lace gown he'd bought her in Broken

Knee. His eyes raked her young, firm body, and she gave a shudder of revulsion.

"I met a man who plans to run for Territorial governor in the next election. He's investing in the mine and going to open a general mercantile in Broken Knee. Soon I will be the richest man in the Southwest." He crawled onto the bed, snuggled against her, stroked her tawny hair, and kissed her very gently on the lips.

"I am very happy for you," she said tonelessly. She'd never hated anyone as she hated him. She'd never feared anyone as she feared him.

"I brought you something," he said cheerfully, as though he were speaking to a woman there of her own accord, one who would not slit his throat if given the chance.

She stared at him.

"Another dress."

Her indifference must have registered in her hazel eyes, for he smiled ruefully and said, "My women do not go around in jeans like you were wearing when we first met — jeans and a ratty old shirt and hat." He chuckled. "No, no, no. My women wear only the finest dresses in the land."

She said nothing to this. She did not like dresses. But then, she didn't like anything about this situation she found herself in, being held prisoner by this madman in his mountaintop adobe house above the village of Broken Knee — his village.

"Don't worry, Marya," he cooed in her ear, blowing her hair back from her neck. "You'll get used to the dresses, as you'll get used to me . . . when you finally realize you have no choice in the matter."

His breath smelled like something dead. She wrinkled her nose and fought back a gag.

She didn't say anything. She wished he would just go ahead and mount her and get it over with.

He stroked her hair again and kissed her. "Have you decided, my pretty, to tell me your little secret?"

She smiled coyly. "What secret?"

He nuzzled her neck. "You know the one."

"Oh, that one." It was hard to speak without the rage and revulsion she felt toward this man who had imprisoned her here and pretended they were more than what they were — captor and captive.

"Yes, that secret." He lifted his head and smiled into her face. His cold eyes sent a shiver up her spine.

It was not only his eyes that made her shiver. She'd seen firsthand the horror he was capable of when he'd killed her old friend, Bert Moriarty. Bert had teamed up with her to look for gold in the Pinaleno Mountains. Only, Bert hadn't realized he'd been leading her off to the prison of Leamon Gay's stony, mountain house, an old hacienda once occupied by a Mexican rancher and situated high to discourage attacks by marauding Apaches.

How could Bert have known?

How could he have known such an evil man existed on earth, much less in the mountains where Bert and Marya were looking for a cache of lost Spanish treasure? How could he have known he'd meet up with such a man who would kill him in the cruelest way possible and imprison young Marya in the hacienda — at the veritable and literal edge of the rocky, sun-seared earth?

Poor Bert . . .

"Yes, that secret," Leamon Gay repeated now. He nipped her neck gently. It hurt only a little, but she recoiled inside. She knew the pain he was capable of inflicting.

"No, I'm not ready to give up that one yet," she said. "A girl can't give up *all* her secrets, you know."

She blinked to clear her vision. Still, she saw Gay thrust his knife into Bert's belly. She saw the blood flow over the hilt, heard

Bert scream. . . .

Gay chuckled. "Oh, you are a little demon, aren't you?" He crawled between her legs, which she opened for him. She wanted him to get on with his ravenous coupling so she could follow through with her plan to avenge Bert's death and to escape this madman once and for all.

Gay kissed her hungrily, nipped her lip as he pulled away. Rising up on his arms, he stared down into her face, only a faint smile now tugging at his thin, sunburned lips. His eyes were at once sharp and merry. "You do know that if you weren't such a lovely little thing you'd be dead by now, don't you?"

She pursed her lips, staring back at him, not saying anything.

Bert's eyes found her, filled with terror and pleading. And then they dimmed and rolled back into his head. . . .

Gay lifted a hand to her right shoulder, slid the strap of her nightgown down her arm, revealing her small, firm breast. He gazed at it wolfishly, his tongue slightly protruding the knife slash of his mouth. His long white hair caressed her skin, which pimpled with revulsion. "I'd have tortured the truth from you and then let you die as our good friend Bert died."

He removed the other strap, laying bare

the other breast. He kissed it, tongued the nipple.

Bert's eyes closed as he stumbled back, clutching at the knife in his belly. Held by two of Gay's men, a knife at her throat, Marya watched her old friend fall to the ground and die.

"You do know that, don't you?"

She nodded, swallowed, trying to get a rein on her fear, on her revulsion. "Yes." Her voice was a whisper.

"Good."

While he grunted on top of her, bunching his ugly face as though in pain, she casually dropped her left hand over the side of the bed. She felt around for the knife she'd smuggled out of the kitchen and hid beneath the mattress. She probed at the mattress with her fingers, moving them up and down and up again, her movements growing frantic. Her heart pounded.

The knife wasn't there!

But it had to be there. She'd put it there just last night, in anticipation of his return from town. . . .

Suddenly he stopped. "What's the matter?"

She snapped her gaze at him, trying to arrange an innocent expression. "What do you mean?"

"What are you looking for?" His voice and eyes were dull.

She shook her head slowly. "I was not looking . . . nothing."

"Is this" — his right hand grabbed something from the rumpled quilts beside him, and he thrust it toward her face so quickly it was all a blur — "what you're looking for?"

She screamed and whipped her head sideways. Missing her face by inches, the knife plunged into her pillow with a popping and tearing sound. Feathers flew. When Marya opened her eyes again, she saw him staring down at her savagely, his face turkey red, the dangling white hair contrasting it sharply.

"Is that what you're looking for?" he raged. Then he laughed madly. "Silly girl — you think I don't know how much you despise me?" He laughed again.

She lay still, her head down, waiting for the final blow, knowing there was nothing she could do to stop him. He was a powerful man. She was only a girl, barely eighteen years old, barely over a hundred pounds.

"No!" she cried, fear overcoming her. "No, please! Don't kill me!"

"No, please, don't keel me!" he mocked

her accent. He grabbed her chin brusquely, turned her head to face him. "Don't worry, my sweet little Russian queen. I'm not going to kill you just yet."

He pulled the knife from the pillow, tossed it on the floor in a cloud of feathers. He went to work on her again, and when he was done, he climbed hastily off.

Staring down at her, he said, "But if you haven't told me where the treasure is in forty-eight hours, I will turn you over to my Mexican miners. And when they're done with you, if there's anything left, they'll sell you to the Apaches. Those red savages will know just how to get the utmost pleasure from a little polecat like you."

Leamon Gay turned, picked up the knife, and padded barefoot out of the room.

Behind him, Marya Roskov drew her arms tight across her breasts, raised her knees, and turned onto her side, sobbing.

The coach squawked and clattered into the little mountain town of Broken Knee later that same day. Sergei was back in the driver's box, and Prophet was back atop Mean and Ugly.

He'd led the way up the trail that wound through the barren, rocky mountains under the scorching desert sun and leveled out finally between two rows of false-fronted buildings so new that the smell of pine still tanged the air. Those buildings constructed from adobe still looked wet. Even the sign standing along the road, proudly announcing BROKEN KNEE, appeared as though it had been painted and erected only yesterday by an optimistic booster. The sun hadn't faded it yet, as it did most things in this neck of the woods.

Prophet felt a bit faded himself, as desert trailing was wont to do to a man. He gazed around at the hustling little town, wondering where he and the Russians would find the countess's sister amidst all these coverall-clad miners and dusty mules and sun-bleached ore wagons and no-account drifters squinting out from under the awnings before saloons, whiskies and warm beers clenched in their hands.

It was loud for such a tiny, haphazard-looking berg nestled between enormous mountains strewn with orange boulders and saguaro cactus. Tin-panny music clattered from several saloons. Whores laughed, men guffawed and whooped, mules brayed, steel-rimmed wheels churned the dusty, packed street, and chickens squawked nearly everywhere. Crows cawed from atop the wood facades.

Above it all rose the raucous thunder of the stamping mill that stood about a hundred yards beyond the other end of town and another hundred yards up the mountain. That's where all the ore wagons appeared to be heading as they trailed in from the west. The empty ones clattered back down Main Street, curving through a narrow pass in the western ridge, into the desert and, presumably, to the mine that had lured this sweaty, dusty humanity and din to these wretched mountains.

Prophet grinned up at a scantily clad whore flaunting her wares from a flophouse balcony as he halted Mean and Ugly, the coach pulling up behind.

"Need some lovin', cowboy?" the whore asked.

She was a hefty blonde with purple feathers in her hair.

"Maybe later," Prophet said. "In the meantime, what's the fanciest hotel in town?"

The whore shrugged and sucked on the wooden tip of her cigarette. "There ain't nothin' fancy in Broken Knee, sugarplum. But the best place is the Gay Inn over yonder. The bedbugs are under ten pounds and the spiders don't charge ye for the stings."

"Why's it called the Gay Inn? They have a lot of fun over there?"

The whore laughed as though it was the funniest thing she'd heard all morning. "Leamon Gay owns it, like everything else in this town."

Prophet considered the information, remembering what Riley Fergus had told him about Leamon Gay. "Much obliged," he told the whore, raising his hat.

"No problem, honey," the woman said. "Come see me sometime. You and your friend."

"We'll do that," Prophet said. He turned to Sergei, who regarded the whore appreciatively. "Why don't we head over there first and make the countess comfortable? I'll take the coach and horses over to the livery barn."

"Do you think it is appropriate for a lady?" Sergei asked, scrutinizing the hotel about forty yards up and across the street.

It was a three-story, unpainted building with a wide veranda. THE GAY INN had been painted above the awning in bright red letters. There was a patio of sorts, covered with gravel and from which a single saguaro jutted, its right arm twisted around behind itself.

"Doubt it," Prophet said.

Sergei nodded grimly, obviously not approving of the town. He waited for a thundering ore wagon to pass, then shook the reins over the bays' backs and headed for the hotel.

When the countess and Sergei had gone into the Gay Inn behind the two young men hefting their luggage, Prophet led the bays to the livery barn and dismounted before the two wide doors that seemed to beckon him into the cool shadows within.

He'd never been so tired of the sun in his life. He secured a couple stalls from the hostler and parked the coach out back, where the hostler assured him it would be safe from the criminal element Prophet knew to be part and parcel of any booming berg like Broken Knee.

"Tell me," Prophet said as he left Mean and Ugly's stall, where he'd watched to make sure the hostler fed the horse plenty of oats and cool well water. "You ever seen this girl?"

Deciding there was no time like the present to get started looking for the countess's sister — the sooner he found her the sooner he could get out of this hellhole — he'd fished Marya Roskov's picture from his shirt pocket. The countess had provided him with the picture of the young blonde with a delicate, fine-featured face and expressive eyes.

"No, never seen that one," the hostler said. His name was Jorge Assante, he'd told Prophet — a barrel-chested Mexican with a round, unshaven face and a floppy straw hat. "I see plenty like her, though. Maybe not that pretty, but cheap. Try the Opera Hat Tavern or, better yet, try the —"

"No," Prophet said, shaking his head. "This girl isn't a whore. She might be looking for gold."

"A girl? Looking for gold, señor?" The Mexican was incredulous. "Not around here. *Muy* dangerous! *Muchos bandidos* and Apaches! Besides, Señor Gay — he doesn't like anyone sniffing around his mountains. Unless they work for him, I mean. No prospectors." Assante shook his head. Eyes wide with gravity, he ran his index finger across his throat.

"That a fact?" Prophet asked, remembering that one of the Miller twins had made the same gesture when speaking of Gay.

Shaking his head slowly, the hostler walked back into the shadows to retrieve the fork he'd been using to muck out the stalls when Prophet had ridden up.

To his back, Prophet said, "So this guy is a pretty big hombre around here, eh?" He was fishing for information — anything at all.

The Mexican didn't say anything. He took up his fork and walked into a stall.

Prophet persisted. "Just how powerful is this Gay fella, anyway?" If Gay didn't like prospectors intruding on what he considered to be his mining rights, he might have been responsible for Marya's disappearance. It was worth looking into, anyway.

The hostler stopped. "Take my advice, señor," he said softly, just loudly enough for Prophet to hear. "Go and enjoy the town. Spend some money. The liquor is good, for a mining town. And the women are not bad. You will have a good time . . . as long as you do not ask about Señor Gay."

Prophet studied the man thoughtfully. Jorge Assante returned to his work, the sunlight angling between the upright boards of the barn's outer walls bisecting him in angles, revealing his dirty denim shirt and snakeskin galluses, the sweat runneling the hay-flecked dust on his face.

Prophet grabbed his saddlebags, Richards ten-gauge, and Winchester, and left the barn. As he turned right, heading for the Gay Inn, he heard a soft whistle. He stopped and turned.

A man was sitting in the alley between the

livery barn and a general store. His back was propped against the barn, between two crates. Prophet could see only a few inches of pin-striped trousers, expensive black boots, and the man's face peering over the barrel between him and Prophet.

Or what was left of the man's face. It had been beaten to a bloody pulp.

13

"Couldn't help overhearing you in there," the man said, jerking his head to indicate the barn behind him, "askin' about Leamon Gay."

"So?"

The man chuckled. Then he frowned and gave a pained grunt. "Ah . . . it hurts to laugh."

"What the hell happened to you?" Prophet asked, wandering over to get a better look at the man.

He wore an expensively cut broadcloth suit with a fawn-colored vest and paisley tie. His brown hair was longish and wavy but badly mussed and streaked with dirt. He was a handsome young man, Prophet could tell through the bruising and swelling of his face.

"Gay's boys," he said, wincing, revealing a silver eyetooth. "You don't want to play the tables here. They're all rigged. I found that out and beat one of the dealers at his own game, you might say. Gay's lieutenants didn't appreciate it — especially when I won back not only every penny of the five hundred I'd lost but tripled it."

Prophet stared down at the young man, frowning at what looked like one hell of an aching noggin. A goose egg had sprouted on his left temple, the color of a Texas thundercloud.

"Let me guess," Prophet said. "After you left the saloon, they jumped you in an alley."

The man shook his head. "They jumped me out in front of the Gay Inn, beat the hell out of me, and stole every dollar I had in my wallet. Even took my watch. It was gold. Bought it in St. Joe after a streak of luck on the gambling boats up from New Orleans."

"Your luck done run out, I'd say."

"You got that right."

"What are you doin' here in the alley?"

"Well, I had a room at the Inn, but found out I wasn't wanted after the little incident in the street. The manager tossed my bag at me." The gambler patted the modest carpetbag beside him, chuckling ruefully. "Went to get my horse so I could get the hell out of town, like I'd been ordered, but didn't have any money to pay the livery bill. That Mex in there don't believe in credit. So I stumbled out here and been here ever since, sleepin' mostly and waitin' for the cobwebs to clear. I been seein' two of everything, but I must be gettin' better. There's only one and a half of you."

"Well, I reckon that's enough of me," Prophet said. "This Leamon Gay — he sounds like a real prince. Any idea where I might be able to find him?"

The gambler chuckled again. He winced at the pain shooting through his head and face. "Yep. But take my word for it. You don't want to find him. And you sure as hell don't want him findin' you."

Prophet squatted down beside the beaten gambler. "How much is your livery bill?"

"Ten dollars."

Prophet raised a brow.

"I been here near two weeks," the gambler said. "Name's Clive Daws."

Prophet shook Daws's extended hand. "Lou Prophet. I reckon if you been here two weeks, Mr. Daws, you probably know quite a bit about this town and our friend, Leamon Gay."

"More than I wanna know, I'll tell you that."

"If I pay your feed bill and buy you a steak

and a couple of stiff drinks, you think you could tell me some more?"

Daws gave Prophet the twice over and squinted one swollen eye. "You don't look like a lawman."

"I ain't."

"What are you, then?"

"Never look a gift horse in the mouth, Mr. Daws." Prophet stood and extended his hand. "Come on. Let's go dip our heads in a trough. My belly could use a fine paddin', and it looks like you could use a bite your ownself."

"A drink might put a little spark back in my veins." Daws accepted Prophet's help up and gingerly dusted himself off. He looked at Prophet warily. "But if Gay's men see me, I'm liable to get us both in a heap of trouble."

Prophet offered the gambler a grin. "Let me worry about that."

The limping Daws led Prophet to a small canvas and wood tent shack situated near a garbage-choked ravine at the north end of town and slightly back from the main drag.

"I haven't been here," Daws said. "Ain't my kinda place. The whiskey's probably half-strychnine and gunpowder, but they probably won't recognize me here, either."

Daws took a bench at the rough-hewn table near the plank bar. Prophet dropped his gear near the bench, then ordered drinks from the grizzled proprietor — a bottle of whiskey, two glasses, and two mugs of beer — and set them on the table. He sat across from Daws, who'd thrown back his first whiskey before Prophet's butt had touched the bench.

Daws rubbed a soiled, beringed paw across his blood-crusted lips. "That's mighty good."

Prophet threw back his own whiskey, then refilled both glasses. "You a gambler by profession, Mr. Daws?"

The well-dressed gent was glancing around, obviously pleased no one seemed to recognize him. There were only two other people in the place — a stocky young black man in the blue, yellow-striped trousers of a federal soldier and a homespun shirt open to his navel, and an old Chinaman with a patch over his right eye. They sat across from each other at a table near the brightly lit doorway, but they weren't speaking.

"That's right," Daws said. "I work the mining camps mostly." He chuckled. "Think I'll stay away from this one in the future."

"Sounds like a good idea," Prophet said, sipping his warm, flat beer and licking the foam from his upper lip. "So tell me about Leamon Gay."

"Hey, keep your voice down, will you?" Daws admonished, leaning toward Prophet and glancing at the barman, who returned the look, frowning askance.

Prophet saw that the black man and the Chinaman were looking at him, as well.

"Sorry," he said to the gambler.

Daws threw back his second whiskey, then refilled his shot glass. In a low voice he said, "What's to tell? He's a penny-ante crook who made it big smuggling horses across the border and selling whiskey and weapons to the Injuns. Also hunted Apache scalps. He put his money into a saloon in Wickenburg and then another saloon and a couple whorehouses in Phoenix, and made a small bundle. When an old prospector discovered gold in these mountains about four years ago, the prospector disappeared of a sudden."

Daws looked at Prophet meaningfully. The whiskey appeared to have loosened his mood as well as the stiff muscles in his face and shoulders. Even some of the swelling around his eyes appeared to have gone down.

"The next thing you know," Daws continued, "Gay leads a caravan of miners and his own band of hardcases up here and builds him a town. Gay himself took over an old Mexican ranch house — haciendas, they call 'em down here — on a mountaintop near the mine. I spied it from a distance through field glasses. Fancy place on a big, grassy shelf jutting out of the mountain. Big shots from all over the Territory ride up here to rub shoulders with the owlhoot."

"What money won't do for a man's reputation."

"They say he has enough for several reputations."

"And all the games in the town are fixed?"

"And all the whores belong to Gay. He gets a percentage — a big one — of every dollar they make."

"In return for what?"

"Protection."

"From?"

Daws grinned without humor. "Gay." He sipped his whiskey, followed it down with a big swallow of the beer. "Any women who come to town and decide they're going to open their own businesses, independent-like, get closed up real quick. They either sign up with Gay, or end up as part of the trash in that ravine yonder."

"Sweet."

"Yep."

"So why'd you stay here so long?"

" 'Cause I'm a poor loser. Decided to figure out how the games were rigged. The dealers are damn good — he must've sent away for them. But I finally figured it out." Daws dabbed at a jellied gash over his upper lip, just right of his nose. "My sin, however, was greed. I should've just won back what I lost and hightailed it. But, no, not me. I thought I'd hit the mother lode."

"Instead, it hit you."

"You got it." Daws was watching Prophet deftly building a cigarette across from him. "So, tell me something. What are you doing here, Prophet?"

"I'm looking for a girl."

"Wife or sister?"

"Neither." Prophet produced the picture of Marya Roskov from his breast pocket and showed it to Daws.

"Pretty," the gambler said.

"Ever see her around here?"

Daws studied the picture, then slowly shook his head. "No, can't say as I have. She's pretty. One like that would stand out in this hole."

"She's Russian," Prophet said, hoping that might jog the gambler's memory.

Daws raised his eyes to Prophet's. He appeared to frown, though it was hard to tell with all that purple swelling around his eyes. "Russian?"

Prophet waited for the gambler's memory gears to click.

In a few seconds they did. "I heard one of the miners mention something about a 'furriner' — a 'purty furriner' — the other night, in one of the saloons. Something about the girl living up at Gay's house . . . as his mistress."

Prophet studied the gambler, waiting for him to continue, his blood quickening in his veins. Had he found Marya? It almost seemed too much to hope for. He'd nearly convinced himself the girl was dead.

Noting Prophet's piqued interest, the gambler spread his hands and said, "That's all I know."

Prophet dragged deeply on his cigarette and sipped his beer. "I reckon there aren't too many 'furrin' girls in these parts."

"Mostly Americans and Mexicans and a few Indians," Daws said. "You think the one up at Gay's might be the one you're looking for?"

"It's worth checking out."

Daws chuckled, the cuts on his lips opening slightly and oozing jellied blood. "Easier said than done, my good man. You'll learn that. Cheers." He threw back the last of his whiskey.

Voices grew outside the tent saloon. Prophet and Daws glanced at the entrance, where two men appeared, ducking inside the flaps.

Daws turned quickly back to Prophet, his face bleaching. "Oh, shit."

"What is it?"

"Those are two of Gay's upstarts."

"You don't say," Prophet said, appraising the two men, who walked between the tables, approaching the makeshift bar. Both were big and burly, one younger than the other by several years. The older man carried a hide-wrapped club from a lanyard on his wide, black belt.

"Hello, Jake. Hello Dan," the bartender said nervously as the men approached.

"Hello, there, Charlie," the older man with the bung starter said. "You got your tax?"

"It's been a week already?" the bartender grumbled.

"Sure has," Dan said without smiling.

"Time sure flies," the bartender said, turning to a wooden lockbox on the shelf behind him. He extracted five one-dollar bills from the box and tossed them on the bar planks. "There ye are — five dollars. What it's for, I'd sure like to know."

"Why, for your protection, Charlie," Jake

said, as though answering a ridiculous question. "I mean, where would you be if it weren't for Mr. Gay? Hell, you'd prob'ly be peddlin' your rotgut whiskey down in Tucson, for a third of what it brings you here."

"That a fact?" Charlie said, unconvinced.

"That's a fact," Dan said grimly. "It'd do you to be a little better mannered next time we come for Mr. Leamon's dues."

"I'll keep that in mind, Dan," the bartender said. His hatred for these men and for Leamon Gay was apparent in his dark eyes and flushed cheeks. He eyed them disdainfully over the bar planks, leaning on his fists.

The men bid the barman a mocking adieu. Turning away, the older man raked his eyes over Prophet and Daws. The gambler was crouched over his empty glasses and staring at the table, trying to make himself small.

Jake froze, frowning at the gambler. "Hey, don't I know you?"

Daws closed his eyes and spread his sore lips in a grimace. He appeared to be trying to turtle his head into his shoulders.

"Hey, Dan," Jake said, nudging the younger man, "don't we know him?"

Dan scrutinized the gambler, who stared at the table, flushing, his haunted eyes like those of a rabbit cornered by two wolves in a privy.

"Why, we sure as hell do," Dan intoned. "We done gave him a scoldin' last night and ordered him out of town."

Prophet lifted his voice. "Nah, it wasn't him."

Both men turned to the bounty hunter.

"Who the hell are you?" Jake asked.

"Name's Prophet." He narrowed his eyes at Jake, who was carrying a double-barreled shotgun. "If you turn that gun any closer to me, friend, you're gonna be wearin' it up your ass."

Dan's laugh was shrill. "What are you tryin' to do, you stupid bastard? Commit suicide?"

"He sure as hell is," Jake said as he leveled his shotgun at Prophet.

The barrel had just come down in his right hand when an explosion rocked the room, blowing Jake two feet in the air and hurdling him back across a table. In nearly two pieces separated by a ragged, red hole in his middle, he rolled off the table and hit the packed-earth floor with a thump and a massive fart.

The second barrel of Prophet's sawed-off coach gun, which he'd swung over the tabletop in the time it took an average man

181

to blink, exploded on the heels of the first blast. Dan was reaching for the Remington on his hip. The gun wasn't halfway out of his holster when a massive, ragged hole opened in his chest. He flew straight backward, slamming his head against a beer keg as he fell. His head hung like a puppet's from a frayed string. His eyes fluttered, found Prophet, fluttered again as his mouth worked, trying to form words. Then he gave up, dropped his chin to his chest, rolled onto the floor, his head touching Jake's, and died.

The Chinaman and the black man had bolted to their feet, shuttling their wide eyes between Prophet and the two dead men. Daws had flung himself to the floor, covering his head with his arms. Now he lowered his arms to peer through the gun smoke. At length, his eyes found Prophet.

"Jesus H. Christ."

The bartender was climbing to his feet behind the bar, lifting his head to inspect Gay's men.

Calmly Prophet glanced at the door as he broke the Richards open, plucked out the smoking wads, and thumbed in two fresh. He snapped the shotgun back together as the barman said, "Oh, my god."

"Prophet," Daws said, gaining his feet, his

face white as freshly fallen snow, "you have any idea what you just did?"

"I reckon it was either them or me," Prophet allowed. His complacent tone belied the fact that he knew he was in a heap of trouble. He needed to hightail it fast, before more of Gay's men arrived.

"Quick," the barman said. "Go out the back." In spite of the mess in his shack, his eyes were bright and his flushed face was grinning. "I'll make up a story."

Prophet stared at the man, skeptical and puzzled.

"Call it payment for ridding the town of these two human blowflies," the barman explained. Turning to the Chinese and the black man, who were still standing, he said, "Will you two back me?"

They looked at each other. The black man shrugged. The Chinaman nodded slowly, a faint smile on his lips.

"Quick!" the barman repeated, waving Prophet and the gambler around behind the bar.

With one last glance at the dead men, Prophet nodded at Daws and hurried out the tent's back flap. Making his way around the barman's army cot, clothesline, and several discarded crates and barrels, Prophet hurried down a greasewood-lined path which appeared to angle toward the ravine.

"We'd better split up," he said. "How much did you say you needed to spring your horse?"

He turned, but the gambler wasn't behind him. Looking around, he saw Daws running through the shrubs farther down the canyon, tripping over rocks and catching the tails of his swallowtail coat on briers.

The gambler ran as though the hounds of hell were on his heels, and then he was gone.

14

Prophet paused in an alley between a drug-store and a tack shop to watch several townsmen, including two men wearing five-pointed sheriff's stars, run down the middle of the street and turn a corner, heading for the saloon tent.

When the men were gone, Prophet waited for an oar wagon and two beleaguered-looking horseback drifters to pass, then hefted his saddlebags on his shoulder, adjusted the Winchester in his right hand, and walked across the street, the ten-gauge Coach gun dangling from the lanyard down his back.

"What's all the commotion?" he asked the old gent sitting on the Gay Inn's front porch, smoking a pipe.

"You got me," the gent said. "I heard two blasts come from thataway, and seen men runnin'. Probably a couple miners fightin' over whores again." The geezer wheezed a laugh and stuck his pipe back in his teeth.

Prophet wagged his head with disgust. "What's the world comin' to, with men fightin' over whores?"

"Oh, I'd say about the same thing it was comin' to about six thousand years ago," the old gent speculated, sucking his pipe stem and exhaling smoke from his nose, gazing across the street with a self-satisfied expression on his craggy face.

Prophet chuckled. "I reckon you're right, old son."

He stepped inside the hotel and paused in the small lobby. An oak desk with cubbyholes and gold key rings behind it sat to the right of the front door. Between the desk and the cubbyholes sat a slender black man on a high stool, reading a Bible open on the desk. He appeared to be in his mid-twenties. His elbows were propped on the desk, pinstriped sleeves rolled up his arms; his brow furrowed and his lips moved as he read, concentrating hard.

Sensing someone standing there, the clerk looked up, his eyes expectant. "Help you, mister?"

He stopped, his features frozen. Then his shoulders sagged and his mahogany, moon-shaped face acquired a pained expression, as though he'd just seen the last person he'd wanted to see in the world.

"Oh, no!" he exclaimed through a half sob, half-shaking, half-nodding his head with great flourish, as though to emphasize his grief.

Prophet smiled. "Hi, Henry."

"Oh, no," the clerk repeated, still wagging his head. "Oh, Lordy, tell me it ain't Lou Prophet standin' there."

Prophet walked to the desk, let his saddle-bags roll off his shoulder onto the hardwood surface, and stuck out his meaty hand. "How ye been?"

Reluctantly the desk clerk shook Prophet's hand. It wasn't really a shake — more of a halfhearted squeeze — before he let his arm drop to his side, hanging off his slumped right shoulder. His brow was still furrowed, his full cheeks still bunched with despair.

Prophet fashioned an injured look across the desk. "Henry, if I didn't know better, I'd say you weren't happy to see me."

"I ain't happy to see you at all, Lou Prophet," Henry whined. "Why, you almost got me killed! More than once, too!"

"Oh, come on now, Henry. Don't you think you're gilding the lily just a little? I saved you from prison time. I didn't have to vouch for you after that holdup you and your gang pulled — tellin' the jury you didn't know what your friends were going to do when they walked into that Billings bank. You thought they were going to make a deposit and were just holdin' their horses!"

Prophet chuckled and shook his head. "Now *that* was gildin' the lily, but I perjured myself because I liked your ma and sensed you had promise."

Henry's ma ran a Billings boardinghouse, the best in town and one which Prophet frequented whenever he was in the area. He sometimes stayed over just for Begonia Appleby's delicious Southern cooking — honest-to-God soul food — a treat which he had few opportunities to enjoy and which always harkened memories of his boyhood before the war.

Henry Appleby gazed at Prophet pointedly, his black pupils yawning with antipathy. "You convinced me to testify against that gang, Lou Prophet! And when they broke jail, they ran me through three states before I finally lost 'em . . . for the time being. No doubt they're still lookin' for me. Hell, they'll probably be lookin' for me till the day I die. That's why I'm here — as far as I could get from Montana without slippin' over into Mexico. I reckon Mexico's next, though, as soon as I see Mad-Dog and Dead-Eye and their passel of polecats ridin' into town."

Prophet glanced away with chagrin. Fingering the flap on his saddlebag, he grumbled, "How was I supposed to know they were going to break jail?"

"I warned you they were gonna break jail, didn't I? I know those boys. There ain't a jail made they can't break."

"You're a hell of a lot better off here than you would be breaking rock in the territorial pen, old son. And for that you have me to thank, you ungrateful little snot. Now give me a room. I'm tired."

His brows ridged with thought, Henry reached under the desk, produced a ledger book, and set it on the desktop with a pencil. He shrugged remorsefully. "I . . . I reckon I do have you to thank for that, Lou." He opened the book and turned the pages. "I mean . . . I reckon I would be in jail 'bout now if you hadn't lied for me. And Mama — she'd have been shamed somethin' awful."

"Yes, she would," Prophet agreed, picking up the pencil as Henry turned the book around to face him. "Imagine her, havin' to explain an incarcerated son to her boarders." Prophet shook his head and sighed as he licked the pencil and signed his name.

"You're right," Henry admitted. "You got

189

me off that racket, and I should be grateful."

"Yes, you should."

"I'm sorry. Thanks, Lou. I don't know how I can ever repay you."

Prophet swung the register around and hefted his saddlebags off the desk. "I'm sure I'll think of something someday. For now, just get me a room near those two Russians that checked in a little while ago, will you?"

"That what they were — Russians?"

Prophet nodded. Henry slid off his chair and turned to retrieve a key from a hook. "Why you ridin' with Russians?"

"I guided 'em down here. Don't tell anybody, Henry, but —" Prophet stopped as a thought occurred to him. A question. He assumed Henry had been here for a while. A savvy young man who had been in and out of petty trouble most of his life, Henry had no doubt sized up the town and its primary booster, Leamon Gay.

Henry dropped the key in Prophet's open hand. "But what?"

"Say, Henry, you know this Leamon Gay fellow?"

Henry stared at Prophet levelly. After a wary pause, he said, "Not personal. I know *of* him. Why?"

"You know where he lives?"

The desk clerk stared at Prophet with dark suspicion. "Yeah," he said slowly. "I know where he lives. Why you askin'?"

"Ever been there?"

"Why you askin'?"

"Oh, come on, Henry. You ever been there?"

Henry's voice rose, a note of the old despair returning. "Yeah, I been there. So what? I work for the mercantile weekends, and once in a while I deliver goods to the place. So what?" Henry's upper lip trembled slightly, and his eyes bore into Prophet's like obsidian arrowheads.

Prophet's eyes lighted, and he grinned cunningly as he grabbed the young man's arm. "Henry, you're a peach. Give me a few minutes of your time, will you?"

Henry wrenched his arm free of Prophet's grip and stepped back from the desk. "What?"

"Just five minutes, Henry, just five minutes," Prophet beseeched the young clerk. "For the guy who saved you from the pen and saved your mama from a shame no woman should bear. . . ."

Henry scowled and canted a squinted eye askance, the epitome of suspicion and fear. "What you up to, Lou Prophet?"

"Just five minutes." Prophet pulled the

young man around the desk and onto the lobby floor. Henry held back, reluctant, telling Prophet he could not leave the desk unattended.

"Just five minutes for the guy who saved you from the rock quarry, Henry," Prophet said.

Spying a blank placard hanging behind the desk, Prophet turned it around. "Back in One Hour," it read.

Slinging his saddlebags over his shoulder, Prophet ushered the young clerk up the narrow staircase to the second story, ignoring Henry's protests and complaints. "If you got something with Mr. Gay, Proph, please don't involve me. I beg you, man. I'm too young to die. Hell, I'd rather the old gang get me than Gay and his boys. . . ."

Henry was practically sobbing by the time Prophet knocked on Sergei's door, the number of which he'd noted in the register book. When the Russian answered the door, Prophet said, "Meet me in the countess's room."

He didn't wait for the Russian to respond. The young, protesting desk clerk in tow, he turned to the door across the hall and knocked.

The countess answered, looking fresh after a sponge bath and a change of gowns. Due to the heat, she wore a sleeveless little form-fitting shirtwaist with ruffles across the bosom. Her hair was down, parted in the middle, with ringlets dancing about her cheeks. She looked as scrumptious as Prophet had ever seen her. But he had serious business to attend.

"Can we come in?" he asked her. Not waiting for her reply, he pushed open the door and shoved Henry before him into the room.

"Hey, hey, Lou — what's goin' on?" Henry complained. He was nearly sobbing. "I can't . . . I can't be in a lady's room. Oh, for mercy sakes!"

"Oh, Henry, straighten up and grow some horns, will you?" Prophet admonished the lad as he deposited his saddlebags and arms in a corner. To the countess, who stood near the door looking incredulous, he said, "This is my old friend Henry Appleby. We go back, Henry and me. Henry — the Countess Natasha Roskov."

"Oh, shit, Prophet — sorry, ma'am," the desk clerk said, flashing an apologetic glance at the countess, "but I can't be in the room of no white countess — whatever a countess is. Jeepers!"

The door opened and the burly Sergei entered, his wet hair and goatee freshly combed. He, too, had changed his clothes and was looking dapper and fresh. His face registered disapproval at the presence of the two other men in the countess's room.

"What is going on here?" he asked, scowling.

"Come on in and sit down, Serge," Prophet said.

"This is the countess's own private room," the Cossack protested, his big face flushing with fury.

Ignoring the remonstration, Prophet introduced the Russian to Henry, whom he shoved into one of the two chairs before the open window, sliding the countess's open trunks out of the way with his foot. He gave the lad a drink of water to calm him, then turned to the countess, who stood holding one post of the four-poster bed, her heavy brow ridged skeptically. Sergei stood beside her, as though to defend her from a sudden attack from the crazy bounty hunter and distressed desk clerk.

Prophet threw back his own glass of water, then, standing by the window, hoping to catch a breeze, he told the countess and Sergei about what he'd learned from the gambler, Daws.

"Marya is living with Leamon Gay!" the countess exclaimed, slapping an exasperated hand to her throat.

"It might not be her," Prophet said. "That's what we have to find out. If it is her, we have to know if she's there because she wants to be or if he's holding her for some reason."

"I guess we should just ride up there and ask," the Cossack suggested. "That would be easiest, no?"

Prophet nodded and poured another glass of water from the pitcher on the washstand. Thoughtfully, he moved back to the window, stepping over and around trunks.

Finally he shook his head. "That might be the easiest way, but not the smartest. If he's got her there against her will, we'd only be tipping our hand, letting him know we're here to get her back." He paused and gave his back to the window. He looked at Sergei. "I'm thinkin' we sneak up there after dark and reconnoiter the situation."

Sergei crossed his bulky arms over his chest, pursed his lips thoughtfully, and nodded. The countess stared at Prophet, her eyes wide and expectant, thrilling to the possibility that her sister had at last been found.

Prophet swerved his gaze to Henry, sitting in the spool-backed chair looking warily up at the trail-dusty, unshaven bounty hunter.

Henry's black face bunched around itself.

"Oh, man! I done heard enough." Climbing to his feet, he added, "It's just like I thought — you got trouble with Mr. Gay, an' I don't want no part of it!"

Prophet grabbed the kid's arm and shoved him gently back in the chair. "Hold on, hold on. All I want you to do, Henry my child, is to tell us where we'll find Gay's lair and draw us a sketch of the compound. I'll also need to know if he has guards and how many."

"Prophet, please, man, I beg you . . ."

"I'm callin' my note due, Henry. All you have to do is sketch me a little map, and we're even Steven." To the countess, he said, "Paper and pencil?"

The countess crouched over a trunk and rummaged around in its contents.

Henry begged Prophet, "You gotta promise that Mr. Gay won't find out I had anything to do with this. You gotta promise! I mean, hell, I work for the man!"

"Oh, quit bawlin'," Prophet groused, shuttling a tablet and a pencil from the countess to Henry. "Now, draw me a map and be quick about it. I'm getting tired of all your fussin'."

When Prophet and Sergei had made plans

to reconnoiter at Gay's hacienda later that night, after dark, Prophet returned to his room and, in spite of the stale heat and droning flies, slept some of the trail weariness from his bones. He woke around six, took a whore's bath, and headed down to the small, square dining room for supper.

The countess and Sergei were already there, looking rested, as well, and Prophet joined them for steak and all the surroundings washed down with hot, black coffee and followed up with an after-dinner whiskey. To the countess's displeasure, the Gay Inn did not have cognac.

Prophet was about to excuse himself and go looking for a bath and then a card game — even if they were crooked, it was something to do while waiting around for good dark — when Sergei nonchalantly stubbed out his cheroot and asked Prophet if he would look after the countess for a few hours. He had some business to tend.

"Business?" Prophet asked.

The Cossack flushed slightly but remained otherwise composed. "Yes. I thought I would try out the gambling tables."

"Remember, they're rigged," Prophet reminded him.

"Yes, but it will give me a chance to appraise the town — with only the countess's best interest in mind, of course. We Cossacks like to be prepared for anything."

"Oh, of course," Prophet said, chewing back a grin. He was more than happy to spend the evening with the countess but tried not to look too eager as the big Cossack donned his slouch hat, asked the countess if she needed anything before he left, and exited the dining room.

The countess chuckled huskily, covering her mouth and looking in the direction Sergei had disappeared.

"What's so funny?" Prophet said. "You ain't buyin' his excuse?"

"Not in the least."

"I reckon it's about time for him to get his ashes hauled again," Prophet speculated.

When he explained the old expression, she tipped her head back, clapped her hands together once, and said, "He is so formal about it and rather shy and awkward. Like a little Cossack boy."

"And a terrible liar."

"Yes. I heard some soiled doves, as you call them, calling up to him as he stood on his balcony earlier, smoking."

"Ah, the call of the wild," Prophet quipped. "He might find a couple to his liking." He smiled across the table at the countess, who looked more ravishing than he'd ever seen her. She wore a pearl neck-lace with a pearl headband holding her chestnut hair in coils atop her head. "I might even find a pretty little lass to my own liking this evenin'."

She regarded him bashfully. "Do you mean me?"

"Of course I mean you."

"Do you find me attractive, Lou?"

"You bet I do." Prophet smiled.

She reached across the table and placed her hand on his. "I know I am not, but I thank you for saying so, anyway."

"Natasha," Prophet said, gazing directly into her eyes, "when you loosen up and smile, you're one of the prettiest women I've ever known. And, not to brag, but I've known a few."

She sank back in her chair, her slanted eyes flashing. "Yes, I imagine you have, Lou Prophet. With your charm, I think you could have any woman you desire." Lowering her voice, she added seductively, "And tonight you will, indeed, have me." She smiled and reached across the table again. "But first, show me around the town a little?"

"It would be my pleasure," Prophet said, standing and pulling out her chair.

She waited in the lobby while he paid for the meal. Outside, he offered the countess his arm, and they strolled east down the street, which had settled down a little since supper. But the ore wagons continued their endless stream. The saloons were busier than ever, and Prophet speculated they'd get busier by the hour, for the sun hadn't even sunk yet. A pretty, coppery light spilled down from the mountains, and purple shadows drew out from the buildings along the street.

The cooling air was velvety and smelled faintly of desert blossoms.

Fleeing the dust kicked up by the ore wagons, Prophet led the countess off down a side street, toward the ravine that cut around the town.

"I am so happy you found Marya," the countess said as they turned around a tangle of greasewood in their path.

"Now, we don't know it's Marya, Countess. Like I said, this might be a long shot."

"Call me Natasha, Lou, and kiss me." She'd stopped and smiled up at him.

When he turned to her, she threw her arms around his neck, rose up on her tiptoes, and kissed him hungrily on the lips. He returned the kiss, having wanted to kiss her ever since their first tryst in the stage. The countess was many things — arrogant, irritating, demanding, to name only a few

— but she was also bewitching and tender and a superb lover. Prophet didn't mind being her whipping boy nearly as much as he had at the start of their journey. In fact, his feelings for her had grown rather complicated.

"You are some kind of woman — you know that?" Prophet asked her now, staring down into her eyes which the fading desert light rendered an iridescent vermilion.

"And you are some kind of man. Thank you very much."

"Are we back on Marya again?"

"Of course. You have found her. I know it. I know such things when they are in my heart." Her smile broadened. "And you will bring her back to me and my family. I know you will."

"Well, first we have to get her away from Leamon Gay."

"That shouldn't be too hard. Marya has never been able to keep a man interested in her for long. She is — what is the word? Strong-headed?"

"Huh," Prophet chuffed with playful mockery. "Imagine that, with such a wall-flower like you for a sister!"

The countess frowned beautifully, fine lines etching above the bridge of her nose, full lips parting. She knew she was being teased but not exactly how. "What is the 'wall flower'?"

Prophet told her, and she laughed. She took his arm again, and they continued along the path, chatting quietly, silently observing how the dying light turned the desert lime green, then blue and then slowly purple. Tiny birds chatted in the grease-wood and mesquite growing along the bone-dry ravine.

"Have you ever been in love, Lou?" the countess asked after a long pause.

Prophet thought about it for a moment, then nodded. "Yes."

"But you never married."

"Nope. Don't intend to, neither."

"Why not?"

"Don't want to be tied down."

"That is because you have never met anyone you would want to 'tie you down,' as you say."

Prophet shrugged. "I can't imagine anyone like that. I like Mean and Ugly too much. Him and me have quite a time ridin' here and there, chasin' owlhoots and laughin' with the girls. Why, if it wasn't for that, I never would've met you, now would I?"

"You have a point," the countess said with a husky chuckle. "But someday you will want to settle down and have children, to continue after you are gone."

"I don't think so, Natasha."

She looked up at him as they strolled, and he noticed that a sad curiosity had seeped into her eyes. "You are a troubled man, Lou Prophet."

"Troubled?" he said, incredulous. "Hell, I ain't troubled. Now, a wife and kids — they'd trouble me."

"You can say what you want, but you are an unhappy man deep down inside. In your soul. I can see it now. I have seen it often when I have watched you secretly."

"Now, that ain't nice — spyin' on a man," he admonished her, teasing.

"What happened? Was it the war in your country, between the States?"

He glanced at her again, then continued walking in silence, pondering her question. "I reckon if there is any trouble in me — and I'm not sayin' there is, but I guess it's possible — it's no doubt because of the War."

"Did you have to kill?"

"Oh, yes."

"And you saw your friends killed?"

"Sure." He stopped suddenly and looked down at her. He had no idea what he was going to say before he'd started in.

"I had to kill one of them, too, one of my

friends. Only he wasn't only a friend — he was a cousin of mine from Tunnel Hill, Georgia, two years younger. We were in a skirmish down near Dalton, just after Chickamauga. We were on a ridge, and this Yankee runnin' up the ridge shot Andy with a musket he'd loaded with buck an' ball. That means he'd poured two cartridge loads of black powder down the barrel — then a double charge on top of the powder. That's twenty-four buckshots — damn near a mortar round — with a sixty-caliber ball rammed down on top of it. And —"

Prophet stopped, suddenly realizing he'd been chewing the rag and she didn't understand any of it, not a word. He could see that in her eyes staring up at him, filled with woe. But she was listening, so he decided just to go ahead and spill the rest of it, get the gall and wormwood out of his blood.

For he'd never told this to anyone before. Had never even really told it to himself. . . .

"Well, that ball with all that mean powder behind it blew poor Andy's insides clear to Kingdom Come, but Andy lingered. He begged me to shoot him, to end his pain, and he handed me his gun." Prophet took a deep breath and let his eyes wander off.

"So I did it," he said, very softly. "Only I couldn't see very well through the tears in my eyes, and I ended up blowing half his jaw away with the first shot. I finally killed him with the second shot, while those eyes were starin' up at me, filled with more misery and pain and torture than I knew even existed before that day."

Prophet's voice broke on the last of this, and he turned away, clearing his throat. She put a hand on his shoulder and just stood there, massaging his shoulder gently while he thought it all through, then sleeved the tears from his eyes.

Finally he said, "Sorry. Listen to me rattle, would you."

"I am glad you told me," she said, putting her arms around his back and pressing her cheek to his chest.

Prophet found his humor again as they headed back toward the hotel, and they were both laughing as they walked down the main street, squinting against the dust still kicked up by the ore wagons.

In the Gay Inn's lobby, Prophet ordered a tub and hot water for the countess's room, giving the countess a furtive wink. When the tub had been brought up and filled by one of the errand boys, Prophet crept out of the countess's closet, where he'd hidden from the errand boy.

He disrobed the countess, then himself,

and they made a night of it, making love in the tub and then in the bed, stopping only to sip his whiskey and to smoke before continuing again, teasing and laughing and making love like it was the last night of the world.

15

Well after dark, Prophet and Sergei saddled their horses in the livery barn and headed off to Gay's hacienda.

The Cossack looked part gambler, part mountain man in his dark cotton shirt, black denims, and boot moccasins. He wore a broad-brimmed Western hat he'd bought in Denver. Characteristically ostentatious, he'd knotted a black kerchief around his neck and secured it with a gold ring.

He had rented a tall buckskin in whose eyes he claimed he saw "hellfire," adding that every good Cossack warrior rode a mount with the fires of hell in its eyes.

Prophet glanced over at the horse's eyes. "That might just be gas."

Following Henry's directions, they followed the pale ribbon of road through the quiet, purple desert, threading their way through a deep valley between jagged, rocky peaks. A coyote yammered from a nearby scarp. The bald, toothy ridges loomed blackly to their right and left, capped by brilliant starlight. Occasional explosions, dynamite detonated by the miners, echoed in the north.

They drifted off the trail when they heard an ore wagon approach from the north, groaning and creaking, the driver cursing and popping a bullwhip over the backs of the four-mule team. When the wagon had passed, they drifted back onto the road and cantered for another mile, until they came to the trail twisting off to the left — a pale line coiling up the western ridge.

About halfway up the ridge sat Gay's hacienda, a small jewel of light shimmering against the mountain.

"Here's where we dismount," Prophet said.

As they'd planned, they tethered their horses in a gully shrouded by mesquite and sage, then walked westward, avoiding the closely guarded trail. When they'd walked a hundred yards, they started climbing the mountain, moving straight up toward the house, gazing around warily for the armed guards Henry had assured them would be spread across the slope.

Their breathing grew heavy. Sweat ran down their backs.

Stealing around boulders, they came upon a shallow trough in the mountainside. The scrub brush was thick enough to offer adequate cover, as long as no guards were perched in the trough. It wasn't likely. Prophet figured most would have been positioned on higher ground, where they had a clearer view of the valley.

Prophet figured wrong. When he and Sergei were two-thirds of the way up the mountain, a man's voice called out from just above. "Who goes there?"

Prophet and the Cossack froze, crouching, hands on their guns, resisting the urge to draw. Firing their weapons would draw the other guards. Prophet's heart tom-tommed.

"I said who's there?" the guard called again, anger rising in his voice. He was a vague shifting of the darkness about twenty yards up the trough. Dull blue starlight shone off a rifle.

"Just me," Prophet said, trying to make his voice sound casual.

The guard said nothing. Prophet had a feeling he was trying to process Prophet's voice. In a second or two he'd realize he hadn't recognized it.

Reacting more than thinking, Prophet reached his right hand up to the back of his neck, shucking his Arkansas toothpick from the scabbard lying flat against his spine. With the same motion, he crouched lower, spread his feet, and snapped his hand out and down, releasing the savage weapon with a snap of his wrist.

The knife disappeared in the darkness, only a silvery flicker marking its passage.

Thump! The guard grunted softly. Prophet saw his silhouette stagger to the right. The rifle clattered to the ground. Another thump and a groan.

Drawing his bowie, Prophet rushed forward. He stopped and crouched over the body of the prone guard. The man lay on his back, hat off, the Arkansas toothpick jutting straight up from his throat. The blood gleamed darkly.

The man's eyes fluttered, then slowly closed.

Prophet turned to Sergei, who'd walked up behind him and was staring down at the dead man. "Not bad, eh?" Prophet said, a proud half-grin on his lips.

Sergei set his mouth and nodded, shrugging one shoulder. "Not bad. I was about to do the same thing, but not bad."

"Not bad?" Prophet chuckled. He crouched down, pulled the Arkansas toothpick from the guard's throat, wiped it off on the man's shirt, and slid it back in its sheath. "Not bad, like hell . . ." With a snort, he started again up the trough.

They made the crest of the shelf about ten minutes later, and scurried over to a wagon shed at the edge of the yard. Fifty yards before them, the hacienda sat behind a low adobe wall, its tall, arched windows blazing.

Starlight spread a silvery sheen on the red clay tiles. Almond and orange trees were spidery silhouettes against the windows.

A black buggy sat out front, at the head of the semicircular driveway marked with stones. A steeldust horse stood in the traces. Two burly men wearing bandoliers across their chests stood on either side of the wall's gated door, smoking and talking, their voices muffled by distance.

Somewhere to Prophet's right, a cicada whirred.

"Let's head around behind, look for a back door," Prophet whispered.

Sergei nodded and stood. Prophet grabbed his forearm. "Wait!"

He gestured at the hacienda. A man had appeared from the house's rear, walking slowly along the wall. He held a rifle across his chest, like a soldier.

Sergei crouched back down and scowled

at Prophet. "I saw him," he grumbled.

"Sorry," Prophet said gently. "I just thought your noble Russian ass might need savin' — again."

"No, no. You misremember. It was I who saved *your* ass."

"As I recall . . . Oh, never mind," Prophet grumbled, watching the guard moving along the wall.

When the man reached the two men guarding the front, he stopped to chat, then drifted on around the other side of the house.

Prophet said, "Come on!"

Crouching, he and Sergei ran across the packed yard, skirting an empty corral and a blacksmith shop. When they reached the wall, they turned their backs to it and whipped looks to their right and left.

Apparently, the guards hadn't seen them. Wasting no time, Prophet stood and hoisted himself over the wall. Sergei did likewise, dropping into the dusty courtyard, just right of a dead orange tree.

Before them, stone steps rose to a second-story door. Wooden cellar doors lay to the bottom right of the stairs.

"You go in through the cellar," Prophet said, keeping his voice down. "I'll take the door above."

"Why must I take the cellar?"

Prophet looked at him dully. "Why not?"

"I think it is more likely she is upstairs than in the cellar. And since it is I who will recognize her, I should take the upper story."

Sergei made for the stairs. Shaking his head, Prophet crouched over the cellar doors. Carefully he lifted the right one by its metal ring, gritting his teeth at the quaking hinges. Slipping inside, in total darkness, he let the door close softly behind him and struck a match.

He found nothing in the cellar but several old wine casks, racks, dry goods, and cobwebs. By matchlight he made his way up the basement stairs and slipped into a hall, easing the door closed behind him. Hearing voices, he edged along the hall, keeping one hand on his Colt.

At the end of the hall he stole a glance around the corner. In the big, circular room before him was a rough wooden table. Around the table sat four men playing cards and drinking — big, sweaty men in dusty trail clothes and with the belligerent, unshaven faces of long riders.

As far as Prophet could tell, they all were armed with pistols. Two carried revolvers in shoulder rigs. Rifles and shotguns lay in easy reach.

Prophet watched for a while, sizing up the group. There was a pillar between him and them. That and their concentration on the game, as well as the whiskey bottle before them, kept their attention on the table.

Hearing laughter behind him, Prophet turned and walked back down the hall, taking exaggerated steps on the balls of his feet, so his spurs wouldn't ching. Near the middle of the hall, on the right, he came to a stout wooden door with strap hinges and a tarnished brass latch. Voices emanated from the door, which was open a foot.

Pressing his back to the wall, Prophet cocked an ear to the door, listening.

". . . just call it a contribution to your reelection campaign."

A man laughed. "Hell, I've already been reelected!"

"For next time, Senator. For next time."

"Well, I reckon thinking ahead couldn't hurt."

"And all you have to do is convince the territorial governor that I'm worthy of a pardon —"

"For all previous offenses," the senator said, haltingly, as though he were pondering the proposition.

"All previous offenses. Surely, he'll see fit.

I mean, I've been damn good for the Territory's economy, have I not?"

Good-natured laughter. "Well, I reckon you have, since you quit robbing the army paymasters!"

There was a pause while the senator's laughter boiled down to silence.

"That's all in the past, Senator," the one who was obviously Leamon Gay said. "All in the past. Now, I've mended my ways, and I'm damn good for this territory."

"Well, uh, how will I get that? In bank draft or — ?"

"Gold."

"Gold?"

"Pure gold. Twenty thousand dollars' worth . . ."

Prophet shook his head. Gay was a rapscallion, all right. A rapscallion and then some. It sounded as though he would soon be a rapscallion amnestied by the Territorial governor. All future crimes would no doubt be sanctioned by the governor himself.

Having heard enough and wanting to find the girl, Prophet moved off down the hall. A few minutes later he came to a narrow, curving stairs. He climbed the stairs, opened a door, and crept down another hall lit by a single bracket lamp. He paused by a closed door on his left, pressed his ear to the wood.

The sound of splashing water rose in the room. Prophet lowered his gaze to the key in the lock. He turned it and pressed the latch, slowly opening the door, again gritting his teeth against squawking hinges. When the door was open a foot, he slid his head through.

A dull light entered his gaze, and the corners of his mouth curved down in a smile. Before him stood a slender girl — no more than nineteen or twenty — standing naked in a copper tub, her back to him. Ash blond hair hung straight down her back. Her butt was small and round and firm, the thighs long and wonderfully sculpted.

Prophet couldn't help pausing a moment to enjoy the view as she sponged her breasts. Suddenly, as though sensing him there, she turned her head, casting a glance over her shoulder.

Seeing him, she gave a clipped, raspy scream and turned, splashing water over the sides of the tub.

Quickly Prophet stepped into the room, closed the door, and faced the girl with his hands spread open before him.

"Easy, easy," he whispered.

She covered her breasts with her elbows and stared at him with her wide, hazel eyes. She was pretty and fine-featured with a high-born nose like the countess's. The family resemblance continued in the wide-spaced eyes and firm, delicate jaw. Her skin was not as creamy, however. This girl — Marya, Prophet assumed — had obviously spent considerable time in the sun. Her arms were long-muscled, her hands slightly corded, neither of which took away from her femininity. The girl was a looker, through and through.

"Who are you?" she snapped, reaching for a towel off the chair beside her and using it to cover herself.

Prophet kept his voice low, his ears pricked for noise outside the door. "I'm Lou Prophet. A friend. Marya Roskov, I assume?"

She studied him, her eyes remaining sharp, the flush still coloring her cheeks. "How do you know my name?" Her tone was accusatory.

"I'm here with your sister, Natasha, and Sergei."

The lines around her eyes disappeared. She stared at him agape. "What?"

"We're gettin' you out of here."

The girl's face now paled as she pinned Prophet with an urgent stare, clutching the towel to her chest. "Where . . . ?"

"Your sister's in Broken Knee. Sergei's in

the house somewhere. I take it you're not here because you want to be?"

Her shoulders drooped. "Oh, god!" she rasped.

"That's what I thought."

Holding the towel over her breasts and hips, the girl stepped out of the slipper tub, revealing one long, creamy leg in turn. She moved toward Prophet urgently and gazed up at his face. "I hoped so much that someone would come."

"Why's Gay holding you here?" Prophet had just finished the question when he heard a spur ching softly outside the door. He turned, listening. Faintly he heard footsteps.

He sidled up to the door and said, just above a whisper, "Sergei?"

"Lou?" came the Russian's lowered voice.

Prophet threw open the door, beckoned the Cossack in, and shut it softly behind him. He turned as Sergei and Marya locked gazes. The girl's eyes widened with relief and joy, and she bounded into the Cossack's arms.

"Oh, Marya!" Sergei exclaimed under his breath, wrapping the girl in his broad-shouldered hug and holding her tightly, gently rocking her from side to side. She'd buried her face in his chest. Her shoulders jerked as she sobbed.

The Cossack said, "I was beginning to wonder if we would ever find you alive."

When she looked up at him, her lovely face was filled with fear and sorrow. "He killed Bert, and he has been holding me for over a month now, locked in this room."

Sergei smoothed a wing of blond hair back from her brow. "But why, *ma chèrie?* Why is he holding you here?"

"He wants the treasure Bert discovered — Bert, my prospector friend. Did Natasha get my map?"

Sergei nodded, but his eyes were puzzled. "We did not understand. It is a map to what?"

"To the gold," Marya said. "I sent it just after we arrived in Broken Knee, in case anything should happen to Bert and me."

Prophet was dubious. "What gold?"

Marya turned to him, still enmeshed in Sergei's arms. "The Lost Morales Gold Cache," she said. "Bert had found it a few years ago, when he was in the cavalry. The Apaches were too thick in the area to retrieve it then, however. When I met Bert, he had just retired from the army and was gathering supplies to retrieve the gold. That's when Gay found us. His men brought us here. He killed Bert. . . ." She squeezed her eyes closed.

"How did he know Bert was going after the gold?" Prophet asked. He stood by the door, an ear cocked toward the corridor. His nerves twanged in every appendage.

Marya shook her head, half-sad, half-disgusted. "It had been rumored that Bert knew where the gold was. He was not sure how the rumor got started, but Bert was a drinker, you see. He sometimes bragged when he drank. He suspected that he must have bragged about having found the gold one time when he was drinking in one of the cantinas. Word must have gotten back to Gay. When he showed up in Broken Knee . . ."

"Gay figured, correctly, that he was here to retrieve the gold," Sergei finished for her.

"What does Gay need with the gold?" Prophet asked with an incredulous grunt. "I mean, he has a whole mine full."

Marya turned to him again, gave her head a single shake. "The gold is disappearing from the ore. I heard him talking to one of his men outside my window. The vein is playing out."

"Ah," Prophet said, nodding. "He's about to go belly up."

Sergei turned to him, curious. "Belly up?"

"Broke."

"Broke?"

Prophet shook his head. "I'd love to explain" — he looked at the girl critically — "and I'd love to know why in the hell you just didn't go ahead and turn over the gold and be on your way, but there's no time. Miss, why don't you get dressed — and I mean fast — and —"

Prophet stopped and turned his ear back to the door. "Shit!" he exclaimed. "Someone's coming."

16

"It's him," Marya said, meaning Gay. "He's coming for me, to show me off to his senator friend."

"Quick!" Prophet said. "Throw something on."

"No — it's too late. If I go with you now, he'll see that I'm gone too soon. We won't get away." She stared at Sergei, her cheeks drawn down with disappointment. "You both go. Out the window. Come for me another time."

"Marya, no!" Sergei said, his face bunching with frustration, showing his teeth.

Prophet listened at the door. Boots clomped up the stairs, growing louder.

Prophet shook his head and bounded past Sergei, nudging the Cossack's shoulder as he made for the large casement window, open to the night air. "She's right. We'll have to spring her some other time."

Sergei stood staring with red-faced frustration at the girl, refusing to move.

Boots thumped in the hall.

"Sergei — go!" she pleaded, jerking his arm toward the window. Prophet was already straddling the casement, one leg outside.

"I cannot leave you," the Russian insisted.

"If you don't leave me now, we will *all* die," she insisted, jerking on his arm, leading him toward the window. "I have been here this long, I can wait longer."

The boots stopped outside the door. The doorknob turned. Marya watched it, her heart in her throat. The door opened, and Leamon Gay's frowning visage appeared. He wore a bowler hat, and his stringy white hair brushed the tops of his shoulders. His face was pink from the sun; a pair of steel-rimmed glasses perched on his nose.

"The door was not locked," he said, standing there, holding the door open and observing the door as if it held the answer to his question.

Marya turned to the window, where the man called Prophet and Sergei had disappeared. She could hear them scurrying down a trellis pole, making slight scuffing sounds, the wood of the pole creaking with their weight.

To cover the noise, she said more loudly

than normal, "You must have forgotten to lock it when you last went out. Too bad I didn't know, or I would be gone. Is your friend still here? I have only just now finished my bath."

Gay turned to her angrily. "What's taking so damn long? You should be dressed and ready by now."

Marya shrugged. "You know how women are. . . ."

Out the window, a soft thud rose from below. Gay shuttled his frown to it. "What was that?"

Marya's heart leaped. She swallowed it down and fashioned a casual expression. "What was what?"

Frowning, Gay moved slowly toward the window.

"I didn't hear anything," Marya said.

With an exaggerated movement, she cast her towel aside and turned to face him. He saw her in the corner of his vision, turned to her. Staring at her naked young body, the pert breasts standing out proudly from her chest, the frown slowly faded from his face, replaced by a vaguely lascivious grin.

"Ah, you are a lovely specimen!" He stooped to nuzzle her right breast. Straightening, he added, "But don't think it's going to keep you from dying if you don't give up your secret. Now, get dressed. You have five minutes to be downstairs!"

He wheeled and marched out of the room.

Marya heaved a relieved sigh, grabbed her towel, and hurried to the window. Looking out, she saw little but the wall and a few dead trees the Mexicans who had once lived here had planted in the cobbled courtyard. A guard was making his slow rounds beyond the wall. Sergei and the man called Prophet must have slipped away safely. From an open window below, she could here the boisterous voices of Gay's men playing cards in the dining room.

She gazed once more across the yard, feeling all the more lonely for having seen Sergei and learning that her beloved sister Natasha was as near as Broken Knee . . .

Prophet and Sergei were hunkered down behind the wall, under the spread limbs of a dead pecan tree, hidden from Marya's window as well as the yard. They waited for the guard to make his way along the wall. When the man finally passed, strolling casually and smoking, his footfalls soft in the hard-packed dust, Prophet and the Cossack hurdled the wall and ran crouching across the yard.

They were halfway to the corral when

Prophet saw movement to their left, in the shadows before a long, low, adobe building he assumed was a bunkhouse. A wagon parked between the bunkhouse and the wall had hidden from view the two men who now appeared standing there casually conversing on the far side of the wagon.

"Drop!" Prophet whispered.

He and Sergei flung themselves down and shot looks out to their left. Prophet knew it was too late even before he heard: "Hey, who in the hell is that?" The man's voice was rough and loud with incredulity.

Prophet spat a curse. He didn't have to say anything to Sergei. The Cossack knew the score. If they didn't claw iron and trigger lead, they'd be dead in seconds.

Simultaneously they raked their guns from their holsters, aimed from their prone positions, and opened up, cutting the two silhouetted figures down in a blaze of muzzle flashes and an acrid cloud of gunsmoke.

Gay's two men were down but still kicking when Prophet and Sergei bounded to their feet and ran like mustangs with cans tied to their tails.

Prophet was running and breathing so hard he only vaguely heard voices rising behind him. Then came the gunfire, tentative at first. It quickly grew insistent, the bullets whistling in the air around Prophet and Sergei, plunking into the ground around their heels.

They didn't take the time to look for the trough they'd taken up the mountain. When they came to the shelf's lip, they bounded straight over the side, losing their footing, dropping and rolling, banging against boulders and tumbling over shrubs.

Both men were on their feet again in seconds, ignoring the bruises incurred in the fall, still descending, knowing Gay's long riders were in hot pursuit, hearing the pistol and rifle pops growing louder behind them. Prophet was inclined to stop and return fire but decided against it; his muzzle flashes would signal his position.

He ran, leaping rocks, twisting around boulders, and bounding through brush. He heard Sergei about fifteen feet to his left, grunting and wheezing, breath raking in and out of his lungs, the Cossack's boots pounding the ground. In several places, where the boulders were thick, they had to slow down and make their way carefully, but then they ran again, picking out obstacles in the starlight.

Meanwhile, guns popped behind them, men cursed. Casting occasional glances over his shoulder, Prophet saw the muzzle flashes of the men descending the mountain, spread out to sweep as much ground as possible. Prophet and Sergei had the advantage of the darkness. Still, several shots came close, twanging off boulders, spraying Prophet with shards of gravel and dirt.

By the time he and the Russian made the foot of the mountain, Prophet's knees ached, and his feet screamed in his boots. Sleeving sweat from his brow, he paused for a two-second breather and saw that the Cossack did likewise, hands on his knees, blowing and puffing.

"Come on," Prophet said, his voice hoarse with exertion.

He moved off to the left, pushing through greasewood bramble, traversing an arroyo, and finally hearing the startled whinny of Mean and Ugly.

"No more joyous sound have I ever heard," he said aloud, his chest on fire.

He headed for the sound, Sergei following. When they found the horses tied where they'd left them, they toed their stirrups, clawed at their horns, and heaved their exhausted bodies into their saddles.

Prophet looked back the way he'd come. The gunfire had silenced. Distant, muffled voices rose in anger and confusion.

"Think we lost 'em — for now," he told the Cossack.

"Yes, for now," Sergei said, sucking a ragged breath. "I doubt we have time for tea, however."

"We can agree on that, at least, ole hoss."

Prophet reined Mean around and spurred him into a trot through the broken desert. When he and Sergei made the road, their horses bounded into a ground-eating gallop for a distant jog of hills.

Knowing that Gay's men might run them down if they headed directly for town, Prophet and Sergei stayed in the desert for three nights, camping in a different place each night and snaring rabbits for food.

On the fourth day they made their way back to Broken Knee, avoiding the main road, approaching the livery barn from the rear. They stabled their horses with the Mexican, who laughed when Prophet told him they'd been hunting.

"What's so funny?" he asked.

"Nothing, señor."

Prophet glanced at Sergei. They were both sunburned, sweaty, and caked with red desert dust. Prophet's pulse pricked at his hands and feet. He wondered if somehow the hostler knew that he and Sergei had invaded the hacienda.

"What is it?"

The Mexican smiled knowingly. "You've been out looking for the Jesuit gold. That is okay — many men have looked for it." Jorge Assante poked a mocking finger in the air. "But no one has ever found it."

Prophet exhaled a relieved breath. He decided to play dumb about the gold. "What Jesuit gold?"

"You know the gold, señor. The Lost Morales Gold. The gold of many legends. Some men believe, some don't believe. I, myself, do not believe, but that does not mean it is not out there somewhere."

Assante wagged his grinning head as he continued rubbing grease into a cracked strip of dry harness leather.

"It is none of my business what you do, señors," he continued. "But beware. If Gay finds you out there, it will go badly for you."

"Oh? Why's that?" Prophet asked, sliding a furtive glance at Sergei.

"Because he is one of the believers. He wants the treasure for himself, you see." Assante shook his head again and held Prophet with a dark, admonishing gaze. "And if he does not get it, then no one gets it. No, no — it is best you stay out of the mountains. If I were you, I would go farther south and look for treasure. There is said to be much gold in *Mejico*."

"Thanks for the advice," Prophet said. "Grain 'em good, will you?"

"*Si*, señor."

On the way to the hotel, keeping an eye out for Gay's men, Sergei said, "The treasure Marya was after."

"Yep." Prophet sleeved sweat-mud from his brow. "I reckon she and her ole friend Bert didn't know what kind of a ring-tailed varmint they'd be tussling with, when they rode into this country looking for their el Dorado."

"Do you believe the gold is really there, Lou?"

"Hell, I don't know," Prophet said. "To tell you the truth, I don't really care. I just want to get the countess's sister off that mountain so I can wash my hands of all of you, including Leamon Gay, and head on down to *Mejico* for a fandango with the senoritas."

They found the countess anxiously waiting for them in her room, where she'd obviously been doing little but smoking, reading, and drinking coffee for the past two days while she worried. Her room was a mess and her features were drawn.

When Prophet and Sergei had filled her in

231

on what had happened at Gay's hacienda, and why they'd been gone so long, Prophet left and found a bathhouse. Bathed, he returned to his hotel room and slept until he heard someone probing his door lock.

He grabbed his Colt from the bedpost, thumbed back the hammer, and waited. The door opened, and the countess appeared, moving stealthily. Seeing the gun aimed at her, she said, "It is only I."

Prophet depressed the Colt's hammer and returned the gun to its holster. "Where'd you get a key?"

"The desk clerk."

Prophet smiled. "That was rather bold, wasn't it?"

"I told him it was for you, that you had lost yours."

His head resting in his hand, he watched as she stripped before him, tossing her clothes on the floor, then removed her barrette, letting her hair spill about her shoulders.

She shook her head, tossing her hair down her back, and lay beside Prophet, who lay on the bed naked, for it was as hot as a shallow desert grave in the room, even with the two windows open. She smiled at him warmly and snuggled against him, curling her legs in his. Her skin shone umber in the slanting afternoon light, her body fine and long.

She kissed him and buried her face in his chest. He caressed her back, nuzzling her neck. Absently she fondled his stiffening member.

"Oh, Lou," she said longingly, "how will you ever be able to bring Marya back to me?"

"I've been wondering the same thing," Prophet said as he softly kissed her shoulder. "But I think I know a way."

She jerked away from him and lifted her startled gaze to his. "What is it?"

He told her.

And then they made love.

Leamon Gay's canopied phaeton clattered up the mountain behind the black Thoroughbred, the canopy's beaded tassels dancing this way and that. Four horseback riders surrounded the buggy, all holding shotguns or rifles.

Leaning back on the reins, the driver pulled the phaeton up to the hacienda's front patio shaded by a vast brush arbor. This late in the day the sprawling adobe structure with its protruding vega poles threw a bleak, vast shadow over the yard, in startling contrast to the rust-colored desert below the mountain.

"We're home, Mr. Gay," the driver said, a big blond German in ratty, dusty clothes, and with a short-barreled shotgun sheathed on his hip.

Behind him, the sleeping Gay stirred in the leather seats. He lifted his head and gazed around, smacking his lips. "Ah, yes, we are at that."

He looked around for his black slouch hat, which had fallen to the floor while he'd slept. It had been a long ride from Tucson, where he'd met yesterday with prospective investors in another mining operation. Finding the hat, he donned it, straightened his cravat, and stepped gracefully down from the buggy, the door of which had already been opened by one of the shotgun-wielding bodyguards who had accompanied him to Tucson.

The guards accompanied him everywhere. The downside of being a wealthy man in this lawless land was that everyone and their brother had it out for you. And that wasn't even taking the ferocious Apaches and Mexican *bandidos* into consideration.

What he'd enjoyed most about being a simple bandit himself, in those long-ago days, was that you at least knew who your enemies were. These days he could never be sure — thus the need for guards everywhere he went.

He was walking across the groomed gravel yard when the hacienda's heavy front door opened and his first lieutenant, Brian Delgado, stepped out, clad in his customary bullhide vest and black gunbelt. Delgado was tall and narrow, like his employer. Unlike Gay, his belly was flat, his face and shoulders broad. His right eye wandered in its socket — a little reminder of Apache Pass.

"Welcome back, *jefe,*" he said, pensively twisting a waxed end of his full, black mustache.

"Yeah, yeah," Gay said, impatient. "How did the tracking go? Did you find them?" He was referring to the two men who had invaded — or had tried to invade — the hacienda three nights ago.

He'd sent out a contingent of men to hunt them down, find out who they were, and then drag them through town as an example to anyone else who considered making an unannounced visit to the hacienda, and kill them.

"Sorry, *jefe.*" Delgado threw his arms defeatedly.

"You lost 'em?"

Delgado shook his head. "We tracked

them into the Pasqualante Hills, and they lost us in a creek bed."

"They lost us in a creek bed." Gay's voice was dully mocking. His eyes bored into his lieutenant's like fire-tipped daggers.

Delgado stared back. His own eyes slitted slightly, wary. He swallowed. "Sorry, *jefe*."

"Sorry, *jefe*," Gay mocked again.

He stood staring at his lieutenant for a full fifteen seconds, the other men looking on, silently tense. Then Gay turned, throwing an arm over Delgado's shoulders and leading the man out into the yard, away from the buggy upon which the driver still sat, slumped, the reins dangling in his hands. He watched Gay and Delgado with flat, knowing eyes, the corners of his mouth turned up slightly.

"Delgado," Gay said, stopping when they were about twenty feet from the buggy and in view of all the men in the yard, including those smoking under the bunkhouse arbor, "I made you my first lieutenant because I thought you would be effective."

Delgado's eyes flickered. He swallowed, tried a smile, and let it go. Flies buzzed about his lips, but he ignored them. "Look, *jefe*, I can track a snake across a flat rock . . . usually. But, *dios*, you cannot expect . . . you cannot expect . . ."

"No, I guess I can't expect you to run down two men who tried invading my hacienda, can I? I see that now." Gay's arm was still draped across Delgado's slumped shoulders. He turned his gaze around the yard, where his roughly dressed battalion of hardcases stared on — some frowning, some smiling, some just smoking and staring with mute interest.

Delgado's eyes dropped to Gay's right hand, which had lowered to the crime boss's pistol butt.

"Now, hold on, *jefe*," Delgado said, wrenching himself free of Gay's right arm. "Just hold on. You can't —"

"Sorry, Brian," Gay said, drawing the Colt from his holster.

Delgado took several steps back. As he did, he clawed his own pistol from its holster. The gun had just cleared leather when Gay's Colt barked, slinging a bullet through Delgado's face, just under his left eye. The lieutenant gave a shriek and twisted around, falling to his hands and knees.

Casually Gay stepped toward his lieutenant, lowered the pistol to the back of the man's head, and drilled another bullet through his hat crown. Delgado jerked and slumped forward on his face, his hat tumbling away, knees curled beneath him, blood and brains trickling from the hole in the back of his head.

A disgusted look on his skeletal face, Gay sheathed his pistol and swung a look around at his men. "You all saw that!" he yelled. "That's how I deal with ineffective riders. Remember it."

He swung his gaze toward the bunkhouse, where a big-gutted man in greasy buckskins and with long salt-and-pepper hair stood smoking with two others. "Mackenna!" Gay yelled to the man. "Delgado's job is now yours. Move your things into the house."

The man standing beside Coon Mackenna grinned and gave Mackenna a chiding elbow. "Just make sure you ain't ineffective, Coon," he jeered.

Mackenna just stared grimly, his face flushing slightly, as Gay swung around and headed past the buggy, leaving Delgado a heaped, dead mass in the yard for all his men to consider.

In the house Gay hurried up the winding stone stairs to the second story. Without knocking, he threw open the door to the girl's room and stood there, puffing the stogie and grinning.

"Ah, there you are."

She sat in an upholstered chair at a round table by the window, dressed in one of the pink gowns he'd ordered from New Orleans. She stared at him now, her face appearing drawn and weary.

She tried a smile, but it didn't touch those slanted eyes. "Here I am, right where you left me."

He took the stogie in his right hand, strolled over to her, and placed his hands on her naked shoulders. "How wonderful it is to have a woman awaiting my return from my tawdry business dealings." He knelt like a royal suitor and lightly kissed her forehead. "I've never had a more beautiful woman than you. You are a treat, do you know that, Marya?"

She smiled, trying her best to play along with his bizarre charade, his ludicrous pantomime, his mockery of genuine love-making. He fingered the arm strap of her gown, slowly jerking it down while he nuzzled her neck. "Decide to share your secret?"

"Yes."

He jerked his head up, blinking, surprised. "What?"

"You heard me."

Skirts rustling, she stood and walked to the carved bureau with its vast, ornate mirror, opened a drawer, and removed a sheet of heavy parchment. "I drew the map from memory. It's all yours. Remember, you promised to let me go when you found the treasure."

He took the paper and studied it. "I hope you have a good memory," he said, all vestiges of his playacting gone, his voice teeming with menace. He snapped his head toward the open door behind him. "Benton!"

After a moment the craggy-faced rider named Liam Benton appeared. He was Gay's personal secretary of sorts, the oldest man on his roll.

"Have McKenna take a company of men and follow the map to the *X*, then report back to me pronto."

"You got it, Mr. Gay." The aging secretary, who had once done time for child molesting, nodded dutifully and accepted the map from Gay.

The secretary was heading back through the door when Gay said suddenly, "Wait! Give that back to me."

Frowning, Benton returned the map to his employer.

"Thanks — you can go."

"Yes, sir." Warily Liam turned and disappeared down the hall.

Marya watched Gay with an expression similar to that of the old secretary. Then she realized the problem.

"What's the matter?" she asked, barely able to conceal her delight at Gay's apprehension. "You do not trust your own men?"

Gay's horsey, effeminate features betrayed mild embarrassment. "I'm going after it myself, in good time. Or, I should say, *we* are — you and me. I didn't get to where I am today by being heedless of men's basic natures — the first and foremost of which is greed." He laid the map on the table, then turned to her, standing by the bureau, regarding him with ill-concealed disdain, arms crossed over her breasts as though she'd turned suddenly cold.

He grinned and yanked off his cravat, tossed it aside, and began unbuttoning his shirt. "The second of which is lust."

17

Prophet and Sergei studied the town for three days, noting the comings and goings of the town's main benefactor, Leamon Gay, who never appeared to go anywhere without a contingent of armed guards. While bathing in Metticord's Tonsorial Parlor, Prophet learned from one of the town's business proprietors that Gay gambled in a small room at the back of his saloon every Tuesday and Thursday nights.

"You don't say," Prophet said, feigning only mild interest.

"And this time, by god," the proprietor exclaimed, bathing in the tub a few feet from Prophet, "I'm not going to let that madman turn my pockets inside out!" A strange expression played over the man's face, and he looked around suspiciously.

"You didn't hear that," he said.

"Hear what?" Prophet smiled.

■ ■ ■ ■

Thursday night found the bounty hunter strolling down the boardwalk, waving away the dust kicked up by another ubiquitous ore wagon and wishing Gay would grade a road around the damn town, or move the stamping mill closer to the mine. He paused at the batwings of the Gay Inn Saloon, which abutted the hotel.

A band blared on the balcony while on the dance floor below, bedraggled miners still in their work clothes twirled spangled and war-painted girls in a kaleidoscopic free-for-all of flying hair and colored gowns. Prophet saw Sergei sitting at a table by the piano, drinking alone. The Russian locked eyes with Prophet briefly, gave a furtive nod, then returned his attention to his drink.

Prophet pushed through the crowd and nudged his way up to the bar, where three harried barmen toiled behind the counter, sweat and pomade running down their faces and soaking their boiled shirts.

"Give me the good stuff!" he yelled at one who finally gave him the nod.

The barman produced a bottle of rye and filled a shot glass on the counter. "One dollar!" the man yelled above the din.

"One dollar!" Prophet exclaimed. "Who do I look like — Jay Gould?"

"The forty-rod's two bits."

"I've tasted the forty-rod in these parts," Prophet said dryly, remembering the hangovers he'd nursed the past two days running. He had nothing against gunpowder in his ammunition, but he'd never been partial to it in whiskey. He dropped a gold eagle on the counter and said, "Leave the bottle."

"You got it, mister," the barman said, snapping up the gold piece and rushing off to another yelling customer.

Prophet stood at the bar and gassed with an old-timer named Hardy Groom, a gandydancer turned hard-rock miner. Because of the din punctuated by occasional gunshots fired triumphantly into the ceiling, he couldn't hear much of Groom's conversation. It didn't matter, for it was a one-sided conversation, anyway. Prophet was more interested in the arrival of Leamon Gay, who finally showed up around nine o'clock. None too soon, for Prophet was having a hard time nursing his bottle of red-eye, which he shared with old Grooms, who, after several shots chased with beer, clung to the bar as though to the rail of a sinking ship.

Nestled amongst his brawny bodyguards, the stringy-haired Gay pushed through the batwings, paused to announce one free drink for each customer, and retreated to a back room to the thunder of whoop-punctuated applause.

"That Leamon Gay?" Prophet asked the miner after the noise had settled back to a steady roar. He knew it was Gay; he wanted to make his act appear genuine.

"Why, sure it is, mister. Who the hell else would buy drinks for the whole damn house?"

"I need to talk to him."

The miner laughed scornfully. "You need to talk to Mr. Gay?"

"That's right."

"How come?"

"I need a job."

"Well, sorry to tell you this, sonny, but Mr. Gay don't do his own hirin' and firin'. You'll have to apply at the mine office like everyone else." Groom slapped Prophet's shoulder with good-natured derision and laughed.

"Well, hell, that double-eagle there was the last o' my roll. I'm lighter than a damn feather and gettin' a might wolfish. I need a job an' I need one now — tonight."

"Don't do anything stupid, sonny," the

245

geezer warned. "Just hole up to the livery and apply at the mine tomorrow. I'm sure they'll have somethin' for you. You ever chip rock before?"

"No, can't say as I have."

"Well, maybe they'll give ye a job hostlin' the mules. Watch the black-eared ones. They're meaner'n a Texas whore with the clap. I know that from experience. . . ."

But Prophet didn't wait for Groom to finish. With a high, dramatic flair, he threw back his glass and slammed it on the mahogany. Swallowing, eyes wide with single-minded purpose, he pushed through the crowd, heading for the rear of the long room.

He gave hard shoves to several miners, who cussed his back. He ignored the come-ons of a red-haired bawd smelling of pilgrim spirits and seemingly oblivious to the plump breast that had flopped free of her incredibly low-cut gown.

At the back of the room he found a door and knocked thrice, hard.

After a minute the door opened and a face appeared, hard as an anvil. The coldly glaring eyes took Prophet's measure. The man lifted his shotgun. "What the hell do you want?"

"I'd like to talk to Mr. Gay," Prophet said,

slapping his hat from his head with feigned politeness and grinning his best dullard's grin.

The man smiled with one side of his mouth and said with mild disgust, "Get the hell out of here."

He started pulling the door closed. Prophet jammed his boot in the way. The man's ruddy face darkened, and a prominent vein in his cheek jumped. "Did you hear what I told you?"

It wasn't hard for Prophet to act drunk after all the whiskey he'd consumed with the old miner. "I heard you just fine, but, by golly, I wanna see Mr. Gay, an' I wanna see him now."

"Get the hell out of here, you crazy son of a bitch!"

The man took a step toward Prophet, readying the shotgun for a swing, when a man behind him said, "What is it, Lynch?"

"Just some drunk, Mr. Gay. I'll take care of him."

"I was wonderin' if I could have a word with you, sir," Prophet said over the bodyguard's right shoulder.

There was a table in the middle of the small but opulently furnished room, covered with cards, chips, glasses, and bottles. A half dozen men sat around the table. Gay's bodyguards stood at intervals around the room, and lounged on sofas and upholstered chairs, smoking. A couple girls hovered over the players.

Everyone in the room frowned at the commotion at the door. A couple of the other guards moved toward Prophet, scowling. All the guards were big men — Prophet's size and bigger — wearing soiled denims and cotton or buckskin shirts. They were well-armed with pistols and knives and with plenty of shells in their cartridge belts. They were ready for marauding Apaches or *bandidos* or anyone else gunning for their boss and his gold.

"I was wondering if I could have a word with you about a job, Mr. Gay. I know this ain't exac'ly the right time, but I'm flat broke, sir. And I wouldn't normally be this brassy, but I've oiled my craw a little, if you know what I mean."

The guard at the door turned his head toward the table. "It's all right, Mr. Gay. I'll get rid of this dimwit." As he turned back to Prophet, again preparing the shotgun for a swing, Prophet stepped toward him, pulling back his fist before swinging it forward and burying it wrist-deep in the bodyguard's gut.

The man's head plunged forward as he

bellowed like a poleaxed bull. Immediately the three other bodyguards sprang toward Prophet, who went to work, kicking one in the balls, ducking a swing from another and swinging his fist into a jutting jaw. As the third man grabbed him from behind, Prophet bent forward and heaved the man over his shoulder and smashed him into the floor with a thunderous bark, making the lanterns tingle.

The first man had climbed painfully to his feet, prying his knees away from his wounded oysters, and grabbed his shotgun off the floor. Prophet kicked the shotgun out of the man's hands and belted him twice in the jaw, throwing him back against the wall.

He was a tough hombre and would not go down. As Prophet swung on him again, the other two grabbed him from behind, each taking an arm and wrestling Prophet across the room and against the wall.

Prophet cursed and raged and flailed his arms exaggeratedly.

"I just wanna talk to Mr. Gay about a job!" he yelled. "I needa job . . . I'll do anything . . . I'm flat broke . . . !"

With that, Prophet flung off one of the bodyguards, sent him tumbling over the gambling table and scattering the cards and players. One of the girls screamed as Prophet belted the other bodyguard with a right haymaker, bouncing the man's head off the wall and dimming the light in his eyes.

He was turning to the third man — the man with the shotgun — when something hard slammed his left temple. He staggered backward, blinking. Before his eyes lost total focus, he saw the man with the shotgun standing before him, a savage smile on his face, holding the greener butt-forward toward Prophet.

He jabbed the butt forward once more, wincing with satisfaction as the brass plate tattooed Prophet's forehead, sending the bounty hunter sprawling across a fainting couch, where one of the girls had taken refuge. She now scurried away in her high heels, shrieking.

In Prophet's ears the girl's screams along with every other sound slowly died until he heard nothing at all. His lids fluttered like a dove's wings over his aching eyes.

"Damn," the bodyguard said, setting his shotgun on the floor and crouching over his aching crotch. "That hurts."

Behind him, Gay stood with his gambling companions, smoking and observing the destruction, looks of keen exasperation manteling their brows. Gay glanced at his men, all in various stages of dishevelment, and yelled, "Get him out of here! What the hell do I pay you for?"

He turned his head to the door, where two men with badges appeared. Behind them, the saloon had grown quiet, and the crowd had gathered around the door, peeking in as though at a street accident.

"What happened here, Mr. Gay?" Sheriff Phil Booth asked, eyeing the human wreckage as well as the demolished poker table with its hodgepodge of chips and cards spread across the rug. The sheriff was a short, gray-haired man with an old Remington on his hip, wearing a cheap frock coat and string tie.

"What's it look like, Phil? This man stormed in here and put the kibosh to four of my best men." Gay raked his angry gaze at his bodyguards, two of whom had climbed to their feet. The other two were still testing their land legs.

"Who is he?" It was Booth's first deputy, Charlie Reed.

"I don't know, but get him the hell out of here!" To the bodyguards, Gay yelled, "You men get this place cleaned up. Good God — look at this mess! We were in the middle of a game!"

While the beleaguered bodyguards gazed around, getting their bearings before slowly moving to clean up the mess, the sheriff and the deputy each grabbed Prophet by an arm, yanked him to his feet, and half-dragged, half-walked him out the door.

"Bodyguards, you call yourselves!" Gay groused at his men. He crouched to retrieve a glass and a bottle from the floor, and turned to his gambling partners. "Who was that son of a bitch, anyway? Anybody here ever seen him before?"

"I saw him in the bathhouse yesterday," piped up the owner of the drugstore, Bill Knott, as he righted his chair and brushed spilled whiskey from his sleeve. "Just a drifter, I reckon. Just like he said here, he was lookin' for a job."

"Looking for a bullet, more like," Gay snapped. He looked at one of the girls — a willowy blonde named Dixie. He sat down and patted his knee. "Come here, my sweet little Dixie peach. Come to your daddy. You didn't get hurt when the table fell, did you?"

"I broke a nail," Dixie said, pouting and wagging the hand as though she'd burned it.

"Let me kiss it," Gay cooed as the blonde scooted onto his lap.

18

"Boy, you got yourself in a whole heap of trouble!"

The voice came from far away, from deep in a tunnel or the bottom of a well. Prophet could barely hear it above the fireworks in his head. There was another sound, like keys jingling, and then a lock rattled. Hinges squawked. He opened his eyes, found himself before a jail cell that stunk of piss and old sweat.

The door was pulled open by a tall young man in a frock coat and wielding a shotgun. He scowled at Prophet as someone else shoved him through the door.

Falling forward on the cot — a strap-iron shelf hanging from the wall by chains — Prophet drew his lips back from his teeth and groaned. He turned his head to the door. A short, gray-haired man with close-set blue eyes and wearing a sheriff's star stood in the open cell door. He wore a hat a shade darker gray than his hair, and his coat had been washed so many times it appeared white in places, its collar frayed.

The old badge-toter took one step forward. "Now, I don't know who in the hell you are or what in the hell you wanted with Mr. Gay, but tomorrow mornin', two of my deputies are going to escort you a mile out of town. From there, you're gonna head east, out of the Territory. Understand? If I catch you back in Broken Knee again, I'll turn you over to Gay himself — and believe me, he won't be near as charitable as yours truly."

There was a short pause.

"You comprendo my lingo, cowboy?" the sheriff asked, his voice sharp with anger.

Apparently it was his job to keep the town free of cutthroats — especially those who might trouble Broken Knee's infamous father and primary booster. Prophet's little fandango at the saloon must have made the sheriff look negligent, and it piss-burned the old man good. He no doubt lived very deep in Gay's pocket and was hoping to stay there, snug as a worm in the dirt.

Prophet grunted.

"What's that?"

Prophet turned his head on the pillow. "I hear you, Sheriff," he said, continuing his down-at-the-heel grubliner routine. "I was just lookin' for a job's all. Didn't mean no harm. Sure am sorry."

"Just you understand you're gettin' the hell out of town tomorrow, and you're never comin' back!"

The door slammed with an iron clatter, and Prophet lifted his head against the reenergized inner explosion, which seemed to vibrate through the pillow. The key clattered in the lock, the light in the cell block died, and Prophet rested his chin on the pillow with a sigh.

"Lou?"

Another, different voice. Prophet only growled at it, his face buried in the pillow that stank of old puke.

"Pssst — Lou?"

The voice was familiar, Prophet realized now. Lifting his head, he opened his eyes. The darkness had given way to a wan, gray light. He turned to the cell door, but no one was there.

"Lou — here," came the voice again, the voice of a Russian speaking stilted, precise English. "At the window."

Noting that the pounding in his head had abated somewhat, and that he must have slept for several hours — the light told him it was nearly dawn — Prophet stood and stepped over to the window. It held no glass, only bars. Just beyond the bars stood the dusky shape of Sergei Andreyevich looking customarily peculiar with his western hat and Russian mustaches and goatee.

"What happened?" the Russian asked. The pearly dawn light lined his frowning eyes under the hat brim.

"Things didn't exactly turn out the way we figured," Prophet confessed. He'd thought that if he could take Gay's bodyguards to the dance, so to speak, he could beat a shortcut to the crime boss's payroll and eventually get close enough to Marya to spring her from the hacienda.

"Gay was not impressed, eh?" Sergei asked glumly.

Prophet winced at the pain in his head. His tone was defensive. "I gave 'em a pretty good fight. It was four against one, for chrissakes."

"I should have been there," Sergei said. "Together, we would have taken the room apart."

Prophet shook his head and rubbed the back of his neck. "Too risky. If we were both in the hoosegow, who'd look after the countess?"

Sergei's silhouette nodded. "Now what happens?"

Prophet sighed. He inspected the goose egg on his forehead with his fingers. It was two eggs, rather — one big one and one small one. The smaller one felt the most tender, shooting sharp pains into his eyes when he touched it.

His cheeks balled with pain, he said, "It looks like they're escortin' me out of town."

The Russian's reply was matter-of-fact and more of a statement than a question. "They are kicking you out of Broken Knee."

"According to the sheriff, I should feel lucky. But don't worry. I ain't givin' up. I'll be back. You and the countess just sit tight up there in the Gay Inn. I'll figure something out yet."

Sergei shook his head disapprovingly.

"It ain't my fault," Prophet groused. "You and the countess thought it would work, too."

Sergei said nothing. He shook his head again and, grumbling, walked away.

Prophet rasped after him, "Hey, where you goin'?" Nothing chafed him more than the Cossack's haughty attitude. "I wasn't the only one thought it would work!" Prophet called too loudly.

Sergei did not reply. Prophet heard only the Cossack's boots grinding gravel as he disappeared around the corner of the jail-house.

"Proddy son of a bitch."

Prophet turned from the window and dippered himself some water from the wooden bucket in the corner. He sat back down on the cot, its wall chains complaining against his weight, and fished in his shirt pocket for his makings sack. He was glad the sheriff had left it alone, for Prophet liked to smoke while he thought, and he had a heap of thinking to do now, in spite of the big heart thumping in his noggin.

How in the hell would he be able to help Sergei and the countess get Marya back after being banished from town? It wasn't like he and Sergei could just storm the hacienda. And they couldn't sneak in again, after they'd been spotted there once by the hacienda guards.

Damn . . .

The sun had risen, flooding Prophet's cell with brassy sunshine, when the cell block door opened. . . . The sheriff appeared carrying a key ring and looking grim.

"Well, son," he said as he stepped before Prophet's cell, "I wasn't expectin' this, but I can't say as I'm surprised."

"About what, Sheriff?"

The sheriff nodded to indicate the front

of the jailhouse. "Mr. Gay's outside, waitin' for you in his buggy."

"In his buggy?" Prophet asked, puzzled. "Why?"

The sheriff poked the key in the lock and turned it. He shook his head. "It don't look good."

"What don't look good?"

"I reckon I shoulda hustled you out of town before Gay got to thinkin' about it."

Prophet was exasperated. "About what!"

"About what you did last night to his men. He musta got to thinkin' about it and decided you couldn't go unpunished. Sets a bad precedent. I'm sorry, old son. He'll probably have his men haul you out in the desert and put a bullet in you. I'm sure it'll be fast, though."

The sheriff swung open the door and drew his Remington, aimed at Prophet.

"You mean you're gonna turn me over to him? So he can kill me?"

"Like I said, I'm sorry. Ain't much I can do about it, though. This is Gay's town."

"And you're just his jailor."

The sheriff nodded grimly. "He pays well, so . . ."

"You dance to his music."

The sheriff waved the gun, and Prophet stepped out of the cell.

"Right on through the cell block door there," the sheriff ordered, falling in behind Prophet, poking his back with his gun barrel to remind him he was covered.

Prophet did as he was told — what else could he do? — and walked into the sheriff's office furnished with a couple of shabby desks and a sheet-iron stove. Two young deputies sat around one of the desks. Seeing Prophet, they smirked and rocked back in their chairs, self-satisfied.

"Reckon this is the end of the line, old son," one of the deputies said, fingering his sparse blond mustache and hitching his holster on his hip.

"Shut up, Jerry," ordered the sheriff. "Right on outside," he said to Prophet.

The bounty hunter stepped out under the brush arbor shading a strip of packed earth before the adobe jailhouse. Gay's phaeton sat in the street. Gay sat on the rear leather seat, resembling a whiskey peddler in a black-checked suit and bowler, his bleached hair hanging straight to his shoulders. Wire-rimmed spectacles were perched on his long, hooked nose. His raptorial features combined with the suit made him look ludicrously evil, an obvious pimp and panderer, crafty vermin who had outrun the law long enough to get rich enough to buy it. He obviously enjoyed playing the role of rich hooligan and boomtown lord.

Four bodyguards — the same ones from last night — sat on their horses around the phaeton. One had a white bandage wrapped around his head and tied under his jaw.

Another sported a swollen eye as purple as spoiled fruit.

Another's arm hung in a sling.

The fourth was sitting on a small, red pillow and leaning slightly forward in his saddle, as if to lighten the load on his crotch.

They scowled at Prophet as though staring into the sun. Gay studied the bounty hunter like a three-card draw.

The sheriff came out behind Prophet. "Here he is, Mr. Gay," he said, pointing out the obvious. "I reckon he's all yours," he added with a note of genuine regret in his voice.

Gay studied Prophet another moment. "Who are you?" he asked tonelessly.

"Me?" Prophet said, hesitant, tipping his head to the side to work the kinks in his neck. "I'm Lou Pepper."

Gay stared as though considering a stucco wall, then blinked his raptor's eyes once. "Where are you from and what have you done?"

Prophet considered his story a moment, then licked his lips and canted his head the other way. "I'm from Georgia and I've done just about everything there is and a little more."

"Can you shoot as well as you can fight with your fists?"

Prophet flicked his eyes at Gay's scowling guards, nodded, and let his upper lip rise, grinning. "Almost."

Gay lifted a gun and cartridge belt off the seat beside him, and slung it toward the bounty hunter. The belt landed in the dust at his feet. It was Prophet's gun, cartridge belt, and bowie knife.

He looked at Gay, wary. The man said, "You got a horse?"

Prophet hesitated. "Yeah . . ."

"Strap your gun on and get it. Then meet me at the mine office. You're hired."

Gay propped a French calfskin boot on the back of the seat before him. "Let's go," he told the driver.

The driver clucked to the horse, and the phaeton clattered away, two guards riding point, two riding drag. All four stared resentfully back at Prophet.

"Well, I'll be damned," said the sheriff. "You gotta be the luckiest sumbitch alive."

Prophet snorted with relief and stared

with wonder at the dwindling caravan. "Took the words right out of my mouth."

19

An hour later Prophet and Sergei reined their horses to a halt on the mine road.

Before them sat the mine's dark gash in a high cliff face, chalky tailings tonguing below the entrance. On a slope far below sat what Prophet figured was the mine office — a barrack-like stone structure with a red tile roof. It was flanked by stables and a wagon shed as well as an enormous corral for the mules that pulled the big Murphy ore wagons to the stamping mill.

Wagons pounded down the switchbacks from the mine, contributing to the brassy dust hanging heavy in the scorched, dry air.

Mules brayed and blacksnakes popped. A couple of brindle hounds barked at the wagons. At a stone repair shop to Prophet's right, a smithy reshaped a bent wheel rim while a mule skinner and a shotgun guard sipped coffee from tin cups and offered counsel.

Prophet gave Sergei a meaningful look, then gigged Mean and Ugly toward the office, turning to avoid a booming wagon and cussing mule skinner. As he and Sergei neared the office, Prophet saw the four bodyguards whose skulls he'd dusted last night sitting in a row of hide-bottom chairs on the porch, shaded by a tin-roofed awning.

They squinted out from under their hat brims as Prophet and the Russian approached the hitch rack. The guards looked none too happy to see Prophet, who grinned and nodded affably.

"Howdy, boys. Doin' all right?"

"Buddy, you think you're smart. Don't get too smart," warned the man Prophet had kicked in the balls.

"Who — me? I'm just a simple Georgia boy tryin' to make a livin'."

A few minutes later a runty clerk ushered Prophet and Sergei into Gay's office at the building's rear. Gay sat behind a big oak desk, smoking a hefty cigar and going over a ledger. His sleeves were rolled up his long, pale, knife-scarred arms.

"Who's this?" he asked, regarding the Cossack disdainfully.

"Friend of mine," Prophet said. "Met him on the trail over east. Can you use him, too,

265

Mr. Gay? He's short but a broad son of a bitch. Look at him."

Gay studied the Russian, obviously impressed by his looks. "Can he fight like you?"

Prophet laughed. "Well, now, I wouldn't say he can fight like me. Not many can. But he can hold his own in a Dodge City barn dance — I'll give him that." He glanced at Sergei, who flashed him an indignant look.

Gay walked around the desk, his cigar smoldering between his slender fingers. He stopped a foot away from Sergei, squinted into the Russian's emotionless brown eyes. Sergei stood stiff-backed, tense as a private given the twice-over by a general.

"What's your name?"

Prophet cleared his throat. "Uh — he don't speak, sir. He's mute. He can write, though. That's how I found out his name is Dick." If Gay heard Sergei's accent, he might tie him to Marya.

"Dick?"

"Dick."

"Dick what?"

"Uh, Dick Lubowski."

"Lubowski."

"Dick here — he's been a bar bouncer and a bodyguard to several governors. Why, he even escorted an English prince West on a huntin' trip. Saved the royal from a scalpin' — held off twelve Injun bucks with nothin' but a six-shooter and a bowie knife!"

Gay stared into the Cossack's eyes, his nostrils twitching as though testing the air for the smell of dung.

"Mighty impressive credentials," he grumbled, and poked the cigar back in his mouth for several thoughtful puffs, his cold eyes narrowing.

"He ain't real smart, though," Prophet added. He noted a slight flush rising in Sergei's cheeks. "No, he ain't a whip like me, but then we can't all be good with our fists *and* smart."

Gay's eyes flickered toward Prophet, and a sneer yanked at his mouth. "He's not as bright as you? What a pity." Gay puffed the stogie. "Well, I haven't seen him fight, but I'd like to see how well he takes a punch."

Gay had barely finished the sentence before he pulled his arm back, making a fist, then swung it forward. Prophet winced and blinked. When he looked again, he saw the stubby, hairy fingers of the Cossack's left hand wrapped around Gay's wrist, Gay's fist barely touching the Russian's belly. Gay's hand was turning pink. He gave a restrained yelp as he pulled back on the captured limb, shuffling to his right.

Prophet elbowed the Cossack. "That's enough, Dick. I think he gets the point."

A few minutes later, massaging his right hand with his left, Gay led Prophet and Sergei outside, where the four bodyguards were still sitting in a grim line on the porch.

"Harland, DeBocha — you're fired," Gay said crisply. "Clean your things out of your quarters and get the hell out of town."

The four men looked at one another, then at their boss, dumbly. "Huh?" one of them grunted, outraged.

"You heard me. Scram! These men have won your jobs."

"He surprised us last night, Boss!" said the guard with shaggy muttonchops and a white bandage around his head. His bib-front shirt was open to the thick matt of dun-colored hair on his chest. He wore an ivory-gripped Colt in a well-worn shoulder rig.

Gay wasn't swayed in the least. "All the more reason for you to scram." The outlaw bent over slightly at the waist. *"Scram! Outta here! Go! Vamoose!"*

Scowling with fury at Prophet and Sergei, the two men scuttled like two scolded dogs down the porch steps.

"Give your shotguns to these two," Gay

ordered, indicating Prophet and the Russian.

The men stopped, glanced at each other. The man with the muttonchops and shoulder rig tossed his shotgun to Prophet. With a curse, the other man — the man with his arm in a sling — tossed his two-bore to Sergei, who grabbed it with one hand. Then both men turned, untied their horses from the hitch rack, mounted up, and rode away cursing and shaking their heads, their faces aflame with malice.

Muttonchops hipped around in his saddle. Glaring at Prophet, he said, "You ain't seen the last of us, you son of a bitch!"

He gigged his horse after the other man, and, passing an oar wagon, they galloped down the mountain trail, their dust sifting behind them.

"Well, then," Gay said, snapping his jacket down and turning to the two bodyguards sitting in their chairs and eyeing their new colleagues skeptically. "Dwight Rosen, Mel Clark — meet Lou Pepper and Dick Lubowski."

Prophet grinned at the two men, and pinched his hat brim. "Hidy-ho."

The guards stared at him and Sergei with ill-concealed disdain.

■ ■ ■ ■

The two new and the two veteran guards loitered around the mine office porch the rest of the day.

After supper at the Inn, Gay and the bodyguards rode up the mountain to the hacienda with its buffer of armed sentinels waving and nodding from the rocks along the mountain. When the phaeton had pulled up to the front patio, which was guarded by a beefy gent smoking a cigar and holding a shotgun, Gay climbed out of the buggy and turned to his four bodyguards.

"Clark, Rosen — show Pepper and Lubowski where they'll be sleeping." With that, Gay headed inside and promptly disappeared — either to Marya's room or his office, Prophet assumed.

"You do it," Rosen told Clark when Gay was out of hearing range. "I'm getting a drink."

Clark cussed at his partner's retreating back, then led Prophet and Sergei through a side entrance under a deep-set portico.

They swung down a dimly lit hall around the north side of the house. They skirted a graveled courtyard with a few benches with rotten wood and rusty iron frames, and a dry adobe fountain with dead leaves and sand piled around its base.

Clark stopped before a stout, wood door with chipped green paint and a tarnished brass latch. The door and five others faced the derelict courtyard that had probably been the sight of many Mexican fandangos in the house's rich Mexican history before Gay and his outlaws had moved in and trashed the place.

"So poor ole Dick can't talk, eh?" Clark asked conversationally, one hand on the door's latch.

"You'd have a longer conversation with a barn wall than ole Dick here, God bless him," Prophet said, cutting his eyes at Sergei, whose nostrils flared disdainfully.

"He lose his tongue to Injuns, or some pigtailed girl cut it out?" Clark asked with a mocking chuckle.

Prophet wagged his head. "You best be careful what you say about ole Dick. Just cause he can't talk don't mean he can't cut loose with a haymaker that would shatter your jaw like china."

They were clomping down the flagstones, spurs chinging. Clark stopped abruptly and turned to the Russian. He was an inch or so taller than Sergei. He puffed up his chest and gritted his teeth.

"Oh, yeah? You a tough guy, Dick?"

Sergei dully returned the man's stare. Prophet watched uneasily, hoping the Russian didn't forget himself and speak.

Sergei knew what the price of that would be, however. He maintained his composure. Clark broke the stare.

"Don't seem all that tough to me," he snarled, running his filthy sleeve across his mouth, turning, and continuing down the courtyard, chuckling. It seemed to make him feel better after what had happened last night and then Prophet and Sergei being rewarded for it with jobs.

The hardcase stopped and threw open a door. "This is it, boys. Home sweet home — for as long as you're gonna be here, anyway." He chuckled again with meaning. "Me and Rosen bunk in the next room there. When he ain't upstairs with his little honey, Mr. Gay stays in that room yonder." Clark gestured to a door just around a corner of the courtyard. A broken sculpture of a Spanish conquistador stood to the door's left, chipped saber raised.

"Gay has a woman here?" Prophet asked, fashioning a curious frown.

"Sure he does. Always keeps at least one around. Sometimes two. He's had as many as three in the house at a time, but it don't work too well with this many men around, if'n you get my drift."

"Who's the girl?"

"That, my friend," Clark said, "is none of your business. She don't wanna be here, though — he keeps her locked in a room upstairs — so if you see her tryin' to sneak out, stop her. Those are orders straight from the boss hisself."

Prophet sensed Sergei's muscles tightening. Ignoring him, Prophet said, "I don't reckon I care what Gay does with his women, as long as I get paid. . . ."

"That's right," Clark agreed. "Just do your job and keep your mouth shut. And you see any strangers around, shoot first and ask questions later. Someone tried sneakin' in the other night."

"That right?" Prophet asked, moving into the room and scraping a match alight on his pistol belt. "Bandits?"

"Prob'ly," Clark said, nibbling his scarred upper lip. "There's always someone out gunnin' for Mr. Gay. But your main job is to guard him when he leaves the hacienda. Inside the house, he's well protected by the other guards spread out across the mountain. But it never hurts to keep your ears pricked and your eyes skinned."

"I s'pose a man like that has made a few

enemies over the years," Prophet speculated, touching the match to a candlewick.

"I reckon he has, but he pays well, and I like the digs here, so I don't ask questions about it or even think about it much. I just keep one hand on my pistol butt and one eye on my backtrail, if'n you know what I'm sayin. Well, I hope you boys are comfortable here." Clark smiled without humor and left, leaving the door open behind him.

Sergei shoved the door closed and turned to Prophet, who threw out a hand, shushing the Russian while he listened at the door.

Confident Clark had drifted off, Prophet said, "Okay."

"I cannot bear the thought of Gay . . . and Marya," Sergei growled, turning and moving slowly, anxiously about the long, narrow room. "I cannot bear the thought of what he does . . . has been doing . . ."

"Well, he won't be doin' it for much longer," Prophet promised. "I say we don't waste any time tryin' to spring her. As soon as everyone in the house has gone to bed, we head upstairs and nab her out of here."

"Yes, yes, yes," Sergei eagerly agreed.

"Only problem is . . ." Prophet said, running a hand thoughtfully along his jaw, letting the sentence trail off.

"Is what?"

"Once we have her, how the hell do we get past all these owlhoots?"

"We will shoot our way, if we have to!"

Prophet winced at the Russian's foolhardy zeal, but he allowed there were few other answers. "I reckon. . . ."

20

Prophet and the Russian sat around and smoked for several hours, not talking much. Killing time, Prophet cleaned his guns, then loaded and unloaded them and loaded them again.

Finally he heard two sets of boots clicking and chinging on the flagstones outside the room. The door of the room abutting theirs opened and closed. That would be Clark and Rosen heading for bed. They'd probably been playing cards at the round table in what had once been a formal dining room.

Prophet noted that he and "Dick" hadn't been invited to play. He smiled.

Later, a single pair of boots clacked in the courtyard, coming from the other direction. Cracking the door, Prophet saw Gay's dimly lit figure, the man's shirt open, belt unbuckled, hat in his hand, coming down the far walk. The crime boss stopped at his bedroom door, opened it with a key, and went in.

Prophet checked his watch. One-thirty.

"He turned in," he told Sergei.

When they'd removed their spurs and stuffed them in their boots, Prophet opened the door and scanned the courtyard. Seeing that all was clear, he and Sergei stepped into the courtyard, and the Russian gently drew the door shut behind them.

Prophet had been considering the route to Marya's room, and now turned right, walking on the balls of his feet. They came to the end of the walk and continued through a winding corridor between two rows of doors, through another courtyard. When they were nearly to a short set of steps, the door on their left squawked.

Prophet grabbed Sergei's arm and pulled the big Russian into the shadows behind a statue of one of the saints. Holding his breath and feeling his heart pound, Prophet watched the door open, gritting his teeth as the hinges squeaked. A big figure appeared, a Mexican yawning and adjusting his shell belt on his broad hips. The man carried a rifle in his right hand. The handle of a large knife jutted from a sheath strapped behind his left shoulder. Probably a night guard assuming his shift.

Wearily the man turned and drew the door closed, then ambled back the way Prophet and Sergei had come, throwing his head back and yawning loudly.

Prophet sighed quietly, glanced at Sergei, and stepped out from behind the saint, again walking on the balls of his feet as he climbed the stone steps, turned, and climbed another, winding set of stairs, disappearing into shadows.

They scurried past three guards in a small room pillared off from a living room with a giant fireplace. Then they slipped up another set of stairs and down a dark hall.

"This is the room, isn't it?" Prophet whispered, stopping before a door.

Sergei nodded. Leaning close, he listened, then glanced down. "The key," he said softly but urgently. "It is not in the lock."

Soft, quick footsteps rose behind the door, like a person running barefoot. The door clicked, and Prophet tensed as it opened. The girl stood there, eyes wide, wearing a thin wrapper over an ornate nightgown. Behind her, a green lamp burned on a table beside the large bed.

"Marya!" Sergei exclaimed under his breath.

"Sergei!" she cried, throwing her arms around the big Cossack's neck, hugging him. "I am so glad you are all right. I thought you might have been injured the other night. I heard the shooting."

"We are fine, my girl," Sergei assured her.

She drew the door wide and beckoned them in, then closed the door. "He took the key, but I fixed the lock so he could not lock it," she explained.

"How in the heck did you manage that?" Prophet asked with an amazed chuckle.

"Marya is a most industrious young lady," Sergei told him, adding dryly, "Sometimes more industrious than what is healthy for a pretty young countess."

The girl shushed them. "Guards pass the door regularly," she said. "After the other night, he tightened the security around the hacienda. How did you get back in?"

"We're on his payroll," Prophet said.

She arched a brow at him.

"Our good Prophet got us positions on Gay's staff," Sergei explained to her. "We are protecting him now." He smiled wryly. "We thought it would be the easiest way to get to you."

She turned to Prophet, an admiring light entering her gaze. "That was a good idea." She sounded surprised.

Prophet gave an ironic grunt. "I've had

one or two in the past. We best get a move on."

"No." Marya shook her head. "I have another way — a safer way."

Prophet frowned, hoping they hadn't risked their necks getting to the girl's room for nothing. "What way is that?"

"The night after next, when the moon is full, I am showing Gay where Bert found the Spanish gold. With your help, I will slip away from him on the trail. Now that you are guards, it should be even easier."

Prophet glanced at Sergei, considering it. He turned to the girl. "Are you sure he's going to take you with him? Why won't he just make you draw him a map?"

"Because he won't trust me. But on the trail, if I don't show him where the treasure is, he can threaten to kill me."

"Which brings me to another question," Prophet said, narrowing his eyes critically. "Why didn't you just go ahead and give the man the gold, for chrissakes? I mean, is it really worth losing your life over?"

The pretty blonde glared at him as though awestruck. "He killed Bert! I couldn't let him get away with killing Bert *and* stealing his gold!" She crossed her arms defensively. "Besides, he would have killed me as soon as he found it. By not telling him, I was extending my life . . . and increasing my chances of getting away."

She smiled smugly.

Prophet shook his head. Another loco royal. That made three. Sergei was guilty by association. "Miss, you're somethin'."

"Yes, she is definitely that," Sergei agreed, frowning, not at all happy about what she had put himself and her family through. Turning to Prophet, he asked, "Do you think her plan will work, or shall we, uh . . . spring her now?"

"Considering all the guards on this mountain, I'd say we'd have a better shot if we waited till they left town together. He might take half his army, but half's better than facing them all right here on their own ground."

Sergei put his hand on her arm. "I do not like leaving you here again, *ma chèrie.* I do not like leaving you here at the mercy of that man for another night."

"It is all right, Serge," she assured him. "I know what you are talking about, but I am all right. In my mind I just slip away. . . ."

He stared at her with deep emotion, then engulfed her in his arms. "Soon, my dear countess Marya, you will be free once and for all."

"Night after next," Prophet assured her. "Now let's break a leg, Russian."

Sergei frowned at him curiously, moving his lips over the expression.

"Never mind," Prophet whispered, and carefully opened the door.

The next morning Prophet, Sergei, and the other two bodyguards escorted the polished phaeton down the mountain and pulled up before Gay's saloon in Broken Knee. Gay had a meeting with several of his business partners in the saloon's back room. He ordered the bodyguards to wait in the main room for him — and to drink nothing but coffee.

So, sipping coffee, playing a few rounds of poker and billiards with the other bodyguards, including the two men who guarded Bill Braddock, who owned another saloon in town and was one of Gay's business partners, the men whiled away a couple of hours.

Around eleven o'clock several buxom women entered the saloon, making eyes at the bodyguards and giggling, the feathers in their hats swaying. A full-hipped brunette greeted Clark lustily and pulled his hat down over his eyes. Then she strolled with the other women into the back room, where the high rollers were meeting.

Prophet glanced at Sergei, arching his brow curiously.

"Right on time, just like always," one of Braddock's men said with a chuckle.

Clark said, "Yeah, Miss Jenny over at the High-Time, she don't let the big shots wait. She sends the girls over at eleven o'clock sharp every Friday!"

A few minutes later the door opened and Gay appeared. The hippy brunette was on his arm, smiling as though she were having the time of her life. A good actress, Prophet thought. The other four men — all with women on their arms — followed Gay out of the room.

As they passed through the tables toward the door, Gay said, "You men stay put. We'll be back in an hour. And remember — nothing but coffee!"

Then he parted the batwings and led the chuckling, giggling procession out of the building. They turned left, apparently headed for the Gay Inn next door, where Gay probably reserved a few rooms.

Prophet looked at Sergei as he lifted his coffee cup and curled his nose. Sergei returned the glance, his gaze dark with understanding. Taking Gay down was going to be a pleasure for them both.

Prophet was about to stroll to the bar for the free lunch the bartender had just spread out, when a man dressed like a mule skinner entered the saloon, his face flushed with gravity.

"Hey, there's been an accident down the street. Someone come quick, will ye? A man needs help!"

"What happened?" Clark asked.

"A man was hit by an ore wagon. He's in a bad way. The sheriff and his deputies ain't in their office. I thought maybe someone here could help."

Imagining the havoc an ore wagon could wreak on a body, Prophet hurried through the batwings and outside. He followed the mule skinner down the boardwalk and around the corner, heading west.

Gazing down the side street, he saw nothing but crates and barrels stacked along the street, and bits of trash scuttling in the breeze. This wasn't really even a street, just a wide space between buildings. Straight ahead lay the rocky desert spotted with sage and greasewood and windblown trash, bald mountains rising in the distance.

The sound of a door slamming jerked his gaze back right, to a closed door at the rear of a tobacco shop. The mule skinner was nowhere in sight. He must have gone through that door and slammed it behind him.

Baffled, Prophet looked around, feeling the hair on the nape of his neck rise. Hearing footsteps behind him, he turned. Sergei was moving toward him, looking around with a baffled gaze similar to Prophet's. Prophet noticed that none of the other bodyguards from the saloon had joined them. He and Sergei were alone.

"Where is this injured man?" Sergei said skeptically, turning his head slowly from left to right.

Prophet's right hand went to the butt of his .45 as his eyes scanned the rooftops. Before he could say anything, a man stepped out from the rear of the store across the empty lot. Another moved out from around a small goat stable, swerved to avoid a pile of fresh manure, and moved toward Prophet and Sergei.

It was Harland. The other man, also moving toward Prophet and Sergei, was De-Bocha. The fired bodyguards were smiling easily now, throwing their dusters back from their gun butts. Their eyes were shaded slits beneath their hat brims.

"I reckon we been duped," Prophet said, glancing behind him again, making sure the other bodyguards weren't back there preparing to catch him and Sergei in a crossfire. Nope. It was just Harland and DeBocha. The others must have gotten word of the ploy and remained in the saloon, not wanting to buy trouble with their boss.

Prophet swung his gaze back to the fired bodyguards. To Sergei, he said, "How's your fast draw?"

They were flanked by the north side of the Gay Inn, and several windows were open. In case anyone inside the hotel was listening, Sergei gave only a grunt, which Prophet took for a restrained Cossack war cry.

"You sons o'bitches ready to die?" Harland asked, his bright green neckerchief blowing up around his chin.

"Today's as good a day as any — that's what me and the Injuns always say," Prophet said with a wry grin, belying his misgivings. He'd never been Billy the Kid with a handgun. But he was willing and accurate, and often that counted for more than speed.

Also, there was his Confederate battle cry — "Eeeeeee-hyah!" The piercing yell froze the bodyguards for the split second it took Prophet to draw his revolver, raise it, and level it at Harland. The bodyguard was only raising his own pistol, a look of consternation furling his brow and widening his eyes, as Prophet triggered the Colt and watched the bullet plunk dust from Harland's shirt on its way through his breastbone to his heart and then out the other side, where it chipped wood from the store wall behind him.

Before Harland hit the ground, Prophet swung his gaze to his left. DeBocha was crouching over the bloody wound in his belly, his hat tumbling forward off his head. The wounded man cussed and began raising his gun again when Sergei fired his shiny Colt again, planting a blood blossom in De-Bocha's forehead. The ex-bodyguard twisted around with another cry and fell, kicking dust.

Prophet looked again at Harland, who lay sprawled on his back, arms flung out, dead. There was a long silence.

"Good shootin'," he told Sergei at last.

"Your yell — it froze them," the Russian said quietly.

"Yep."

"Was that fair fighting, Lou?"

Prophet turned and started back for the saloon. He grinned as he passed Sergei. "Nope."

The other bodyguards had gathered at the corner of the boardwalk to watch the festivities. None of them looked very pleased at the outcome. "Sorry, boys," Prophet said as he pushed through the crowd and headed for the batwings.

Above the vacant lot, in a second-story window, Leamon Gay stood naked, the brunette beside him, resting her chin on his shoulder. She was nude, as well. Staring down at the two dead men in the empty lot, Gay grinned.

"Those two might prove worthy of the salary I'm paying them yet," he told the whore.

In the next room to Gay's right, Gay's business partner, Bill Braddock, sat on the edge of his bed. He, too, was staring out the window, down at the two men in the lot. Unlike Gay, Braddock was frowning.

"I can't stand looking at that stuff — all that shooting," the naked whore said behind him. "This is a savage town." She'd turned away from the grisly scene and was facing the wall.

"Shut up," Braddock told her. "I'm trying to think."

"About what?"

Braddock's voice rose with impatience. "Shut up, will you?"

He watched the stocky, black-haired gent, Gay's mute bodyguard, stroll back toward Main Street. But his mind was on the other man who'd already left the alley — the tall, sandy-haired hombre with the easy stride and careless manner. Braddock had recognized him — or thought he had. He'd seen that catlike stroll before, the easy set of those broad shoulders. The off-putting grin that only slightly camouflaged the man's kill-devil nature.

Braddock lowered his head and ran his hand through his thinning gray hair. Where, oh where, had he seen that man before? It was right at the tip of his tongue. . . .

Braddock raised his head, a slow grin drawing at his thin lips capped with a pencil-thin mustache. Oh, yes. Oh, yes . . .

He remembered the bounty hunter who'd tracked him and his partner, Edwin Harrol, into Idaho several years ago, after they'd robbed a bank in Bannock, Montana Territory. He'd been a relentless son of a bitch, tracking them through a winter storm in the mountains. He'd killed Edwin with a short-barreled shotgun. Cut him in half when Edwin had drawn on him in a farmer's barn outside Idaho Falls.

Braddock had spent a year in prison after that . . . before he and two others had dug their way out. . . .

"Who's who?" the whore said, still facing the wall.

"That man who was down there. The big,

grinning bastard with the sandy hair."

"What about him?"

"I just figured out who he is."

"Who?"

"Prophet," Braddock said, smiling out the window. "Lou Prophet." Braddock chuckled, thoroughly delighted with himself. "Gay's new guard, Lou Pepper, is a god-damn Rebel bounty hunter!"

21

The next morning, in her room in the Gay Inn, the countess penned a note to her mother back in Boston, informing the widow about the search for Marya. Describing the roguish westerner she and Sergei had hired to guide them to Arizona, she smiled devilishly, leaving out the parts about her and Prophet's mad couplings, which would not only have scandalized the elder noblewoman but probably given her a heart stroke, as well.

Since the death of her husband, Count Roskov, Countess Tatayanna had become most protective of her daughters' honor. They'd had to flee Russia like vagabonds; thus, in the elder countess's view, the honor of their name was virtually all they had left, and it was to be protected at all costs.

The countess rolled her eyes. No one in America gave a rat's ass about the Roskovs, much less their "honor." Feeling pleased with the vulgarism, one of the many she'd picked up from the irreverent Prophet, she returned her gold-tipped pen to its holder.

She left the missive unfinished, hoping to complete it later with news of the trip's success — that Marya had been freed from Gay and that she, Natasha, and Sergei were returning home together.

The joy of the prospect was tempered by only the fact that once they had freed Marya from Leamon Gay, they would be separating from Prophet, the garrulous bounty hunter with whom the countess believed she was now in love. . . .

Willing her thoughts away from Prophet — his flinty green eyes and wolfish smile and the way his big brown hands had massaged her shoulders and breasts — she put away her writing supplies and placed the letter in a leather portfolio.

Then, feeling aimless and depressed, wondering how she'd spend the rest of this day, waiting for Lou and Sergei and Marya to appear, she strolled to the window and stared down at the street. It was crowded with bullwackers and salesmen and scarlet women parading their fleshy wares on corners and from balconies. Two boys in tattered clothes — probably sired by drunken miners and abandoned by prostitutes — ran down the street, laughing, chased by a sleek black mongrel with one white front paw.

This was indeed a savage place. The countess could not understand what had possessed Marya to come here. She'd always been the adventurous sort and a prideful, willful child, but Natasha couldn't help believing that this hellhole, as Prophet had called it, was more adventure than even Marya had bargained for.

"Oh, Marya," Natasha whispered as she stared through the fly-specked window, "please be safe. . . ."

She was about to start downstairs for lunch, when she saw something out the corner of her eye. Turning back to the window, she gazed south down the street, blinking as if to clear her eyes, her heart fluttering in her chest.

A polished black buggy was approaching the inn. Four armed men surrounded it, two of whom were Lou Prophet and Sergei. Seeing them was a wonderful surprise, but what surprised Natasha most of all was that riding behind the buggy's formally attired driver and beside a pale man smoking a thick cigar was none other than the Countess Marya Roskov herself!

"Oh, my God!" Natasha whispered, unable to believe what she was seeing. She placed both her hands on the window, as if to move closer to her long-lost sibling. "Marya . . . is it really you?"

It was. There was no doubt about it, the countess realized to her shock and amazement. She would have known that proud, lovely face anywhere — that flaxen hair falling from beneath Marya's green felt hat, those self-possessed eyes that now betrayed fear, yes, but also a defiance even stronger than usual.

The way Leamon Gay sat beside her, insouciantly smoking and glancing off as the carriage pulled up to the hitch rail, it was obvious to Natasha that he possessed Marya, or thought he did. But from Marya's demeanor, he may have possessed her body, but he did not possess her soul.

"Oh, Marya!" Natasha cried under her breath, moving her face even closer to the window. She wanted so much for her sister to see her that it took all her willpower to keep from pounding the window.

Befuddlement assailed her. What was happening? Why was Gay coming here with Marya? How did this mesh with Lou and Sergei's plan? Or did it?

Then something occurred to her: Maybe Gay was bringing Marya here to see her,

Natasha.

Could it be?

As improbable as it seemed, could it be that Marya was with Leamon Gay of her own free will and that, having learned from Lou and Sergei that her sister was here in Broken Knee, Gay was bringing Marya here for a visit with Natasha?

The countess did not consciously analyze the wishful speculation, but only reacted to the possibility, nervously running her hands through her hair, which she had not yet coiled and fastened atop her head. Then she hurried out of her room and down the dim, carpeted hall, and turned down the stairs.

Halfway down, she stopped, her heart leaping into her throat when she saw Marya passing to the right of the stairs — less than fifteen feet away! Her hand was wedged in the crook of Gay's arm, as if he feared she might run away if he released her.

Following behind were two bodyguards, rough-looking men in buckskins and denims and carrying several guns apiece. One of them passed beyond the stairs. The other stopped and gazed up at her, a lascivious smile lighting his face. Finally he winked, pinched his hat brim at her, and continued past the stairs and into the dining room.

A moment later the countess became

aware of two sets of eyes on her. She saw Lou and Sergei standing where the body-guard had stood, in the lobby, to the right of the stairs. They were both gazing up at her with expressions of contained anger and anxiety.

Prophet glanced at Sergei, whispered something, then continued after Gay and Marya, heading for the dining room. Mean-while, Sergei hurried up the stairs, taking the steps two at a time.

Stopping before the countess, he clutched her elbow and whispered in her ear, "Please go back to your room, Countess!"

"That . . . that was Marya," she stammered with delight.

"Yes, that was Marya, and very soon now, she will be free. Go back to your room and wait for us there. Please, Countess!"

With that, the big Cossack wheeled, hurried back down the stairs, and moderated his pace, taking several calming breaths as he walked across the lobby and disappeared into the dining room.

"Very soon now, she will be free," he had said.

The encouraging words resounded in the countess's head, lightening her heart, as she turned and willed herself back to her room.

■ ■ ■ ■

"That's one purty little filly there!" Rosen said, whistling under his breath.

He, Clark, Prophet, and Sergei sat together several tables away from their boss and his "chosen," as Gay ironically called Marya. There were several other diners in the room, and their conversations covered the bodyguards' remarks.

"Yeah, she shore is," Clark agreed. "I don't see why he hasn't brought her down to the town before now. A man has a fine little damsel like that, you'd think he'd wanna parade her around a might. Show her off."

"Not if she knows where the Morales Gold Cache is," Rosen said. "Someone's liable to kidnap her, make her show him where the gold is."

Clark laughed as he spooned split-pea soup in his mouth. "Shee-it. Wild horses and a string of Missouri mules couldn't drag that out of her. She's a polecat, that one. The only reason she's talkin' now is cause she got bored, moonin' around that hacienda the last three weeks."

"She could moon around my hacienda anytime," Rosen said, staring across the room, where Gay and Marya sat eating in silence.

Prophet saw the angry look boiling up on Sergei's features. The Cossack had taken offense at the way the two bodyguards were ogling Marya and making comments. Fortunately, the men were too distracted to notice the Russian's displeasure. Prophet gave Sergei a kick under the table. Cowed, the Russian stuffed bread in his mouth and followed it down with coffee.

A few minutes later the head waiter appeared from the kitchen, toting a long wicker basket draped with oilcloth. He set it on Gay's table with a flourish, then showed the crime lord a bottle of wine, to which Gay nodded his approval, and deposited the bottle in the basket. Gay smiled and nodded — a macabre caricature of a romantic lover about to take his betrothed on a picnic in the hills.

Dressed in a pale green riding habit — another gift from Gay — Marya sat stiffly in her chair, staring off.

When the waiter had disappeared, Gay turned to the bodyguards and nodded.

"Here we go, boys," Clark said, shucking off his napkin.

As had been decided earlier, when the official orders had come down, including the plan for Gay and Marya to have a quiet lunch at the hotel before heading into the mountains, Prophet went out and drove Gay's carriage over to the livery barn.

Two fine, black saddle horses were waiting before the open doors, fully rigged. A packhorse stood there as well, its panniers sagging with the weight of four days' worth of supplies. Taking the reins of all three horses, Prophet led them back to the hotel just as Gay and Marya emerged, surrounded by Clark, Rosen, and Sergei.

But what caught Prophet's attention and made him wince were the four other men sitting their mounts in the street before the hotel. They were well armed, and, saddlebags bulging, appeared ready for a long ride.

Additional riders.

"Are your horses well fed and watered?" Gay asked them as he and Marya strode to the two saddle horses Prophet had led from the livery barn.

"All ready and rarin' to go, Boss," one of the guards said with a nod.

"Good. Be sure to keep your eyes peeled, all of you," Gay added, shuttling his glance around his men. "Apaches have been spotted in the area we'll be traversing. Small bands of them, but Apaches nevertheless, and I think you all know what that means."

"We sure do, Boss," Clark said as he swung up onto his saddle. "But with this many of us, I doubt they'll attack."

"You just keep your eyes peeled, mister," Gay said gruffly. "You hear?"

"You got it, Boss," Clark said, cutting his eyes around sheepishly.

Prophet was staring at Sergei, as if to say, "What the hell do we do now?" With this many bodyguards, he and Prophet were badly outnumbered. It was going to be some trick to get Marya away from Gay.

Locking stares with Prophet, Sergei chewed his mustache and grimaced.

"Here, let me give you a hand, miss," Prophet said to Marya as she came around her horse. She gave him her hand with a taut smile that said she hadn't been expecting this many guards, either.

"Get away from there, mister!" Gay intervened. "I'll help her up on her damn horse. See to your own!"

"Yes, Mr. Gay," Prophet said, truckling. "Whatever you say, sir."

He climbed aboard Mean. When Gay had swung up onto his own mount, he trotted ahead of the group, his chin jutting self-importantly. Marya fell in behind him as Gay called, "Let's go!"

The bodyguards gigged their horses after

their boss. Prophet hung back with Sergei. They stared after the six well-armed body-guards.

Finally Prophet sighed and brushed Mean with his heels. "Well, you heard the man, mister," he said with irony. "Let's ride."

Across the street two men stepped out of the Pink Pig Saloon. One of the men was the Pink Pig's owner, Bill Braddock, clad in a cheap business suit and bowler, his thin mustache freshly trimmed and waxed.

Behind Braddock stood one of Braddock's men, a snake named Tony Roma. Roma shook his long black hair from his Indian-featured face with its multiple scars and pits, and glanced at his boss expectantly.

"Have the men ready to ride in ten min-utes," Braddock said tightly, staring after Gay.

Roma hitched his cartridge belts on his lean hips and ambled casually away.

"Go!" Braddock raged behind him. "Move your half-breed ass!"

Clutching his hat to his head, Roma bolted down the boardwalk.

In her hotel room Natasha Roskov anxiously paced the floor between her bed and the grimy window.

Since watching Gay's group ride out of

town a half hour before, her stomach had been a nest of writing snakes. With that many men accompanying the crime boss, how in the world could Prophet and Sergei rescue Marya? Surely Gay would have men watching her at all times. Even if they did manage to get her away from Gay, surely Gay's men would run them down in the desert and kill them!

"Oh, Marya!" the countess whispered, feeling a painful tightness in her chest.

She didn't know what to do with herself. She couldn't stay in her room. The waiting and wondering would drive her crazy.

But what else could she do?

At her wits end, she suddenly stopped pacing, her restless eyes freezing as an idea occurred to her, a plan working itself out in her mind. She would ride out after the group.

She realized it was an impulsive, foolhardy idea. She'd never fired a gun in her life; she could be no help to Prophet and Sergei. Still, she could not remain here without going insane, and she felt an overwhelming need to be close to Marya.

Turning to one of the turtleback trunks, she began filling a carpetbag. She changed into a simple, light blue riding dress and a cream hat she'd bought in Denver because it looked distinctly Western. It was more than a mere memento to her now, however. Now it would protect her from the fierce desert sun.

Bag in hand, she went out and locked the door behind her. Dropping the key in her pocket, she went downstairs and asked the man standing behind the desk where she could rent a horse. On his direction, she headed for the livery barn.

The Mexican hostler took one look at the countess — one long, smoldering look followed by a grin — and told her sure, he had a horse she could rent.

"Put a sidesaddle on him for me, please."

"Do you not want to know how much he costs, señora?"

"No, just saddle him," the countess said, rummaging around in her carpetbag for her money.

She rode out on a high-stepping pinto a few minutes later. Behind her, the hostler grinned as he counted the wad of greenbacks she'd thrust into his hand.

The countess did not know where Prophet and Sergei were going, but from her window she'd seen them head south from town. Since there were few trails that way, and few riders came or went in that direction, she figured their horse tracks would be fairly easy to follow.

She was right. The fresh tracks were clearly marked in the finely sifted dust of the trail that rose and fell across the rocky desert, angling around mesquite thickets and boulders and rising through passes between buttes.

She rode for over an hour, the sun slanting westward, when she suddenly became confused. The trail forked, and both forks were scored with recent hoofprints. The trail had narrowed considerably the past mile or so, the hooves overlapping, so she couldn't tell by counting the sets which fork Gay's group had taken.

Deciding that the left fork looked the more promising, she gigged the pinto ahead, climbing a gradual slope rising to saguaro-studded hills shaded by higher rimrocks. The sky was cloudless. The sun turned rusty as it sank toward the western horizon. Occasional roadrunners crossed Natasha's trail, and once she startled two wild pigs — *javelinas,* she believed they were called — that had been sleeping in the shade of a low upthrust of rock. They scampered off, squealing and startling the countess's horse.

The noise scared Natasha, as well. The dying light, her distance from town, and the yawning, empty silence of this vast wilderness spawned a deep apprehension. This was a foreign land to her, alien as the moon. Afflicted with a terrible sense of her aloneness and vulnerability out here — were there wolves or even bears here, and were those coyotes yipping from that ridge over there? — she resisted the urge to turn back. It was so late in the day, it would be dark long before she returned to Broken Knee, and in the dark she might easily get herself irrevocably lost.

No, she'd started this foolish trek. She must continue. She hoped she would find Prophet and Sergei soon, though what she would do then, she had no idea.

She also hoped she'd taken the correct fork in the trail, and that she was following Prophet and Sergei and not a group of prospectors — or highwaymen, or, worse yet, Indians. . . .

Fifteen minutes later the trail dipped into a ravine in which she could hear a spring gurgling. A horse's whinny sent an electric jolt through her spine, and she reined the pinto to a halt, staring ahead through the darkness. A fire guttered low, about forty yards away amidst rocks and spindly trees. Near the fire a horse flicked its tail.

A camp!

She was pondering a plan when something knocked her out of her saddle. She hit the ground with a squelched cry as the air was hammered from her lungs and her ears rang from the throbbing in her skull.

Blinking her eyes, she stared upward, dazed. A man climbed to his knees and hovered over her, blocking out the stars. It was a savage face — flat and dark-eyed and framed by long black hair. His labored breath was fetid with alcohol, his teeth black from rot.

The dull eyes inspected her like those of an animal inspecting a prospective meal. Grinning, he lifted his head and yelled, "Hey! It's a woman!"

22

The sound of boots crunching gravel rose around the countess. A hand appeared on the dark man's collar, jerking him back on his hands and heels.

"Get away there, Roma," another man growled. "Let me see."

Another face appeared — a snake-eyed face with a two-day growth of beard. The man wore a bowler and a white shirt unbuttoned halfway down his chest. "Who in the hell are you?" he asked the countess gruffly but appraising her with interest.

Her face creased with pain, she glanced around to see four other men standing around her, regarding her with varying degrees of lust and curiosity in their hard, wild eyes. They wore filthy riding clothes and guns on their hips. One man — a short, fat man with red-Irish features — had several bandoliers draped across his chest and two revolvers in the cross-draw position on his thighs. The foul odor of the men's sweaty bodies was thick in the countess's nose.

"Answer me, you bitch, or I'll shoot you right here!" The thin man wearing the bowler was obviously their leader. He had a big revolver and a wide-bladed knife on his hip. Neither went with his city clothes.

Natasha recoiled, terrified. Quietly she heard her voice say, "I am . . . Natasha Roskov."

"Ah, Russian." The man in the bowler smiled. "Any relation to that Russian gal of Gay's?"

Natasha said nothing. She stared at the man fearfully, wondering what kind of malignant mess she'd stumbled upon and suddenly wishing she'd remained in Broken Knee. Getting herself killed wasn't going to do Marya any good.

When she said nothing, the man called Roma chuckled. "Hey, she's purty! We can have a hell of a good time with her."

"Shut up, Roma!" the leader scolded. He knelt down before the countess and grabbed her hair, pulling her head brusquely back. "I asked you a question, miss. Is Gay's girl the one you're lookin' for?"

Struggling against the man's painful grip, the countess nodded.

"She's your sister?"

"Yes."

The leader thought for several seconds while the other men looked on with mute interest. "You in with Prophet and the short black-haired gent?"

Tears of pain oozing from her eyes and rolling down her cheeks as the man tightened his grip on her hair, the countess looked at him with vague bewilderment. How did he know Lou? How did he know that Lou and Sergei were not bona fide bodyguards?

Apparently, Natasha's expression was answer enough.

"Thought so," the man said, grabbing her by her arm and jerking her to her feet. He called to one of the men to fetch a rope. "I'm gonna tie her to this tree over here," he said, brusquely leading the countess to a tall mesquite not far from the fire.

"What we gonna do with her, Boss?" Roma eagerly asked.

Ignoring the question, the leader directed one of his own to Natasha. "You belong to Prophet or the other man?"

The countess had no time to absorb the question, for he dragged her along quickly, causing her to trip over rocks and small branches. When he threw her down at the base of a mesquite tree, about ten feet from the fire, he spoke again. "You heard me. You must belong to one of 'em — pretty little thing like you. Which one?"

She sat against the prickly tree, catching her breath, watching the leader accept a length of rope from one of the other men. After a second's consideration she chose to let the man believe she was Prophet's woman. If he knew of Prophet's reputation, he might spare her, fearing the bounty hunter's retribution.

It was worth a try.

"I . . . I belong to Lou Prophet," she said, meeting his gaze with proud defiance. "I am Lou Prophet's woman."

"What the hell you doin' all alone out here?" He was cutting the rope with a wide-bladed knife. The other men had gathered around him, still watching Natasha with lascivious interest.

"I came here from Broken Knee, looking for him and my sister."

"Prophet after the gold, too?"

The countess stared at him, genuinely bewildered. "What gold?"

"The gold Gay's after. The gold your sister has a map to." The man grinned as he tied the countess's wrists together. "The gold I'm after."

Natasha blinked, distractedly watching the rope loop around her wrists, wincing as he yanked it tight. So that's what this man and his men were out here for. The treasure marked on Marya's map.

"Lou and Sergei are only trying to free my sister from Gay's grip. They do not care about gold. I do not care about gold. I care only about my sister."

The man tied a knot in the rope and looked at her, measuring her expression against her story.

"I do not care about gold," Natasha repeated beseechingly. "You can have the gold. I want only my sister."

The man stared evenly at her. Finally he cut off another, longer length of rope. He looped it around her waist and tied it behind the tree. Confronting her again, he nodded.

"Well, you might get your sister back," he said, nodding again, his expression vaguely mocking. "If she's still alive after tomorrow, that is. 'Cause, you see, we're going after Gay tomorrow. And we're going to get that map of your sister's — one way or another."

He straightened and dusted off the knees of his broadcloth trousers. "Not only that, but I'm gonna kill me a conniving ~~goddamn~~ bounty man by the name of Lou Prophet,

too . . . after I've tortured him real good."
He winked and turned away.

The words resounded in Natasha's ears,
pricking the tender skin along her spine,
causing her heart to throb against her ribs.
Not only did Prophet and Sergei have to
worry about Gay's bodyguards, they would
have to contend with these men, as well.

The countess fought back a sob. *Oh,
Marya . . .*

The leader was talking to his men. "You
two get back on watch, for chrissakes. Don't
you know this is Apache country!"

Another man said, "What about her,
Boss?"

"What about her?"

"Aren't we gonna . . . you know . . . ?"

The leader chuckled. "Well, I just might,
but you boys won't. Hell, you'd probably
kill her, and then we wouldn't have her for
tomorrow."

"What're we gonna do with her tomorrow, Mr. Braddock?" another man asked as
he stood near the fire, staring down at Natasha and hungrily bunching the thighs of
his buckskin pants in his fists.

"She's gonna be riding with us when we
ride up to Gay and his crew. I figure if they
see a woman in our party, they'll hesitate
before they shoot." Braddock grinned and

nodded and clapped one of his men on the shoulder. "And if she really is Prophet's woman, which I don't doubt — that big Georgia bastard has a weakness for good-looking women — Prophet'll hesitate, too. Even if it's only for half a second, that's all the time we'll need."

An hour earlier Prophet rode drag on Gay's crew, climbing the eastern foothills of the Penalino Mountains, a long, rocky range buttressed by two tall, bald peaks that looked like match flames as their crests caught the last of the day's light.

Prophet was deep in thought, ruminating over their predicament. Six bodyguards lay between him and Marya. Seven counting Gay, who may have considered himself a civilized businessman now but had probably been handy with a six-shooter not all that long ago, and likely still was.

When Prophet had thought Clark and Rosen would be the only other guards, he figured they'd be able to snatch Marya away relatively easily, not far from town. But with these extra guards, that plan was out the window.

Thinking it over now, watching Marya and Gay riding ahead of the pack of bodyguards filing up a twisting game trail, Prophet decided their best choice was to try and slip her out of the camp later that night. Gay would have guards posted, watching for Indians, but Prophet thought if he and Sergei were crafty and quiet enough, they might be able to slip away without anyone noticing.

Then they'd head back to Broken Knee, pick up the countess, and get the hell out of Dodge, so to speak. Of course, Gay would trail them, but Prophet had eluded more than one pesky tracker in his day.

When Sergei drifted back in the pack, sidling up to Prophet, he turned a questioning glance at the bounty hunter. Prophet got out his makings sack and rolled a smoke as he spoke softly, telling Sergei his plan. When he was done, the Russian only nodded, not risking a reply, and gigged his horse ahead.

"We'll stop here for the night," Gay announced sometime later.

He reined his horse to a halt in a wide arroyo abutted by a high stone wall and bordered by low shrubs and mesquite trees. A spring bubbled up between two of the trees, and a couple of the bodyguards quickly strung a rope around it for the horses.

When camp had been made, Prophet

saw Marya say something to Gay, then walk off down the arroyo. Prophet was rubbing Mean and Ugly down with a handful of brome that grew thick along the spring.

He looked around. Only three bodyguards sat around the fire. Gay sipped wine from a long-stemmed glass and sat on a log, looking wan. Apparently, he didn't often ride a saddle these days. The old outlaw had gotten soft.

The other men had been posted around the camp, on the lookout for Apaches. They'd revolve the watch every two hours until dawn.

No one appeared to be watching Prophet, so he dropped to the grass and slipped casually into the arroyo and stepped quietly across the stones, taking his time in the darkness, heading in the direction Marya had gone.

When he'd walked around a bend, her voice rose on his right. "Who's there?"

Quietly he replied, "It's Prophet."

A moment later he heard stones crunch and brush rustle, and then she appeared, a vague form of a girl in the thickening darkness.

"Sorry to bother you," he said, knowing she'd probably slipped off to tend nature.

"But I didn't know when else we could talk."

"It is all right," she whispered, looking around warily. "Are you sure we are alone? I expected him to follow me. He doesn't think I'll try to escape out here, with Indians around, but he's very jealous."

"I'll make this quick," Prophet said, moving to her so he could keep his voice low.

He told Marya the plan. "How heavy do you sleep?" he asked her.

"Not very . . . anymore," she added with a grimace.

"Don't worry," Prophet told her. "We'll get you free of that varmint."

He squeezed her arm reassuringly and turned to make his way back to the camp. He stopped when Marya grabbed his elbow. "When I am free, will you help me find the treasure?"

Prophet turned back to her. Her face was vaguely defined in the gathering darkness, but he could see that her eyes were wide with appeal. He chuffed a mirthless laugh.

How in the hell could the girl think of searching for lost treasure after all she'd been through? Most would have wanted nothing more than to hightail it home.

"We'll talk about it later," he told her, having no intention of going after the so-called treasure. When he and Sergei had sprung Marya from the camp, they would make a beeline for Broken Knee, where they'd retrieve the countess and make another beeline for Denver. Then Prophet would ship the three Russians home, once and for all.

The countess was one pretty woman, but no woman was worth this much trouble. . . .

When he got back to his horse, he was startled by Gay's voice. "Where have you been, Pepper?"

Gay was standing in the darkness, his wineglass reflecting light from the kindling stars. "I've been looking for you."

"Just off tendin' nature, is all."

Gay studied him, though Prophet couldn't see his face. Finally Gay moved toward the bounty hunter. "Let me warn you, Pepper. Any of my men I find with my women are done for. Do you hear? And I don't mean they're just fired." He was close enough now that Prophet could see him blink, smell the wine on his breath. "Do I make myself clear?"

"Very clear, sir," Prophet said, making a mental note to cut this uppity outlaw's throat tonight before he left.

"Good."

Before he could walk away, a man carrying a rifle came up behind him. "Boss, we got trouble." The man was breathing hard, his clothes soaked from sweat, as if he'd run a good distance.

"What is it?"

"Injuns. I seen three of 'em just before the sun went down, two ridges over south."

Gay cursed. "They know we're here?"

"Probably," the man said, swallowing. "I fought those bastards with ole Crook, and believe me, they're wily. And by the way they were skulking around that ridge, I'd say they're tryin' to get close to our bivouac."

"Shit!" Gay swung on his heel to the fire.

"What do you wanna do, Mr. Gay?" asked one of the bodyguards sitting by the fire, a note of fear in his voice. It was obvious he was all for returning to Broken Knee.

"Douse those flames," Gay ordered. "And everyone stay alert."

One of the other men by the fire cleared his throat tentatively. "You don't think we should head back to town? Maybe try this another time?"

"No, I don't," Gay said with conviction. "I fought Apaches myself, when I was running horses across the border. They will not attack at night. At first light tomorrow we move out as planned." He looked at the last man who had spoken. "Unless you're afraid, McNab?"

"No, no, sir — I ain't afraid" — McNab concocted a snicker — "of a few 'Paches."

"Good," Gay said, walking away. "Marya, where are you, my dear?" he called, his voice dwindling with distance.

Prophet turned to pick up his saddle and saw Sergei standing on the other side of Mean and Ugly. "Indians, eh?"

"Yep," Prophet growled, not liking it one bit.

"What does that mean for us, Lou?"

Prophet kept his voice low. "It means we don't leave tonight. The Apaches probably have us surrounded, and we'd run into them in the dark. Besides that" — he chuckled ironically and with great frustration — "we're now probably safer with Gay than without him."

"What about Marya?"

"Good question," Prophet said.

23

Later that night, drunk and reeling from alcohol, Braddock led the countess away from the camp to rape her.

He threw her down and ripped her shirt-waist. She struggled against him, kicking and clawing at his face. He slapped her once with the flat of his hand, then balled his fist and punched her in the temple.

"Now, then," Braddock wheezed, his sweat dripping into her face, "that should settle you down, eh? I just want a little fun. Just a little." His words were slurred by drink, and he swayed from side to side as he straddled her on his knees. "I'm gonna get it one way or another; you might as well give it up. Go easy on yourself."

"Go to hell," she spat at him, struggling against his weight. He'd pinned her hands above her head with one hand while he worked his way into her chemise with the other, roughly fondling her breasts.

She kicked her legs futilely. "I would rather die!"

"That can be arranged, you little Russian bitch!" he yelled, and punched her again.

That took the air out of her lungs and the fight out of her arms and legs. Her head swirled, and she felt a searing pain between her eyes. From the fire, she could dimly hear the snickers and laughs of Braddock's men.

He would rape her, and there was nothing she could do about it. This realization nearly coincided with the realization that Braddock had passed out on top of her. He'd slumped forward, buried his face in her chest, and had fallen sound asleep, snoring.

She lay there tensely, not moving, fearful of waking him up lest he continue what he'd started.

She stared at the constellations revolving above her, listening to the chatter and spats and grunts of Braddock's men around the fire, then later to their snores and to the snorts and blows of the sleeping horses and to the dry scuttles of burrowing creatures. Her eye swelled where Braddock had hit her, and blood trickled from her lip before it dried on her chin.

He lay heavy upon her, snoring, putting her limbs to sleep, until, with painstaking ease, she managed to slide him off her left side. She was trying to slip out from under his arm when he grunted, blinked his eyes, and wagged his head. Natasha froze, stared at him in terror.

His eyes closed. Soon his snores resumed. Afraid to move and possibly wake him again, she lay stiff on her back, his left arm draped over her belly, alternately dozing and waking with her heart pounding.

Finally, after what had seemed an eternity, when the dawn was a pearl wash in the east and the birds had begun their raucous morning cries, he snorted and grunted, gave a moan, and lifted his head.

"Wh-where . . . what . . ." He blinked at her dully. He winced and raised up on his hands, ran them over his face and through his hair. "Well, I'll be ~~goddamned~~," he said. "I fell asleep!"

"You are an animal," the countess scolded. She pushed herself into a sitting position, brushing sand and pine needles from her bare arms.

Braddock looked at her, noting the torn shirtwaist. "Did we . . . did I . . . ?"

"I did nothing," the countess said with taut-jawed disdain. If he thought he'd had his pleasure, he might leave her alone now. "It was all you. And then you passed out. You are a savage beast."

Braddock chuckled and climbed to his feet. "Yeah, I've been called a beast a time or two." He staggered, clutched his head with his hands. "Ahh . . . my head . . ." He looked at her and formed a lascivious grin. "Too bad I don't remember last night, though. I bet you were fun."

"Are you going to let me go, now that you have had your fun?" she asked hopefully.

"Shut up." Braddock winced again at the pain in his head, spat, and brushed dust from his broadcloth trousers and sweat-stained white shirt. "I still got plans for you and your Mr. Prophet." He reached down and jerked her to her feet. "We got some riding to do this morning."

From his perch above Gay's camp, Prophet watched the sun rise. As the huge lemon orb rose above the distant knobs, a sharp dread rose in his loins and belly.

It was daylight. The Apaches could attack at any time.

Prophet had been on guard here, on the south side of the camp, since two o'clock, and he'd seen or heard no sign of the red devils. But that didn't mean they weren't there. In fact, the prickling along his spine told him they were near, sure as hell.

Prophet adjusted his Colt and bowie knife

on his hip and climbed down the rocky upthrust toward the remuda, where Sergei and several other men were rigging up their mounts. Marya was still sitting with Gay on a log, nibbling a biscuit. She sent Prophet a questioning look; neither he nor Sergei had been able to inform her of the change in plans, and her glance told him she was wondering why they hadn't snatched her from the camp last night.

In reply to her silent inquiry, Prophet gave his head a brief shake, then turned to Mean and Ugly with the horse's bridle in his hand. When the other men had led their horses from the remuda, leaving only Sergei and Prophet, Prophet swung his saddlebags over Mean's back and said under his breath, "Keep your eyes peeled, Serge. If they attack, we grab the girl and hightail it."

Sergei nodded at Prophet over his horse's saddle.

When they all were mounted, Marya led off, following the map in her head. Prophet hoped she remembered it correctly and that they arrived at the "treasure" soon. He didn't know what in the hell would happen once they got there and Gay saw that there was no treasure. He figured he'd cross that bridge when they came to it.

In the meantime, Apaches . . .

All morning the column threaded its way through canyons and washes. At one point they dead-ended in a box canyon, and Gay threw a fit, asking his "chosen" if she actually knew where she was going or did she want a bullet in her pretty temple?

Marya regarded the crime boss boldly. "I made a mistake. Have you not ever made a mistake, Mr. Gay?"

"I told you to call me Leamon," he muttered under his breath, self-consciously cutting his eyes around at his men. "After all, I am your chosen, aren't I, my dear?"

Marya did not answer. As she turned her horse around and rode back past Prophet and Sergei, she rolled her eyes.

Prophet glanced at Sergei. "Spunky as a front-tit calf, ain't she?"

Sergei shrugged and reined his buckskin around.

Following an arroyo, they entered another canyon. Riding at the rear of the column with Sergei, Prophet scanned the cliff tops rising on both sides of the arroyo. Again he felt a prickling, as if some witch were stitching his spine.

"Be ready," he told Sergei.

The Russian frowned at him.

"I got a sense about these things," Prophet said, looking straight ahead, sweeping the cliff tops with his eyes. "You ride ahead, try to get as close to the girl as you can. When those bastards attack, grab her horse and head back this way. We'll ride back down the arroyo."

As they entered the shadows that the cliffs canted onto the rocky bed of the arroyo, the prickling along Prophet's spine increased, reaching into his ass and thighs. He adjusted his Colt, then reached down and unsheathed his Winchester. He levered a round in the chamber, uncocked the hammer, and rode with the rifle's butt snugged against his hip.

"What the hell's the matter with you, Pepper?" one of the mine guards asked — a stocky German named Klein. "Losin' your nerve?"

"Yeah, that's it," Prophet grumbled, keeping his eyes on the cliffs. "Now, shut up and keep your eyes peeled, unless you want an arrow in your back."

"Hey, don't tell me to shut up, you —"

Klein was cut off by Gay's voice rising from the head of the column. "Whooooah!"

Prophet cocked his Winchester's hammer as the column slowed to a halt. His gaze caught on a small group of riders gathered on a ledge about thirty yards ahead, where the cliffs opened again.

The fact that the riders weren't Indians

lightened Prophet's mood a little. Then he saw the woman at the head of the group, sitting a black horse with her hands apparently tied behind her back. A thin man in a bowler hat was holding a shotgun to her head.

Prophet couldn't see her clearly from this far away, but he thought she looked like the countess. The realization flooded his gut with bile and set his heart hammering and his vision swimming.

What in the hell was she doing out here?

The two groups of riders sat staring at each other for nearly a minute. Then the other group rode toward Gay's — slowly, the lead rider keeping the shotgun on the countess's head. Gay sat at the head of his column in befuddled silence.

"What the hell's goin' on?" someone near Prophet muttered.

"It's Braddock," Prophet said as the other group approached.

Gay called out, "What the hell is going on here, Bill? What are you doing out here?"

"Same thing you are, Leamon."

"What's that?"

"I'm out here for the gold." Braddock grinned, his unshaven cheeks looking muddy in the bold light, his dusty bowler tipped at an angle over his left eye.

"Thought we might make a little swap. This woman here for yours. You must be getting tired of yours by now, aren't you? I know you, Leamon." Braddock chuckled.

Marya tensed in her saddle. Prophet heard her say in a voice pinched with shock, "Natasha!"

"Marya, stay there — I am all right," the countess said timidly.

The crime boss rose up in his saddle, his face flushing with anger. "Bill, what is the meaning of this?"

Prophet and Sergei gigged their horses up in the procession, until they both sat near Marya and Gay.

"You heard what the meaning is, Leamon," Braddock said. "I want the map to the gold."

Before Gay could respond, Braddock cut his eyes at Prophet. "That's what that bounty hunter you have working for you's after, too."

"What bounty hunter?" Gay said, brows beetling as he glanced around, confused.

"Prophet," Braddock said.

"You mean Pepper?"

"Is that the handle he gave you?" Braddock laughed. "Hell, his name's Prophet. Headhunter. He's after your gold, Leamon. Him and that gent there" — he canted his head to indicate Sergei — "and these two women."

Gay turned to Sergei and Prophet. "Why, you sons of bitches," he spat. Then he turned his crimson face back to Braddock and the five men surrounding him.

"And you, Bill," he castigated. "You pathetic, double-crossing bastard. I don't know what makes you think I'm going to trade this girl for that one, when that one doesn't even have a treasure map!"

With that, Gay reached for his revolver. But before he'd lifted it, Braddock gave a spine-melting yell and arched his back, tripping a trigger of his double-barrel shotgun, which exploded in the air above Natasha's head.

Braddock's horse turned, crow-hopping, revealing the Apache war lance protruding from its rider's back. Above him, an Apache stood on a rocky shelf jutting out from the cliff. Reaching for an arrow from the quiver on his back, the brave cut loose with an ear-rattling war cry.

"Countess!" Sergei yelled, bolting forward at a gallop.

24

Screaming like witches released from hell, a dozen Apaches slipped and slid down the rocky cliff wall, their hide-red faces pinched with animal fury. Several loosed arrows into the canyon. Men from Braddock's and Gay's group cried out as the arrows split the air and knocked them off their mounts.

Holding taut to his horse's reins with one hand, Prophet fired the rifle with the other. Mean was in a frenzy, as the other horses screamed and the other men began opening up with their pistols and rifles. Prophet could not draw an accurate bead. He fired three more times, anyway, to cover Sergei as the Russian galloped toward the Countess Natasha's frightened mount.

Dodging and ducking under whistling arrows, Prophet whipped Mean over to Marya, whose horse danced amidst the gunfire that rose up from the arroyo around them. Several of Braddock's and Gay's men had dismounted to kneel in the arroyo, triggering bullets at the cliff bristling with Indians.

"Come on, girl, let's ride!" Prophet shouted, flailing for the bridle of Marya's rearing mount.

Marya cursed the horse, sawing back on the reins. As the horse whinnied and plunged forward, bolting into Mean, Prophet grabbed the bridle and reined his own mount left, heading back down the arroyo.

"Keep your head down!" he yelled to Marya as arrows and lances clattered in the rocks around them.

Prophet had ripped the reins from the girl's hands and was now leading her galloping mount down the arroyo, swerving around confused, riderless horses.

Sergei's deep voice boomed above the Indian whoops and the gunfire. "Go, Lou! I've got the countess!"

Prophet looked back. The hairy-faced Russian was galloping down the arroyo, trailing Natasha's mount, upon which the countess rode sidesaddle, her skirts and hair whipping in the wind as she cast anxious looks at the skirmish behind them.

Prophet didn't have to rake Mean with his spurs; the horse knew the score, and he'd never liked Indians to begin with. Headlong, the horse galloped down the arroyo, its hooves slipping slightly in the sand as he curved around rock-walled bends.

Twisted around in his saddle, Prophet triggered his six-shooter at the several Apaches pursuing them on foot. A couple wielded old-style revolvers that misfired or threw their slugs wide of their targets.

Prophet plugged one in the belly, another in his right kneecap. Both went down, wailing. Another stopped running and lifted his bow. The arrow whistled over Prophet's head. The warrior quickly notched another and let fly. The arrow arced through the dusty air, brushed Natasha's right shoulder, and plunged into Sergei's lower back.

The Russian gave a grieved shout and stiffened in his saddle.

"Sergei!" Natasha cried.

The Cossack shook his head and shouted, "Keep going, Countess! Ride!"

When they were out of range of the Indians, Prophet holstered his revolver and faced forward in his saddle. Mean galloped over the rocks, leaping over cacti, shrubs, and mesquite branches.

Prophet had tossed Marya her reins, and she now rode abreast of him, crouched over her horse's head and flicking her reins back over the mount's rump, urging more speed. Her face was flushed with fear. Having lost her hat, her blond hair flew out in the wind.

Several yards behind her, Sergei rode slumped forward in his saddle, head down, his right hand reaching behind for the arrow in his back. His horse was losing speed.

"We have to stop!" It was Natasha, whose own horse had caught up to Sergei.

Cursing, Prophet reined Mean to a sliding halt. Sergei's horse had already stopped. Natasha had ridden over and was crouched over Sergei, speaking in Russian.

"How bad is it?" Prophet cast a glance at their backtrail. The shooting was growing faint. No Indians appeared to be trailing them.

"It is buried in his back!" the countess cried, scowling at the arrow protruding about two inches right of his spine. "Oh, Lou, can you do something?"

Sidling Mean up to Sergei's fidgeting horse, Prophet said, "How you doin', hoss?"

"I have been . . . better, Lou," the Russian said in a pain-pinched voice.

"Let me see what you got there in your back, you big lummox. A souvenir, eh? Well . . ."

The arrow's tip was buried about four inches deep. Prophet gave it a pull, but it wouldn't budge. Sergei lifted his head with a pained grunt.

"She's in there good," Prophet said. Glancing around, he added, "He can't ride much further. Losin' a lot of blood. We have to hole up somewhere."

"I know a place," Marya said. "Follow me."

Prophet frowned at her, skeptical.

"Follow me!" the young countess insisted.

Prophet glanced at Natasha, who returned the puzzled look. He shrugged and grabbed the reins of Sergei's horse.

"Hold tight, hoss," he told the Russian. "We got a woman driver. Let's see where in the hell she leads us. Can't be much worse off than we are now, though, eh?"

"No!" the Cossack objected. "Leave me. Save yourselves!"

"We aren't leaving you, Sergei!" the countess cried.

"Lou, leave me!"

Prophet shook his head and and kneed Mean into a trot, pulling the Russian's horse behind him. "Shut up or I just might."

"Please go," the Cossack said, casting a worried look behind. "The Indians . . . they will be following."

Ignoring the Russian's pleas, Prophet cantered his horse back down the arroyo behind Marya. Turning left between two boulders, they followed what looked like a feeder ravine. It was a narrow canyon with high walls occasionally narrowing to no more than six feet, occasionally widening to twenty or thirty.

Cliff swallows screeched above them. The sun was blocked by the sheer stone walls, and the air smelled cool and earthy.

"There!" Marya cried, bringing her horse to a stop and whipping around in her saddle. "We can hide in that cave. We can even hide the horses."

Prophet looked where she was pointing. A cave opened on the cliff wall. It was a big opening — about the size of a modest settler's cabin.

Prophet slipped out of his saddle, dropped Mean's reins, and walked back to Sergei, who was crouched over his horse's neck. His face was sweat-beaded and pale.

"Come on, hoss," Prophet said, reaching up to give the big Russian a hand down.

Marya and Natasha had dismounted and now hurried over to help. Together, the three of them pulled Sergei from his saddle and led him up a slight grade to the cave entrance. Prophet paused a moment, Sergei propped against him. He couldn't see very far inside, but what he could see — merely stone walls and an uneven floor littered with bird and bat shit and slender dried leaves — looked friendly enough. At least it was shelter.

"Let's set him down over here," Prophet said, and led the Russian to the left wall.

He and the women eased Sergei down. Squatting on his haunches, Prophet helped him lie prone. Sergei muttered what could only have been Russian curses while Prophet probed gently at the Apache arrow protruding from his back.

"What can you do?" Marya asked Prophet. She and Natasha both sat near Sergei, their dusty, sunburned faces wan with fear and anxiety.

"Well, first thing I have to do" — Prophet carefully grabbed the bloody arrow in his right hand and snapped it off — "is break off the end."

Sergei lifted his chin from the cave floor and shouted something that sounded like *"Rumashkahaven!"* But then everything Russian sounded alike to Prophet.

"There." The bounty hunter nodded, satisfied. "Now, you women gather some wood and build us a fire. Just a small one. We don't need much smoke with those Indians around. I'm going to get our horses and gear."

"Why do I always have to be the one who gets shot, Lou?" Sergei called as Prophet headed out of the cave.

"Reckon you just don't live right, pard," Prophet said with a grin.

When the fire had been built and water boiled, Prophet sterilized his narrow-bladed knife, gave Sergei several sips of whiskey, and went to work cutting the arrowhead from the Russian's back. Sergei tensed and grunted and took several more slugs from the bottle while Prophet worked, cutting with his right hand and probing around the arrowhead with the other.

The women gazed on, faces creased with horror.

"Are you sure you know what you are doing, Lou?" the countess asked, one hand on Prophet's shoulder.

"Well, that's the thing," Prophet said, wincing with concentration as he probed the flinty arrowhead, which had lodged between two flat tendons. "I really don't, but since there ain't no sawbones around, what else can we do . . . ?"

Finally the arrow came free. Sergei gave a groan.

"There it is," Prophet said, setting the flint head and six-inch shaft on the cave floor, where Sergei could see it. "There's your souvenir, hoss."

The Russian muttered another curse.

When he'd covered Sergei with a blanket, Prophet turned to Marya. She and Natasha were holding each other and speaking softly, grateful to be in each other's company once again.

"Tell me, Miss Roskov," Prophet said to Marya. "How did you know about this cave?"

Marya released her sister and rested her back against the wall. She smiled mysteriously. "Because this is the treasure cave."

"Huh?" Prophet asked.

At the same time Natasha turned to her younger sister and said, "What?"

With an ethereal smile Marya rose and made her way back into the cave's deepest shadows. "Bert told me it was back here somewhere. Around a ledge." Her voice grew fainter.

"Marya," the countess called, worried.

"I'm all right," the girl returned, her voice sounding as though it were coming from halfway down a well, echoing off the stone walls.

Prophet stood and gazed anxiously into the shadows. "You better not go back very far, miss. Never know —"

"I found it!" Marya cried. "I did! I really

did! The trunk is here, just like Bert said!"

Prophet looked at Natasha, who looked back at him, one eyebrow arched. Prophet shrugged and walked back into the shadows, running his right hand along the wall and holding the left one out before him, feeling his way.

"It has a lock on it," Marya said from what he judged to be about thirty feet away.

"Hold on," Prophet said.

A scream rose behind him, freezing his blood.

He stopped and wheeled around. "Countess?"

She screamed again. Prophet grabbed his .45 from his holster and ran back the way he had come. "Natasha!"

As he neared the cave entrance, he saw two figures silhouetted against the bright opening. One was a man. One was a woman — the countess. The man had his left arm around her neck, holding her tight. In the other hand he held a gun to her temple.

Still in the cave's shadows, Prophet dropped to one knee and extended the Colt.

"Don't shoot, Pepper!" Leamon Gay yelled. "Or Prophet, I should say. Or I'll blow her head off."

Prophet knelt there, gun extended, heart racing. He was trying to figure out what to do and could come up with nothing. Damn. He'd thought for sure that Gay had been killed by the Indians. He was wondering how many more of his men were out there, when a shadow appeared on the sunlit cave wall.

A man stepped into the opening, his revolver extended. It was Clark, hatless, clothes torn, blood streaming from a cut on his brow.

"Don't shoot her," Prophet said. "There's no point."

"Drop your gun!" Gay commanded.

"All right, I'm putting it down," Prophet said, setting the gun on the ground by his boot.

"Now kick it over toward me. Gently."

Prophet kicked the gun toward Gay. Holding his hand chest high, he straightened. He heard footsteps and knew Marya was coming up behind him. She stopped near his right shoulder.

"Hey, baby doll," Gay said, grinning.

In the harsh sunlight Prophet saw the sweat and blood on his face. It looked as if he'd taken an arrow in his right arm, just above his elbow. He'd broken off the end so that only a couple inches protruded from his bloody sleeve. He'd knotted a tattered handkerchief above it. His broadcloth trousers were dust-caked.

"Did you find our treasure?" he asked Marya with mocking humor.

"Please let her go," Marya pleaded. "Please, Leamon . . . I'll do anything!"

"Marya, you will not!" the countess shot back.

"I will, Natasha. This is all my fault. I didn't mean to involve you and Sergei. I should not have sent you the map! I only wanted to keep it safe from *him!*"

Before the countess could reply, Gay said, "This is all real sweet, but I wanna know where the treasure is. You have three seconds to tell me, and then I paint the walls of this cave with your sister's brains! One . . ."

Before Gay could get to two, Marya cried, "It's back here!" and jutted a hand out behind her.

Gay stared, blinked. "Huh?"

"It's back here," Marya said, quietly this time. "It's back here in the cave, right where Bert left it."

Gay glanced at Clark. Frowning he stared at Marya. "This a trick?"

"No, it's no trick," Marya said. "We've been circling around it. I could not bring myself to —" She shook her head. "Please . . . just take it and go."

Gay turned to Clark again. "Come on,"

he said. Shoving the countess ahead of him while maintaining a stranglehold on her neck, he took three steps forward, as did Clark. Then Gay stopped.

"Clark," he snapped, "kill Prophet. Get the sneaky bastard out of my way."

Clark grinned and turned his revolver on Prophet. "Be my pleasure, Boss. Been wantin' to do that for a long time. . . ."

The barrel of Clark's revolver yawned wide at Prophet's face. Prophet's insides boiled.

He was trying to decide which way to dodge when Clark suddenly yelled and grabbed his left leg, bending at both knees. His gun barked, the slug ricocheting off the ceiling above Prophet's head and into the floor behind him.

Instinctively Prophet ducked and saw Sergei's hand come away from Clark's leg, leaving the six-inch arrow Prophet had removed from the Russian's back in the side of the bodyguard's thigh. Wasting no time, Prophet dived for his gun as Gay turned his own revolver on him and fired.

The bullet spanged off the floor behind Prophet. Gay fired again. Prophet grabbed his Colt and rolled right, avoiding the second slug. He stopped and, propped on his right shoulder, extended the gun, aimed carefully so he wouldn't hit the countess, and fired.

The Colt jumped, spitting smoke and fire. The bullet took Gay just below his hairline. The crime boss gave a grunt and flew backward off his feet. He landed half in and half out of the cave, his dead eyes staring wide at the sun.

Prophet turned to Clark, who'd fallen to both knees but who was now cursing furiously as he swung his revolver on Prophet. Prophet snapped his Colt around and shot Clark twice in the chest, laying him out against the cave wall. Clark dropped his gun. His boots twitched, and then he lay still.

When Prophet shot Gay, the countess had dropped to her knees and covered her head with her arms. Now Prophet looked at her.

"You okay?"

Slowly she lowered her arms and nodded. Marya ran to her older sister, dropped to her knees, and engulfed her in her arms.

"I am so sorry, my sister!" the younger countess exclaimed. "I am so, so sorry. I nearly got you killed!"

Meanwhile, Prophet turned to Sergei, who had propped himself against the cave wall, wincing painfully but his color improving. "Thanks, hoss," Prophet said.

Sergei waved it off. "What was I supposed to do, my dear Prophet? Lie around while you got your ass shot?"

The Western slang sounded ridiculous, voiced in the halting, Russian-accented English. Prophet chuckled and walked to the cave entrance, looking cautiously around. He saw no other men, no other horses but the two standing about fifty yards up the canyon, nibbling a tuft of bunch grass.

"Do not feel so bad, Marya," Sergei said behind Prophet. "At least you did find your treasure, no?" The Russian chuckled.

Marya pulled away from Natasha, her face brightening. "Yes! It is not all for nothing. I found the treasure. We will be rich forever!"

Natasha smiled. "At least, you think you found the treasure, *ma chèrie.*"

"Oh, I did, I did!" Marya climbed to her feet and turned to Prophet. "Will you help me open the chest, Mr. Prophet?"

"Be happy to, miss."

He followed the girl back into the cave shadows. A moment later they returned, Prophet carrying the treasure chest by its two leather end straps. The chest was a little bigger than a good-sized toolbox. Prophet figured it weighed nearly seventy pounds.

He set it down with a grunt, in the sunlight

at the cave's entrance. He inspected the rusty padlock and drew his Colt. "Everyone turn away."

He aimed at the lock and fired. The lock clattered as the bullet pierced it. Prophet gave it a yank, and it fell from the hasps.

He turned to Marya. "It's all yours," he said, and sidled away to give her room.

Marya glanced meaningfully at Natasha, then at Sergei, her eyes bright with expectation. Rubbing her hands on her thighs, she said, "I am almost afraid to open it."

"Open it, Marya," Natasha urged. She appeared as eager as her younger sister to see what was inside the chest.

Marya looked up at Prophet, grinning. Then she turned to the chest, placed her hands on the lid, and opened it.

The girl's eyes widened and her face blanched. She blinked several times, as if to clear her vision. She said something in Russian which Prophet translated as "Oh, my god!"

Prophet looked inside the chest. "Well, I'll be jiggered," he said.

"What is it? What is it?" Natasha cried, crawling over to peer inside.

When she did, her eyes lost their luster.

"Is it gold?" Sergei asked from his place against the wall.

Silence hung heavy in the cave for nearly a minute as Prophet, Marya, and Natasha stared dully into the treasure chest. Flies buzzed, the sun beat down, and cicadas whined outside.

Prophet gave a slow nod, his features flat. "Yeah, you're rich, all right," he said slowly. He reached into the chest and dipped up several handfuls of Marya's "treasure."

"Rich in horseshit and rocks," he said, letting the dried horse manure and stones fall back into the chest.

Marya stared at it. Slowly her eyes welled with tears. "No!" she cried, dropping to the cave floor and covering her head with her arms. *"No! It cannot be!"*

Prophet shook his head, sifting through the rocks and horse manure. "No treasure in here," he said, feeling sorry for the girl. "Not even a pinch of gold dust."

"Bert . . . he would not do this to me!" Marya cried. "He would not!"

"Come, little sister," the countess said, kneeling down beside the crying girl. "Let us go outside and get some air."

Natasha was giving her sister a hand up, when Prophet, still sifting through the dried dung in the chest, said, "Wait."

The women turned to him, as did Sergei, who arched an eyebrow.

346

Prophet clawed out several handfuls of the dust. "Seems to be a false bottom to this thing," he said, leaning back to look at the outside of the chest, then clawing out more dung and rocks. He'd thought the chest had seemed inordinately heavy for only shit and stones.

"Sure as hell," he said at last. "There is."

"What?" Marya said with gravity, her eyes regaining some of their luster as she pulled away from Natasha and knelt down again beside Prophet.

She sat there in hopeful silence, hands on her knees, as Prophet used his bowie knife to pry up the chest's false bottom — a thin wood plank. As he lifted it out, his eyes widened and the muscles of his face re-shaped themselves into soft lines.

Marya sat with a similar expression, her jaw dropping.

She said nothing for several seconds as Prophet lifted out one gold bar and then another and another, until four bars, spar-kling brassily in the desert sunlight, sat before the awestruck young countess. Marya's eyes seemed to sparkle of an inner gold light of their own.

Prophet cuffed his hat back on his head and stared down at the gold. "Hellfire and damnation," he said, blowing a long breath through puffed cheeks. "Would you look at that!"

25

"What I want to know," Prophet said to Marya over dinner two nights later, "is why your prospector friend didn't take out the Morales gold as soon as he found it."

The four of them — Prophet, Sergei, and the two countesses — sat together in the Gay Inn's posh dining room. They'd made it back to Broken Knee the day before without incident.

Sergei was still shaky, and he drank vodka with a Russian's abandon, but the wound was healing nicely. They'd reported to the sheriff only that Gay and the other bodyguards had been killed by Apaches. In spite of the crime boss having owned ninety percent of the town, no one had seemed all that distraught.

Marya's gold was hidden away in one of the Countess Natasha's turtlebacked steamer trunks, awaiting departure for Denver and then back East. Prophet figured the bars were worth at least a hundred thousand dollars.

Marya wiped her mouth with a cloth napkin and turned to Prophet. "He thought that, with all the bandits in the area, it was safer right where it was, until he mustered out of the army. Unfortunately, Bert imbibed too much too often, and bragged about the find in a Broken Knee saloon. Apparently, one of Gay's men overheard. I was with Bert when Gay attacked us, on our way here from the fort. One of Gay's men killed him."

Natasha swallowed a chunk of steak and asked, "How was it you found yourself with Bert, *chèrie?*"

Marya shrugged. "I worked in restaurants and hotels to finance occasional prospecting trips in the mountains. I had a wonderful time . . . until I ran out of money and couldn't find a job." She sighed.

"I had no money and nowhere to go but back home." She turned to her sister, a beseeching expression on her pretty, hazel-eyed face. "I love you and momma and you, too, Serge, but I was not yet ready to go home. I wanted still to be in the American West. I love the West, and I was afraid that if I left, I would never come back."

"So you stayed without telling us where

you were," Natasha said, her tone lightly castigating. "But I still do not understand how you came to know Bert."

"Bert found me camping alone in a dry riverbed down near Bisbee. He was very kind. He taught me how to ride, to pan, and to use a rifle and a single jack, and where to find different minerals. The Indians left us alone. He'd been a soldier, but the Apaches had known him for his kindness and generosity." Marya's voice grew quiet and sad, her eyes pensive.

Brightening, she added, "Once, we even camped with a band of Pimas."

The Countess Natasha stared at her sister with mute amazement, shaking her head. "Marya, you are the black goat of our family."

"That's . . . sheep," Prophet corrected. "Black sheep."

"Whatever," Natasha said, still regarding her sister with befuddlement and wonder. "You will never cease to amaze me, my sister." She pulled Marya close to her and kissed her temple.

"We are rich," Marya said. "If we invest wisely, we will never have to worry again about money."

"Yes, after we give Lou his share, we will have more than enough to make the family secure in Boston," Natasha said, pouring herself a fresh cup of coffee from the silver pot.

"Wait a minute, wait a minute," Prophet cut in, turning to Natasha. "I told you, that's your money. I don't want anything more than the fee we agreed on in Denver."

Sergei spooned sugar into his coffee and regarded Prophet skeptically. "What do you have against money, my friend Lou? You have earned an equal portion of the gold."

"No offense," Prophet said. "But not on your life. Do you realize what that kind of money would do to a man like me? Why, between the booze and the women and the gambling sprees, I'd be dead within the year!" He shook his head. "A man like me needs only enough money to keep him and his horse fed. And for a few drinks with the ladies on weekends, of course."

Prophet winked at Sergei, who threw his head back, laughing.

Later, they filed out of the hotel, Natasha and Marya walking arm-in-arm, still catching up in hushed French and Russian. The countess's stage was parked before the hitchrack, the two matched bays looking ready and rarin' for the long trek back to Denver. Prophet had agreed to accompany the trio back north, scouting the way and riding shotgun.

Prophet didn't mind. The money was good, and it was too hot for him in this country, anyway. The señoritas could wait. Besides, he'd gotten rather attached to his and the countess's late-night trysts.

As he untied Mean and Ugly from the hitchrack, the horse, as he often did, gave Prophet's shoulder a playful nip.

"Ouch! ~~Goddamn~~it, Mean. Why in the hell did you do that?"

The horse flicked its ears and shook its head, pleased with itself. Prophet was about to give the dun a good sock in the jaw when Sergei sidled up to him.

"Uh, Lou," the Russian said in a low voice, watching the women board the stage, holding the hems of their traveling skirts above their ankles. "I just wanted to thank you." He seemed to hesitate.

"For what, Serge? Diggin' that arrow out of your back? You done already thanked me."

The big Russian smoothed his thick, black mustache down with his right hand, thoughtful.

"No," he said. "You see, I know that the countess Natasha is, well, very beautiful. And I know that she has — how do you say? — eyes for you. I just wanted to thank you,

you know, for not letting your man's lust get the best of you."

He clapped Prophet on the shoulder. "You know what I am saying, Lou? I am thanking you for not taking advantage of the countess's innocence."

Prophet arched a brow. "Her innocence. Yes. Well, Sergei, never let it be said that Lou Prophet ever took advantage of a girl's innocence."

"You are a man of honor, my friend."

Prophet clapped his hand on the Cossack's back. "You have no idea how honorable I am, Serge. No idea."

Sergei smiled. "Well, shall we kick up a little dust and horse piss, Lou?"

"Uh, that's horse *sweat*, Serge, and I'm ready if you are."

The Cossack nodded and climbed atop the stage. A few minutes later, he shook the reins over the horses' backs, and the stage creaked into the street, heading south where it would pick up the eastern trail to New Mexico territory. The countess stuck her head out the window, smiling at Prophet.

He gigged Mean up to the stage and took the countess's extended hand.

"Later, Lou?" the delectable Russian royal asked with a devilish grin.

"Oh, yeah," Prophet said, giving her a

wink and squeezing her hand. "You can count on that."

Inside the stage, Marya was watching her older sister curiously. "Later?"

Natasha smiled and cocked an eyebrow at her younger sibling. "Just never you mind, *ma chèrie.* You're not the only one in the family with a sense of adventure."

Smiling to herself, the countess shuttled her gaze back out the window. She watched the big bounty hunter in worn denims and buckskin tunic jog his hammerheaded horse out front of the stage.

As Prophet rode, he threw his head back, singing, "Jeff Davis built a wagon and on it put a name. Beauregard was driver, and Secession was the name . . ."

ABOUT THE AUTHOR

Peter Brandvold was born and raised in North Dakota. He's lived in Arizona, Montana, and Minnesota, and currently resides in the Rocky Mountains near Fort Collins, Colorado. Since his first book, *Once a Marshal,* was published in 1998, he's become popular with both readers and critics alike. His writing is known for its realistic characters, authentic historical details, and lightning-fast pace. Visit his Web site at www .peterbrandvold.com or drop him an E-mail at pgbrandvold@msn.com.

B